A Southern Season

Four Stories from a Front Porch Swing

by

Eva Marie Everson, Claire Fullerton,
Ane Mulligan, Linda W. Yezak

A SOUTHERN SEASON: FOUR STORIES FROM A FRONT PORCH SWING BY EVA MARIE EVERSON, CLAIRE FULLERTON, ANE MULLIGAN, LINDA W. YEZAK
Published by Firefly Southern Fiction
an imprint of Lighthouse Publishing of the Carolinas
2333 Barton Oaks Dr., Raleigh, NC 27614

ISBN: 978-1-946016-38-6
Copyright © 2018
Cover design by Elaina Lee
Interior design by Karthick Srinivasan

Available in print from your local bookstore, online, or from the publisher at:
ShopLPC.com

For more information on this book and the author, visit: EvaMarieEversonAuthor.com, ClaireFullerton.com, AneMulligan.com, LindaWYezak.com

All rights reserved. Non-commercial interests may reproduce portions of this book without the express written permission of Lighthouse Publishing of the Carolinas, provided the text does not exceed 500 words. When reproducing text from this book, include the following credit line: "*A Southern Season: Four Stories from a Front Porch Swing* by Eva Marie Everson, Claire Fullerton, Ane Mulligan, and Linda W. Yezak published by Lighthouse Publishing of the Carolinas. Used by permission."

Commercial interests: No part of this publication may be reproduced in any form, stored in a retrieval system, or transmitted in any form by any means—electronic, photocopy, recording, or otherwise—without prior written permission of the publisher, except as provided by the United States of America copyright law.

This is a work of fiction. Names, characters, and incidents are all products of the author's imagination or are used for fictional purposes. Any mentioned brand names, places, and trademarks remain the property of their respective owners, bear no association with the author or the publisher, and are used for fictional purposes only.

All Scripture quotations, unless otherwise indicated, are taken from the Holy Bible, New International Version®, NIV®. Copyright ©1973, 1978, 1984, 2011 by Biblica, Inc.™. Used by permission of Zondervan. All rights reserved worldwide. www.zondervan.com. "NIV" and "New International Version" are trademarks registered in the United States Patent and Trademark Office by Biblica, Inc.™

Brought to you by the creative team at Lighthouse Publishing of the Carolinas (LPCBooks.com): Eddie Jones, Eva Marie Everson, Jennifer Uhlarik, Christy Distler, Jennifer Leo, and Kay Coulter

Library of Congress Cataloging-in-Publication Data
Everson, Eva Marie; Fullerton, Claire; Mulligan, Ane; Yezak, Linda W.
A Southern Season: Four Stories from a Front Porch Swing / Eva Marie Everson, Claire Fullerton, Ane Mulligan, Linda W. Yezak 1st ed.

Printed in the United States of America

Praise for *The Final Ride* in the Circle Bar Ranch series by Linda Yezak (*Ice Melts in Spring*):

If you like Texas, romance and cowboys — and who doesn't?! — then you will love *The Final Ride*. From the first page to the last, Linda Yezak had me wondering what would happen next. With the fabulous interaction between the characters—sparks did fly!—and the make-you-smile ending, I couldn't get enough!

~**Kathleen Y'Barbo**
Best-selling and award-winning author of
historical and contemporary Christian romance

Praise for *The Ornament Keeper* by Eva Marie Everson (*Lillie Beth in Summer*):

I love *The Ornament Keeper*. For such a little Christmas book, it packs a big literary wallop for everyday life. It is a strong, powerful, raw story with a deeply moving message of forgiveness that I believe will literally save marriages. Don't miss it!

~**Brian Bird**
Screenwriter and Executive Producer
When Calls the Heart and *The Case for Christ*

Praise for *Mourning Dove* by Claire Fullerton (*Through an Autumn Window*):

Set against the backdrop of a complicated 1970s South – one both forward-looking and still in love with the past – and seen through the eyes of a Minnesota girl struggling to flourish in Memphis society, *Mourning Dove* is the story of two unforgettable siblings with a bond so strong even death can't break it. Claire Fullerton has given us a wise, relatable narrator in Millie. Like a trusted friend, she guides us through the confounding tale of her dazzling brother Finley, their beguiling mother Posey, and a town where shiny surfaces often belie reality. Like those surfaces, Fullerton's prose sparkles even as she leads us into dark places, posing profound questions without any easy answers.

~**Margaret Evans**
Editor, Lowcountry Weekly, Beaufort, SC
Former Assistant Editor to the author Pat Conroy

Praise for *Life in Chapel Springs* by Ane Mulligan (*A Magnolia Blooms in Winter*):

Pour yourself a tall glass of sweet tea and head out onto the porch with this richly woven tale of life in a small, but suddenly booming southern town. Mulligan's characters are warm and engaging, not to mention delightfully human, as they struggle to navigate problems both big and small, proving in the end that nothing is impossible when we hold tight to faith and keep our hearts open.

~**Barbara Davis**
Bestselling author
When Never Comes

Ice Melts in Spring

Linda W. Yezak

Dedication

*To Jen, John, and Amelia, who know the value of salvation.
I love you all tremendously.*

Chapter 1

The simple taste of salt water on her lips resuscitated Kerry Graham's most painful memories. It had happened so many years ago. Neither had apologized. Then Mark was gone, and neither could. They'd been newlyweds, kids arguing over stupid things. Until the big one came, the monster argument about fidelity and lies and *where were you last night?* Hurt feelings and wounded pride eroded the feeble foundation of a two-year marriage.

Each new wave roared with memories of cruel words. Each soft rasp of water over the sand whispered apologies that never came. Seagulls and pelicans skimming the surface of the ocean searched for his capsized boat, just as the Coast Guard planes had long ago.

Kerry had left after that. The Gulf of Mexico could keep its dead. She'd moved inland, deeper into Texas, with no intent of tasting salt water again. But God called her back to the bay for a reason. If she didn't need her job, would she have come?

Her Labrador retriever, Puddin, abandoned her to chase a wave, then nose a crab as it crawled to safety. The crab snapped its claws. Puddin jerked back. Even a dog knew to protect itself from pain.

She retrieved her buzzing cell phone from her pocket and checked the screen. Her boss. "Hi, Alan."

"You there?" Alan Samuels never wasted time on niceties.

"Arrived a half hour ago."

"Have you met our benefactor yet?"

"I drove to the address you gave me. She wasn't there." If Elena Marino had been home, Kerry wouldn't have had so much time on her hands to take that treacherous walk down memory lane. "I'll try back later, as soon as I get settled in."

"How do you like the place she rented for you?"

She faced the bright aqua house in a row of other colorful houses built after the hurricane had demolished the area. A quiet neighborhood on a private beach. Perfect. "It's nice. Two bedrooms, full kitchen. All the conveniences of home. Though why she didn't offer me a room in her house is beyond me. It's one of the few places in town that survived the hurricane, and it's huge. Surely, she has a spare bedroom. She could've saved a lot of money, and I would've been able to work my own hours."

"She doesn't like dogs."

"Oh." Renting a house for her where pets were allowed illustrated Mrs. Marino's generosity even more than the donation she intended to make to the museum.

"Besides," Alan said, "she's notorious for guarding her privacy. I'm surprised she'll even let you into her house."

"I'm surprised she asked for me specifically."

"Me too. We have far more experienced and capable personnel."

"Gee. Thanks."

He cleared his throat. "Yeah, that didn't come out right, but you know what I mean."

"Yes, I know what you mean." Everyone in the Poets and Authors of Texas Museum had more experience. At thirty-two, Kerry should've had a few years under her belt—and would have, except for the wedding and the funeral and the years of floundering as if she were the one lost at sea. The ink on her degree had barely dried when Elena Marino requested her help.

"Just be careful to respect her privacy. What she's offering is a small percentage of what she has to offer a museum like ours, so stay in her good graces. And if you have any questions or doubts, call. You have my number."

"I will." Kerry disconnected and whistled for Puddin. "C'mon, boy. Let's go unpack."

Puddin nabbed a stick from the waves, probably burnt wood from a recent bonfire, and trotted toward her with hope in his eyes. He dropped the stick at her feet and sprayed her with the salt water he shook from his fur.

"You always want to play." She scratched his wet ears. "Okay, just for a few minutes, then we'll go inside."

She tossed the stick, and Puddin waited for the wave to fetch it before chasing it into the water and trotting back with it trapped in his goofy canine grin. Laughing, she threw it one more time.

"Great dog."

The man coming toward her wore dirty white shorts and a grungy blue pullover. His stained deck shoes kicked up sand as he walked, and the nearer he got, the stronger the odor of dead fish became. She might have, in moments of lunacy, missed the smell of the sea, but she never missed the other scents associated with it.

He stopped beside her and told her again she had a great dog, as if she hadn't heard him the first time. "What's his name?"

When Puddin saw the stranger standing beside her, he raced back and plopped his bottom right between them. Good boy.

"His name is Puddin."

"Oh, I get it. Chocolate lab, chocolate pudding." He reached out and gave the dog a good whiff of fish innards, then shoved both hands into his front pockets. "Haven't seen you around here before. This is a private beach."

"Yeah, that's what the lease said."

He smiled then. "So, you're the one who's renting the house next door to me."

The soft yellow beach bungalow he nodded toward bore a white trim, making the house look sunny and inviting. Several miles down the beach, she and Mark had owned one similar. They'd argued about the color. He wanted a brighter yellow; she wanted the softer hue. She won, and he'd admitted she was right. It was probably gone now.

The man in front of her offered his hand, but changed his mind and rubbed it on his shirt. "I'm Quinn Russell."

"The beach police?"

"No, just nosy." His sheepish expression worked for him. The sun-bleached hair dipping over his brow and his friendly blue eyes complemented the pink tinge in his cheeks. "This early in the spring, there's not that many newcomers around here, unless they stray down from the public beach."

"Now that we have that straight, I need to get Puddin dry and inside so we can settle in. Nice to meet you." She walked away, slapping her thigh. "C'mon, Puddin."

Quinn called, "Do you need help?"

"I'm fine, thanks."

With Puddin loping ahead of her, she jogged toward her rental. He trotted up the stairs to the balcony, already aware which house would be their home for the next month or so. She yanked the keys from her pocket and ordered him to stay while she retrieved an old towel from inside.

As she rubbed away sand and salt water from the lab's coat, she watched Quinn amble toward his own house. When Mark was deep in thought, he would walk like that, with his head down and his hands in his pockets. Then he would look up, catch her eye, and dazzle her with his brilliant smile. If only she could see that smile again.

Quinn glanced her way once before disappearing from her line of sight. He probably noticed she hadn't given him her name. As long as he could take a hint, they'd get along fine.

She opened the door and let Puddin inside. His claws clicked over the laminate wood-grain floor as he followed his nose in exploration. The message light blinked from the landline phone. She poked the button.

Elena Marino's alto voice greeted her briefly and left orders for her to arrive at Terrapin House by eight in the morning. "And do not be late. I cannot abide tardiness."

Chapter 2

Perhaps sometime in the past, the yard at Terrapin House had been loved and tended. Spires of lavender anise hyssop and globed blooms of allium punctuated green Lady's Mantle beds, providing interest and texture. But these and other plants were unkempt, their beds unruly. Sand reclaimed much of the lawn, but a few patches of grass had survived and turned green with the spring rains. The two-story cream colonial and its seafoam Bermuda shutters needed a fresh coat of paint. At one time, the house and yard had undoubtedly been charming, but their current state of neglect left them depressing at best, foreboding at worst.

Regardless, Kerry would work here for the next couple of months, cataloging whatever treasures and memorabilia Elena Marino cared to donate to the museum. A prolific writer, Mrs. Marino had conducted research for her novels all over the world, in exotic countries women today would be fearful to enter alone. Her promise to donate to the museum had sent Alan on a frenzied search for a construction contractor to develop a wing specifically for her.

Why someone of her prominence in the literary world would entrust her treasures to a newbie like Kerry still confused her.

She adjusted her laptop bag's strap over her shoulder and unhooked the latch on the wrought-iron gate, then cringed as it squealed open on rusty hinges. Next time, she'd bring a can of spray oil to avoid the grating announcement of her presence.

The front door swung open, and the recluse herself beckoned her inside. "Well, do not stand there. Come in. Do not dawdle. The neighbors see everything."

Kerry scurried up the porch steps and through the door. Mrs. Marino shut it behind her, then crossed her arms and scrutinized her as if memorizing every square inch. She seemed barely older than Kerry's mother, and the way she had her dark hair pulled back made the most of the silver shocks at either temple. Behind the lenses of her tortoiseshell glasses, dark brown eyes seemed to miss nothing. Her beige suit was outdated but elegant—tailored and professional, with a mauve blouse peeking from its buttoned jacket. Too business-formal for a day at home with a museum nerd. Compared to her, Kerry was underdressed in her denim clamdiggers and green-striped pullover.

She shifted her weight from one foot to the other. "Thank you for this opportunity and the house you rented for me. It's perfect."

Mrs. Marino offered a curt nod. "Come this way."

She led Kerry through a maze of African masks, pot-bellied Buddhas, and displays of spears and swords from a variety of cultures. Discerning the particulars about the house itself became impossible because of the clutter, but the clutter fascinated her. She itched to touch an Indian sari, feel its gold trim and the silkiness of its vivid red cloth. She slowed to examine the spines of classic books and novels from the world over. Then she picked up her pace to follow her hostess from room to room, with one hand clutching her computer bag and the other shoved deep into her pocket lest she gave in to the urge to feel, fondle, and caress everything in sight.

Mrs. Marino stopped in what must've been the solarium, judging by the number of windows and skylights. She clasped her hands before her like a dowager. "We shall begin here, in the Asia room. You will find everything in order of the books they represent."

She stepped toward an ornately beaded headdress mounted on a child-sized Styrofoam head. "For instance, this is from Thailand. It was given to me while I researched for *The Blue Haze of Pai*." She waved toward the other side of the room. "Over there are gifts from my trip to Seoul to research for *The Yellow Moon of Korea*."

The poster above the display featured an image of the book cover with its title written in Korean. In the corner, an exquisitely woven basket held an arrangement of pink hibiscus.

This would be fun work. With so many amazing things in this room, who could decide what to examine first? "Everything's so beautifully arranged in here. This will make my job much easier."

"Yes, this will be the easiest of the rooms. The day my assistant left will become evident as we venture through the house."

The response left more questions than explanation, but Kerry didn't know the woman well enough to dig. As time progressed, she might dare ask the questions nagging at her—why she was chosen for this job, for example—but for now, she would simply do her job. "You discussed with Alan how this would work, right?"

"Yes. You are to catalog, then a company will package and ship my things to the museum a little at a time. We decided that would be the most pragmatic approach, since I have not quite decided how much with which I am willing to part."

The woman's formal speech sounded odd to the ear, particularly since she wasn't old enough to be so proper. People today didn't use such correct grammar. Sad, in a way. No one Kerry knew would remember how to construct a decent sentence.

An irrelevant point and a time-waster.

"Where may I set up my computer?"

Mrs. Marino apparently hadn't thought of this. She glanced around the room with her fingers splayed over her lips. Finally, she walked toward a desk and chair of simple design but intricate decoration. "This will have to do for now. An artisan in Tibet made it especially for me. It is one of the things I do not wish to donate."

The surface held a flawless, satiny gleam that would be a shame to mar. "Do you have something we can lay across the top to protect it?"

"Oh. Yes. That would be wise, would it not?" She left for a moment, then returned with a linen place mat. "Is this sufficient?"

"Yes, it will do quite nicely." Good heavens, Mrs. Marino's speech patterns were wearing off on her. Would she ever utter another contraction?

She set to work, examining each object, large and small. The need to research unfamiliar items slowed her progress, but who cared? The work fascinated her to the point she would have missed lunch had Mrs. Marino not insisted she join her in the dining room.

The table held a clutter of books, magazines, and papers, but mats similar to the one covering the desk and the matching napkins marked the place settings in front of two spindle-backed chairs, one at the head of the table and one to the right of it. Kerry sat in the second one.

Mrs. Marino entered from the kitchen with two china plates, each holding a sandwich and a handful of plain potato chips. "I do hope chicken salad appeals to you."

"Yes ma'am. It's fine."

She placed the plates on the mats, then clasped her hands together. "And tea. Is tea to your liking?"

"Yes ma'am. May I help you?"

"No, thank you. This will take only a minute."

As Mrs. Marino returned to the kitchen, Kerry examined the sandwich. Plain white bread cut in wedges. Undoubtedly canned chicken bathing in far too much mayonnaise with a few bits of hard-boiled egg and tiny nubbins of celery. Mrs. Marino was an author, not a chef. Definitely not a chef.

She returned with two crystal goblets filled with ice and a weak-looking liquid. "The tea is unsweetened. If you desire otherwise, you must provide your own sweetener. I have none here."

"I'm sure it'll be just fine." Kerry took a sip. Colored water. It would do.

She reached for her sandwich, but Mrs. Marino cleared her throat, then folded her hands and bowed her head. Kerry followed suit because she didn't know what else to do. She hadn't prayed since …

It had been a while.

*

Kerry replaced the last of the objects from Korea and stretched, arching her back to work out the kinks. A distant chime announced the hour—six o'clock. Puddin would be frantic by the time she got home.

She loaded her laptop into its bag and exited the solarium. Mrs. Marino had disappeared soon after lunch. Should she call out to her, or just follow the trail through the clutter to the front door? Only the rhythmic ticking of the clock broke the silence, and shouting into the stillness would feel like sacrilege. She opted for following the trail.

When she arrived home, Puddin whined and pawed at the window. He squirmed urgently as she unlocked the door and released him to freedom.

"I am so sorry, sweet Puddin. I won't let it happen again."

The dog pushed past her and darted down the stairs to the nearest patch of green where he could raise a leg. He hadn't even bothered to sniff first. By the time she caught up, he had found something new to water.

The museum had distinct business hours, but work at Mrs. Marino's so engrossed Kerry that the clock seemed irrelevant. The ten-hour day had flown by for her, but unless Puddin gained the sense and ability to let himself out and back in again, she'd have to pay more attention to the time.

Quinn greeted her as Puddin made a dash for the beach. The dog's dark coat disappeared in the shadows of the dune, but she caught a glimpse of him on the shore in the marmalade light of the setting sun.

She headed to the beach with Quinn in step beside her.

"You must've had a long day," he said.

"What gave me away?"

He nodded toward Puddin, who chased waves and nosed curiosities. "Heard him whining when I came home."

She winced. "Yeah. Time flies, and I wasn't paying attention."

As they neared the water, Puddin raced toward her, sniffed Quinn to assure himself she was safe, and darted off again. So much energy to work off, and so little time for him to do it before she locked them both in for the night. She'd do better tomorrow.

"So, what do you do?" He looked better this evening, clean clothes, combed hair. Too bad about the hair. Its unruliness in the breeze held a certain attraction.

"I'm an acquisitions agent for a small museum."

"Ah. That explains why you were at Mrs. Marino's house today."

She scowled at the ground as she walked. How could she have forgotten the speed of small-town grapevines? "Are you following me?"

"No, I saw your car." He leaned down and retrieved a tiny pink shell, still hinged together, and handed it to her. "How is the old lady?"

"Private."

"She's not the only one."

"Is the bay area crawling with recluses?"

"Just people who value their privacy. You, for instance." The breeze had finally caught his hair, and a lock wisped over his forehead. Combined with his cocked brow and impish gaze, he looked like a blond Clark Gable in his role as Rhett Butler. "You have yet to tell me your name."

She reached for another shell, a blue one, and examined it. "People who wish to remain anonymous should know better than to come to a small town. Few people tend to mind their own business."

He released a delightful baritone laughter that almost made her smile. Almost. Any sign of enjoying his company would only encourage his presence. Not an unpleasant thought, but also not in line with her mission. She needed to do her job and return inland, where the screech of the gulls and the smell of the surf didn't remind her of what she'd lost.

"In a town the size of this one, few people are capable of minding their own business," he said. "It's hard not to see things, not to notice something different, when our surroundings are disrupted by change."

"Sorry to be such a disruption."

"No need to apologize. I'm glad you're here."

His eyes held a warmth that would defrost the ordinary heart. Hers wasn't ordinary. It was out there somewhere, burrowed into the sandy bottom of the Gulf of Mexico.

She turned her face and allowed the breeze to blow the hair from her eyes. "What do you do out here? Are you a recluse too?"

"No, but I feed their inexhaustible appetite for shrimp. The season will open soon."

"You don't talk much like a fisherman."

That laugh again, easily released. How could anyone be so carefree?

"You caught me. I'm not just a fisherman, though I could never imagine giving it up. I'm the pastor at Community Bible. I have a doctorate in theology."

"A doctorate. Simple church attendance isn't enough for you?"

"People tend to pursue their passions," he said. "Look at you. You're here, pursuing yours."

No, she was here because she needed her job. A twist of God's knife in her back.

Chapter 3

The next day, Kerry finished with Thailand and moved to South Korea, one of the few changes from the day before, the others being tuna salad instead of chicken and an earlier departure to rescue Puddin from his bladder. The week continued like that, shifting from one country to another, from chicken salad to tuna, from engrossing work to quiet home. She hadn't seen Quinn again, as if he had finally caught the hint she'd rather be alone, finally noticed she had yet to tell him her name.

Why hadn't she? Why couldn't she open up at least that much? Had she grown so dead inside that even her identity fought for existence?

Grabbing her computer bag, she climbed from her car in rote movements established during a few short days. Mrs. Marino had announced a five-day workweek ending Friday at five, as if sifting through her things were a regular business with regular business hours. Her declaration meant Kerry would suffer through a long weekend.

She walked through the breezeway to the back door—no more attracting attention with a front-door entrance. At Mrs. Marino's request, she'd parked in the carport at the back of the house instead of at the curb in front, as if that could keep small-town tongues from wagging.

Mrs. Marino didn't greet her at the door as usual, but it was unlocked. Kerry stepped inside and clicked the door shut behind her. She slipped out of her wrap—April decided to be cool this year—and headed to the Eastern Europe room. The author had won several awards with *Romanian Nights,* and its movie had been a contender for an Oscar.

Muffled sobs drifted down from upstairs. She stopped near the first step and glanced up. The sound evoked a curiosity she squelched. As private as Mrs. Marino was, any attempt she made to comfort her would be considered an intrusion. And if curiosity were the only reason she offered comfort, the attempt would definitely be an intrusion. She ducked her head and slipped as softly as the squeaky floorboards allowed to her workstation.

The items from Mrs. Marino's Romania years took up the bulk of the Eastern Europe room. Ornately carved wooden spoons, exquisite glassware, brightly colored traditional costumes, and intricately painted eggs covered every surface. Only one small corner had been devoted to *The Long Train to St. Petersburg*, her Russian novel that didn't make much of a splash in America. *Romanian Nights*, on the other hand, had been an international best seller.

She had apparently conducted her research for *Romanian Nights* as a young woman, while the nation was still suffering under the heavy hand of the Ceaușescu regime. She had stayed in Sibiu, northwest of Bucharest. Images portrayed her with a man of her age at the time, standing before great spires of ancient gothic churches. Kerry found very little about Mrs. Marino's time in Sibiu on the internet, though the search engines provided page after page about the book and its subsequent movie. She had never seen the movie, but it wasn't that old. Not compared to what she saw in the pictures, none of which had any inscriptions on the back to indicate where they were taken or when or with whom. Either Hollywood had picked it up late or—

Mrs. Marino entered the room, her tearful morning evident only in her red, slightly puffy eyes. Dressed in a navy blue suit, with a white jacquard blouse and blue pumps, she appeared businesslike, unruffled. She noticed the photographs Kerry had arranged around her, then swiftly redirected her gaze to something across the room.

"Would you care to join me for brunch? Afterward, I think it would be wise for you to take the remainder of the day off."

"Off?" Filling the weekend hours would be difficult enough. Why add half a day to them? "Mrs. Marino, the sooner I can finish, the sooner I can be out of your hair."

She folded her hands together at her waist. "Your presence here is no bother. You are not … in my hair, as you put it."

"But, I've just begun to catalog—"

"Perhaps you can take your work with you. You may return everything on Monday. Now, shall we enjoy our brunch?" She waved her hand in an invitation to precede her.

Kerry cast another glance at the photos, then led Mrs. Marino from the room. The woman was professional, punctual, and no-nonsense, so how could she insist on taking away Kerry's work hours? How did that advance the plan of expediency?

Brunch consisted of lightly toasted white bread and two hard-boiled eggs. Mrs. Marino served milk instead of coffee or tea and a prayer far shorter than any she had offered all week. "Thank you, Father. Amen."

Kerry peeked up from her clasped hands. Her hostess had already unfolded her linen napkin and was cutting an egg in two. That was it?

Mrs. Marino didn't utter another word until after their meal. "Feel free to go now. Have a nice weekend. I will see you bright and early Monday morning."

Go? She'd barely arrived. But before she could form a sentence of polite protest, Mrs. Marino pushed her chair to the table and left.

Kerry gathered her wits and scurried after her, catching her as she ascended the stairs. "Mrs. Marino?"

Her hostess continued to the second-floor landing without a backward glance.

Well, okay then.

Kerry returned to the Eastern Europe room. To take the work with her, as Mrs. Marino had suggested, she'd need a box. She didn't have one, couldn't see one available, and couldn't ask for one because the venerable author had disappeared into the bowels of the house with an unexplained dismissal. So, the first thing she needed to do during her enforced holiday was to get a box, preferably a plastic one with a lid, for the next time she found herself having to work from home.

She shut down her computer and slipped it into her bag. Too many days like this would increase the amount of time she'd be forced to stay here. Maybe whatever had upset Mrs. Marino pertained to today alone, and this wouldn't happen again.

One could hope.

She fished her keys from her pocket and grabbed her computer bag. Before she left, she took one last look at the photographs remaining on her workstation. At the very least, she could scan them and identify the locations, maybe even some of the people posing with Mrs. Marino.

She gathered them and slipped them into a pocket of her computer bag.

*

By the time she got back to the beach house, she'd loaded her car with boxes, groceries, and toys for Puddin. He gave her his usual Jell-O wiggle from tail to tongue, then started nosing the grocery bags dangling from her hands by their cotton handles. Since she hadn't thought to pack reusable bags, she'd had to buy some, all of which were filled with the results of shopping while hungry. She put everything away, fed Puddin, then made herself lunch—a real sandwich, with deli-sliced ham, cheese, lettuce, and tomatoes, and a side of avocado—and carried it to the Plexiglass table on the balcony. Puddin rested on his haunches beside her and envied her for each bite she took of her meal. She tossed him some cheese. He caught it midair.

Barely two hours had passed since her dismissal from Terrapin House for the day. If she spent the afternoon doing the sole project she'd brought home with her, she'd be in for a long evening. Not that her evenings weren't long anyway, but at least she endured them with the fatigue of eight or nine hours of work. Television could be truly mind-dulling if she wasn't tired.

So she'd have to get tired.

She took one more bite of her sandwich, then gave the last of it to Puddin before heading inside to change clothes and put on her running shoes. On the way out again, she grabbed Puddin's favorite ball. "Let's go."

After a good run along the shore and several games of fetch, her plan tired Puddin before it did her. She sat beside him on the sand and tilted her face toward the sun. The roar of the waves served as white noise that allowed her mind to go blank, until the giggles of children filtered through.

Three little ones traipsed ahead of a young woman down the path to the beach from a two-tone blue house. All three looked under the age of ten, and the mother—if she was their mother—was about Kerry's age.

How many children would she have had if the ocean hadn't swallowed her husband? One, for certain. The one she'd carried until her body could no longer feed both the fetus and her grief. A girl. Probably a green-eyed, tow-headed darling who would have looked like her father. She would've been six now. Would she have enjoyed learning, as her mother did? Or would she have been athletic, like her father?

Her heart ached with that familiar pain dulled by time but never entirely gone. Had he really cheated? Looking back now, the evidence seemed shaky, his explanation feasible. Oh, the horrible things she'd said to him—they'd said to each other. And she couldn't take them back. She could never take them back.

She took a breath through her nose to ease the pain, but the smell of the same sea that murdered her husband sharpened the ache instead. Why had she come here? Why had God required it of her? She fisted sand in each hand, working it through her fingers until her nails bit into her palms and one pain soothed the other. She would do her job and go home, back to the safe, numbing rigidity of her rut.

"That's Hope Goodman and her kids."

Quinn stood to her left. The sand must've muffled his approach, and Puddin's deep sleep kept him from sounding the alarm. The dog's legs twitched as if he were still chasing his ball through the waves. Some help.

"She homeschools her kids. That's Mason, the oldest, and Harper"—he pointed at each one— "and the little cutie with the ruffled swimsuit is Mia. She's four."

"She's adorable."

He flopped down beside her and stretched his long legs out in front of him. "They're all good kids. Sweet. Jeff Goodman is the associate pastor at our church when he's not being a cop."

"I didn't realize a town this small had a police force."

"A force to match its size. Two cops, one car, one secretary-slash-dispatcher."

"Quiet community."

"Usually."

A little farther down the beach, the two older Goodman children played in the shallows while little Mia plowed sand into her pink bucket. Apparently, their giggles had crashed through Puddin's dreams. He raised his head, whimpering as he watched them.

Quinn rubbed the dog's ears and was rewarded with a wet kiss. "You weren't ready to wake up yet, were you?"

"Oh, he was ready. He just wants to play with the kids. He's a favorite at the dog park back home."

"And where's that?"

Puddin couldn't stand it any longer. The kids' laughter drew him quicker than any kibble could. He was loping toward them before Kerry could grab his collar.

"Puddin!" She dashed after him, but by the time she caught up, he was already sniffing his new friends and sharing his goofy grin. They formed a pact to be playmates and chased each other to the waves.

"He's harmless," she told their mother. "He loves kids and got away from me before I could stop him."

"The kids seem to love him too." Hope introduced herself. "Are you our new neighbor?"

"For a couple of months, anyway. I'm Kerry Graham."

As he approached, Quinn raised a brow. So now he knew her name. She had no idea why she hadn't told him yet.

"Kerry's working for Mrs. Marino while she's here," he said.

"I saw her not long ago. That poor woman. So sad. This time of year is always rough on her." Hope waved at her kids. "Mason, y'all come back closer to shore."

Kerry hollered for Puddin to come closer too. If he came in, the kids would follow. After children and dog returned to a safer range, she asked, "What's sad about Mrs. Marino?"

"She hasn't told you?" Quinn shaded his eyes from the late-afternoon sun behind her. "No, I guess she wouldn't. She's a mighty private person."

"After some of the things she's been through, it only makes sense," Hope said. "That book of hers—you've heard of *Romanian Nights*?—I believe it's autobiographical. Have you read it?"

"Not yet."

"You should," Quinn said. "It's about the political uproar in Romania that lead to the toppling of Ceaușescu's regime and ultimately his execution. But I think it's about more than that. I think it's about how she lost her husband."

"How long ago was that?" And how could she not know this? In preparation for this assignment, Kerry had done extensive research into Elena Marino. She'd read of her travels and awards, the critiques of her books and the movies made from them, but nothing personal. Just like her quick research at Terrapin House earlier—she'd found nothing personal, as if all the records had been sealed and the entire world had signed a non-disclosure agreement.

Chapter 4

Puddin grumbled and jumped off the bed. Soon his claws clattered over the laminate floor. Kerry rolled to her side, and her Kindle slid off her stomach, its darkened screen saving her place in *Romanian Nights*. What an incredible, bittersweet story. If any part of it was autobiographical, Mrs. Marino had found a true and wonderful love. Kerry hadn't read as far as the loss of that love, but she knew it was coming. She dreaded it with all her heart, but that wouldn't stop her from reading it. The novel was too good for her not to finish.

A timid knock sounded at the door, and Puddin barked. Ten in the morning. Kerry had overslept, but then she'd spent most of the night reading. She untangled herself from the sheets and padded to the door. Mason and Harper stood on the other side of the glass panel, with Mia peeking around them, thumb in mouth. Kerry opened the door and Puddin darted out, greeting the kids with his full-bodied wriggle.

"Hello, little munchkins. What brings you here this morning?"

Mason rubbed her dog's neck, making his collar tags jingle, and looked up at her. "Can Puddin come play?"

"Are you going to stay on the beach?"

"Yes ma'am."

"Then have fun." As they ran off, she called, "I'll be out before too long."

She showered, grabbed an apple and a bottled water from the fridge, then settled on the sofa in front of a coffee table littered with images of Elena Marino's Romanian memories. The one of her in front of the church with the young man always drew her attention. Was this him? Her co-star in *Romanian Nights*?

She bit into the apple, then scanned the photo into her computer and got an instant hit in her search. Andrei Dinescu, an interpreter for the city of Sibiu's tourist department in the 1970s and early '80s. Born 1957, died 1988, leaving behind a wife, Italian-American journalist Elena Maria Evangelista Dinescu. They'd been married five years.

Cause of death wasn't mentioned, but if anything in *Romanian Nights* was true, his death had been suspect.

Kerry grabbed the Kindle from her bed and poked it to life. The copyright on *Romanian Nights* was 2010. From a woman who published a book a year, the twenty-two-year wait for this one must mean something. Had it taken her that long to finally pen the memories? Had it taken her that long to heal?

How long would it take Kerry? Six years had gone by …

She returned to her computer and searched for Andrei's specific date of death, then flopped back against the sofa. Today was the anniversary.

Her phone rang, and Alan greeted her from the other end. "How are you and our favorite author getting along?"

"As good as can be expected for a couple of recluses. She talks funny."

"Funny how?"

"Formal. Proper. Grammatically correct."

"Makes sense, doesn't it? Considering how much she traveled, she was probably dealing with interpreters who'd learned English from textbooks. When was the last time you spoke textbook English?"

"Never." She picked up the picture of Andrei. He'd been a handsome man; they'd been a handsome couple. "How's construction going on the new wing?"

"Slow. When can we expect our first shipment of Marino memorabilia?"

"I just finished the Asia room—"

"A whole room devoted to Asia?"

"Each room in the house is devoted to some country or region she worked in. Should help you organize her section of the museum. Anyway, you can expect that shipment sometime next week. I'll be working on Eastern Europe this coming week, and it's in the largest room in the house. May take me a while." She looked at the picture again. "Did you know she married her interpreter in Romania?"

"Didn't know she'd ever married. You should ask her about it."

"Do you think she'll tell me?"

"Won't know if you don't try."

Considering the author's behavior yesterday, Kerry didn't expect a successful inquiry.

After they disconnected, she slipped on her shoes and headed out to retrieve her dog. By now, the kids might be inside for lunch, and if so, Puddin would be chasing waves until he wore himself out. He saw her coming and charged toward her. She knelt to rub his ears and got her face washed.

Hope joined them and rubbed her hand down his back. "He's a good dog. He's really good with the kids."

"Yes." Kerry stood and slapped her hands together, sending tufts of dark fur floating on the breeze. "I don't know where he gets it from. He's not usually around children except at the park, but he obviously loves them."

The kids joined them, and little Mia wrapped her arms around Hope's leg. The image tangled Kerry's heartstrings. Would her little one have done the same?

Hope caressed Mia's hair. "We're having a beach party later to celebrate one of the few quiet weekends before school lets out next month and tourists start swarming the beach. Want to come?"

"And bring Puddin." Harper put her hand out for him to show his appreciation.

Kerry's favorite memories were wrapped around the beach parties from a few miles farther south on the coast and a few years farther back from her pain. A time when love was still new and God was still good. She and Mark and all their friends had grown up together and could never dream of leaving their hometown. Those days had been full of happiness and laughter, of affection between her and her husband. How she needed these good memories to shield her from the awful ones.

Maybe it was time. Maybe she could create new ones to help her regain her love of the ocean. "What should I bring?"

*

At four o'clock, Kerry and Puddin strode down the shore to the three blue canopies standing adjacent to each other in front of the Goodman home. Hope and someone Kerry didn't know set up a table and stretched across it a plastic cloth splattered with images of watermelon, lemonade, and colorful beach balls. Ice chests held sodas and snacks, and as Puddin darted off to greet the kids, Kerry added her lemon poppy seed loaf to the collection—the only cake recipe she could bake from memory.

Hope introduced Bethany Kennedy, who pointed out her children, Travis and Kendall. The two were Mason's and Harper's ages. They grouped together with Puddin, leaving Mia to scoop sand into her pail where the water lapped the shore. Downwind from the canopies, Quinn and two other men stacked wood for a fire. A smoking barbecue pit stood nearby.

A van bearing the side-panel sign "Community Bible Church" arrived. The church's youth group scrambled out as soon as it parked. Not what she'd bargained for, but she should've expected it, considering Quinn's and Jeff Goodman's positions in the church. The six teenagers played with Puddin—who was in doggy heaven with all the attention—then went for quick swims, and finally set up a volleyball net. Kerry hadn't played volleyball in years, but Quinn dragged her into the game; she played on one side of the net, he played on the other. By the end of the game, the score was tight. She was still spitting sand from her mouth, but her diving save hadn't been enough to push her team to the win.

After everyone had feasted on a twilight supper of hamburgers and hotdogs, Quinn and the guys set fire to the wood they'd assembled. Kerry found the perfect place to sit, away from the smoke but still warmed by the flames, where she could watch both the fire and the sunset. She brought her legs underneath her and draped an arm over her tuckered lab. In their regular life, Puddin never got the workout he'd had today, nor was he allowed to eat as much as was tossed to him during supper. He released a sigh as he flopped to his belly and rested his chin on his paws.

The others grouped around the bonfire, happy but tired. The little ones found parental laps and stared droopy-eyed into the flames. The older kids huddled together, talking and laughing, the sounds of their voices drifting away on the breeze.

This time of day had always been Kerry's favorite on the beach. The roar of the surf, the crackle of the fire, the laughter of friends she'd held dear. Did any of them still live there? Did they have children and church groups and PTA meetings?

Quinn sat beside her and wrapped his arms around his legs. "You're quite a volleyball player. Tough."

"We could get pretty competitive back in the day."

"We?"

Truly the fisherman, this one. Always fishing for information. But the day had been a good one, thanks to him and Hope and the others. She felt more relaxed than she had in ages. Treating him like a friend instead of an intruder seemed only fair.

"I grew up south of here. It's been a few years, but we used to play all the time. I was on the high school girls' team the year we won the state championship."

He released a low whistle. "Glad it's been a few years, then. We wouldn't have stood a chance."

A couple of the teenagers sprinted up to the van and returned with guitars. Before long, the quiet evening turned into a contemporary Christian music concert. She didn't recognize the songs, and even if she did, she wouldn't have been comfortable singing them. She didn't feel comfortable listening to them. The God they praised wasn't the one she knew. Songs of His love and compassion and forgiveness—they made no sense to her. Not anymore.

"Don't you sing?" Quinn spoke into her ear to be heard over a particularly riotous song and all the hand-clapping and amen-shouting that went along with it. Joyful, he would call it.

"Not in a long time." She stood and brushed the sand off her legs. Why stay and put herself through this? "I guess Puddin and I ought to be heading in."

"So early?" He stood too. "Big meeting tonight?"

"No, but I do have some work that won't get done without me."

"You've got tomorrow."

"Well, you know, why put off until tomorrow …"

He shrugged. "Want me to walk you back?"

The kids shifted to another song, a softer melody, and harmonies rose into the night air.

"No, stay here and enjoy the music. I'll be fine. I've got all the protection I need right here." She rested her hand on Puddin's head. He gave her the dopey grin of a dog who would rather chase butterflies than confront a bad guy.

"Yeah, he's fierce." He gave Puddin a pat. "Watch out for her, buddy."

After saying goodbye to Hope and waving to the others, she jogged home. She let herself and Puddin inside, then closed the door and leaned back against it. The music drifted through the walls. Exuberant praises followed worshipful intonations. The songs might be different from when she was in a youth group, but their meanings were the same.

What had she done wrong? Why had He punished her so? All those days after, and He never spoke one word of comfort to her aching heart. She never felt His presence. And now she wasn't sure she cared. He'd abandoned her. She had to deal with it and move on.

Even if she wanted to go back to Him, she didn't know how.

Chapter 5

Now that she knew how to research the reclusive author—not as Elena Marino, but as Elena Evangelista—the world opened for her. Elena Maria Evangelista had been born in 1959 to Italian immigrants to the United States. She studied journalism at a college that no longer offered it and became a freelance writer, selling her articles to major magazines all over the world. In 1982, during the Reagan Administration when the actor-turned-president began his rhetoric against the Soviet Union, she'd taken the first plane to Eastern Europe and made a name for herself with personal interest stories. She'd been twenty-three, fresh out of college.

Kerry found records of her short marriage to Andrei Dinescu. The wedding ceremony occurred in 1983, only five years before he died. No children on record. Beyond that, details were sketchy. A few articles in international magazines, a photo shoot for an American mag—which included the shot of her and Andrei in front of the church— but not much else. After Andrei died, Elena Dinescu dropped off the planet. Kerry found nothing pertaining to either Elena Evangelista or Elena Dinescu after 1988, but Elena Marino's first novel debuted in 2000: *The Blue Haze of Pai*.

Between 1988 and 2000 … nothing. Not even a magazine article.

Had she married and lost a Mr. Marino? Were there other loves and lovers during that time? Had she ever had children? She'd be a grandmother by now, just as Kerry's mother should've been.

Kerry backtracked and took a different direction, tracing Mrs. Marino's parents instead, and still came up empty of anything substantial. Andrei's family was as much of a mystery. The supposed son of a famous Romanian journalist, he lived with his mother, a factory worker, until he graduated from the university. She died under suspicious circumstances just a year before the tyrant who had ruled their nation was executed.

And, again, Kerry hit a wall.

If *Romanian Nights* was autobiographical, it might be the only record of the missing years.

Puddin whined and gave her his *aren't you ever going to feed me* look. The morning had disappeared in fruitless research, and now it was past noon. She'd meant to feed him and take him out for their run before the neighborhood church members returned home. She poured a measure of dry dog food for him, then retreated to her bedroom to look out the window. If Quinn's pickup wasn't in his drive, she might have a chance to take her run unnoticed.

The truck wasn't there, but beyond the small neighborhood, heavy, massive clouds darkened the western sky. In the distance, lightning cut a path through the atmosphere and no doubt incinerated whatever it had hit. Though she counted several *Mississippis* before she heard the thunder, its deep-throated rumble still seemed loud enough to frighten little children.

She grabbed Puddin's harness leash and called him to her. He took one look at the leash and twirled in his happy dance. Poor guy figured they were going for a ride—which was one of the reasons she preferred the harness for him. The other was because of his bullheadedness. Whether or not he obeyed her depended entirely upon whether her commands were okay with him. Silly dog.

They trotted downstairs, but went only as far as the dunes. She kept a tight rein on him when he started for the shore and the churning waves crashing upon it. The wind blew her hair into her eyes and threatened to push her farther than she intended to go.

"C'mon, buddy. Do your business and let's go in."

After a few exploratory sniffs, he complied, but *go in* wasn't in his plans until the thunder grew more boisterous and the lightning more threatening. Then she could barely keep up with him as he dashed back to the house, all but dragging her with him. They returned to the rental's driveway just as the first fat raindrops cut loose from the slate-colored sky. Street lamps flickered on in the middle of the afternoon, and wind whistled through the breezeway and whipped decorative flags into a frenzy. Hurricane season was months away, but the last one still left her heart raw and her nerves taut. She'd watched from the safety of her inland home as news clips showed mile after mile of devastation in the very region of Texas she both loved and hated.

A blinding flash, and the ground shook, rumbling from the impact of lightning on a transformer. Kerry sprinted up the stairs behind Puddin, who darted to his doggy bed in the corner of the main room. He circled in it a couple of times, then laid down and quivered as he watched her with his worried-puppy expression.

"It'll be okay. We're fine and dry. It'll be all right." For now. Come nightfall, it would be dark and creepy. No telling when the transformer would be fixed.

She used the light on her phone to rummage through the supply closet for a flashlight, but found candles and matches instead. Good enough.

Once she settled on the sofa facing the windows, Puddin jumped up beside her and curled against her leg. The gray curtain of rainfall blocked her view of the gulf for almost an hour until it finally eased to a spring shower. Even then, the heavier flow continued to pummel the coastline toward the east as far as she could see. She should overcome her aversion to watching news broadcasts; maybe she would have known to expect this.

The dog's ears perked up, then he lunged from the couch and ran to the door, barking at whatever had captured his attention. Soon Quinn stepped in front of the window, covered in a yellow rain slicker. He held up a pizza box with a question in his eyes. She let him in.

Puddin danced around him as he handed her the box. He gave the lab's head a rub, then said to Kerry, "I didn't know if you'd eaten or not. Power went out all over town just as we left the church."

"How'd you get the pizza?"

"Remy's got a brick pizza oven at the restaurant, so he doesn't have to rely on electric stoves like the rest of us." He knelt and gave the dog a more vigorous rubbing. "Refrigeration is his problem now. He's practically giving away pizzas."

"Thanks for thinking of me." She set the warm box on the counter and lifted the lid. Hawaiian style. One of her favorites. "It looks great. Care to share with me?"

"Hoping you'd ask." He hung his slicker on a peg by the door and left it to drip on the floor mat while he joined her in the open kitchen.

As they ate, Puddin sat on the floor beside her and whined. "Uh-uh, little man. I know how you get when you've eaten greasy food."

"Poor guy. He doesn't know what he's missing." Quinn sipped his tea, then put the glass down. "I meant to ask you last night to join us today. Have you found a church to attend while you're here?"

"No, I don't go."

He quirked a brow. "Atheist?"

"No, not at all. I know He exists. I'm more like a …" How should she put this? Atheist didn't fit at all, but neither did agnostic. "Deist. I guess that best describes it."

"So you believe God exists just because it makes sense that some god must exist, right?"

"Creation demands a creator, don't you think? It's too far-fetched for me to believe that the human eye, for instance, is a total accident. A fluke of some sort. It was created by design by someone who understood its function." She waved toward the window. "We can look out and see a panoramic view, or we can focus on that one raindrop falling from the roof. We can gaze at the entire beach, or we can study a single grain of sand. That's too amazing, too intricate, to believe vision came about by accident. I believe it was created by God. Jehovah. The great I Am. There's really no other valid explanation."

"But you don't believe He is involved in our lives. That you can have a personal relationship with Him." He wasn't asking her; he knew the philosophy and simply quoted it back to her.

"I don't think He cares about us—or maybe He doesn't have time. The guy's got a universe to run, you know."

"What about His Son's sacrifice on the cross? You don't believe in that either?"

"Of course I do. It's a matter of historical record."

"But you don't believe He died for you."

No. She didn't. Not anymore. The deist attitude fit. God created everything, then He stepped back and watched all the little ants run around, tending to their own survival. If one was crushed, what did He care? There were others to amuse Him.

"He did, you know," Quinn said. "He is able to save to the uttermost those who come to Him through Christ. Jesus is in constant intercession for us. Nothing can take us from His hand."

"There's a verse in Romans—not death or life or principalities or powers or yada, yada, yada. It doesn't mention that we can't separate ourselves from Him. That we can't step away from someone who doesn't care anyway."

He studied her for a moment, and she raised her chin. She would not squirm under the scrutiny of the local preacher. He had no clue what she'd gone through, no inkling of how cold that Being he worshiped could be.

"You know your Bible," he said. "You should know that He promised He'd never leave you or forsake you. Doesn't matter if a person is faithless to Him, He remains faithful. He can't go back on His promises."

Oh, but He could, and He had, and she'd given up waiting for Him to offer some measure of comfort.

"The rain has stopped," she said. "I'll be glad when the lights come on again."

Chapter 6

At ten o'clock the next morning, Kerry slipped through the side door at Terrapin House. Whatever time the power returned last night, she hadn't been aware of it until nine this morning. She'd read *Romanian Nights* on her Kindle, finishing it before she drifted off to sleep on the sofa. It hadn't dawned on her to set an alarm on her phone. Now she was two hours late.

The woman who could not abide tardiness worked in the kitchen, singing as she prepared something hidden from view. She wore a dress today instead of a suit. A yellow shirtwaist dress with a floral border that heralded the spring, despite the chill in the air remaining from yesterday's storm.

Kerry slipped off her light jacket and hung it on the hook by the door. "I'm so sorry I'm late. I—"

"Do not be concerned. The storm threw everything off kilter, did it not?" Mrs. Marino turned from whatever she was doing and offered her first real smile. An undeniable joy resonated from her and enveloped Kerry like a warm hug. How could this woman be the same melancholy wraith who'd haunted the house the week before?

"Yes ma'am. A bit off kilter." Kerry adjusted her computer bag's strap on her shoulder. "I'll just go get started. Maybe I can finish with Romania this week."

"No, I think not."

"Ma'am?"

"I have added to the collection. After lunch, we will go through it together. But you have two hours before we eat. A good start, I believe, despite the unavoidable tardiness."

She returned to her preparations and hummed a tune that sounded familiar. Whatever had happened over the weekend turned her into an entirely different person.

Kerry returned to the Eastern Europe room. The only thing new was the dome-lidded letter box sitting on her workstation. Unusual wood; brass-studded. Exceptional craftsmanship. Locked.

This should be good.

She returned the photos to the box where she'd found them and began to catalog the other items in the room, one of which was a tall smoky-glass urn in a beautifully shaped pewter stand. A pewter vine twined around the urn and released a cluster of leaves and grapes at its lip. A card had been tucked inside. The inscription was in Romanian, but under it Mrs. Marino had penned "wedding gift from Andrei, 1983."

She had described the urn in *Romanian Nights*. The couple hid messages to each other inside it. Love letters at first. Then more cryptic notes—dates and times, opportunities when the two could see each other in passing as he worked with the underground to topple an evil ruler. They lived apart for two years, under carefully orchestrated rumors that they'd separated. The housekeeper would leave his notes for her in the urn and somehow deliver to him her notes. Their times alone had been short and bittersweet, until he was arrested and she never saw him alive again. A heart-wrenching story, assuming it was autobiographical. But Mrs. Marino had written the novel with such a raw gut-level emotion that it must've been true.

A shelf above the urn held copies of the book's earlier editions in different languages. On the flyleaf of the 2010 English translation, she had written, "Whom have I in heaven but thee. And besides thee, I desire nothing on earth."

Kerry rubbed her thumb over the words. What a deep love Elena and Andrei Dinescu must have had for each other in such a short amount of time. Over twenty years after his death, Mrs. Marino still felt such loss that it oozed throughout the pages of her novel. And if her tears from Friday were any indication, the pain hadn't eased.

She read the words again. Had she loved that deeply? Six years from the accident, and still her strongest emotions were regret and bitterness. Perhaps, given more time back then, she could have learned to love with this measure of intensity. If she had, they would never have had the argument.

Mrs. Marino stepped in, and the room brightened in her presence. "Come. Join me for lunch. It is special today."

How had Kerry missed the smell of home-baked bread and other tempting aromas that now drew her obediently in line behind Mrs. Marino? Maybe the woman could cook after all.

They took their places in the dining room. Everything on the table hid in covered dishes—a large tureen, a smaller bowl, and bread in a basket topped with a linen napkin. But the covers couldn't hide all the wonderful scents.

Mrs. Marino bowed her head. "Dearest Father, how can mortals offer adequate thanks for the bounty which you provide for us? We are humbled that You supply our needs with such generosity and that You love us with a depth we cannot fathom. Please accept our feeble attempt at love and appreciation in return. For Yours is the kingdom, and we are honored to be in Your presence. In Your Son's most holy and precious name, amen."

"Now," she said to Kerry with a gleam of anticipation in her eyes, "I will treat you to *ciulama de pui*, a recipe I learned while I was in Romania." She lifted the lid from the tureen and revealed a scrumptious-looking creamed chicken with onions, mushrooms, and carrots. "I hope you like it."

"I'm certain I will." How could she not, when it smelled like something from her own grandmother's kitchen?

"Years ago, I learned that enough is good enough and any more is a blessing." She lifted the lid from a bowl of hot buttered rice, and unfolded the napkin from over a golden loaf of bread. "But today, we celebrate."

"What's the occasion?"

"My love, my husband, Andrei, has been reunited with his heavenly Father for thirty years. This is his anniversary. We will celebrate his happiness." She passed the rice. "Please, fill your plate."

As Kerry complied, she tested the conversational waters. "I finished reading *Romanian Nights* last night. Was it … Is it autobiographical? Was Romica actually Andrei?"

"Yes. Have some chicken."

Kerry found a thigh and dished it out, along with a generous spoonful of cream gravy and vegetables, then broke off a piece of the bread. After a bite of the delectable paprika-spiced chicken, she dabbed her lips. Mrs. Marino might not be overly talkative, but more so than a week ago. No telling what mood she'd be in tomorrow. "I did some more research on you over the weekend. Some of what I found in the public records didn't match what I read in the book. According to the records, the charges against Andrei—"

"The public records are lies. What good is truth in a nation that does not value it? What is one more lie added to the mountain?"

"So what was he really arrested for?"

"He was a Christian, an enemy of the State. He and some others in the underground trusted someone." Her lips tightened. "They should not have. They were arrested for distributing subversive material."

"What kind of material?"

"New Testaments," she said. "In those days in the Soviet Union and all its satellite nations, Christianity was not permitted. 'Religion is the opiate of the people.' This is what they believed, this precept of Marxism. So they replaced worship of God with worship of the State and punished everyone who did not bend the knee, as if they could change attitudes and beliefs by decree and force. But those who know the truth cling to it. Here"—she tapped her forehead—

"and here"—her chest—"are the only places we are truly free. Guard your mind and heart."

Kerry had heard of atrocities committed behind the Iron Curtain. No denomination was safe—Lutheran, Greek and Roman Catholics, Eastern Orthodox. Jews especially, but not even Muslims were safe from persecution. The very idea that a government and its society could dictate religious beliefs boggled the mind.

"I couldn't find anything about you for several years after Andrei died. When did you marry Mr. Marino? What happened to him?"

"He does not exist," she said. "The police discovered I fed information to the underground and helped many dissenters escape from Romania. Before I escaped myself, an arrest warrant had been issued against me for treason. Andrei insisted I leave him and flee to Italy. I moved to Portofino and changed my identity." She shrugged. "Elena Marino is a common name."

Kerry had read the harrowing scenes in *Romanian Nights* of Crina and Romica smuggling Jews and Christians out of the country and into the hands of others who would lead them to freedom. "All this must've been horrible for you."

"More so for him. He was the one in prison."

The scenes of the unimaginable brutality Andrei had suffered still tightened Kerry's stomach. "I don't know how you did it. How either of you did it. It all sounds so horrible."

"It was. But God was with us." She used her fork to pick the meat from a drumstick and a piece of bread to sop the gravy that went with it. As she chewed, she focused on something in the distance with an inscrutable expression. She'd retreated into herself.

Conversation over.

God was with them. Despite evidence to the contrary, she believed God was with them. Kerry had read of how Andrei died; she'd read of how all the political and religious prisoners had been treated at the time. The tortures they'd endured were inhumane. How anyone could inflict pain on another with such feral viciousness confounded her. But no one had denounced God to save their lives or the lives of their families, and that confounded her too. It tiptoed the line of believability.

After the meal, Kerry helped with the dishes, then followed Mrs. Marino back into the Eastern Europe room. As they neared, the author's step became less purposeful, her posture less erect. She could back out at any time, but she wouldn't. The woman who had seen horrors in Romania would face whatever she must in her memories.

She brought her shoulders back as she crossed the threshold. "I see you have found the box."

"Yes ma'am. It's beautiful. And locked."

"Yes, though there is no need. Everything is written in Romanian, which is not a language you studied, I believe."

"No. Only Spanish, French, and Italian." The Romance languages of Western Europe. She'd had a different kind of museum in mind when she graduated. "You researched me too?"

"Yes." She slipped a tiny key from her pocket and unlocked the box, but hesitated before lifting the lid. "I had not planned to share these yet, but I have watched you. I have noticed the interest you hold for all the things I have accumulated and the care with which you treat them. I believe I can entrust these to you."

"You know they'll become public in the library. Your identity will be revealed. You'll lose your privacy, your anonymity."

"Yes. It is time. Those who wanted me dead are powerless now or dead themselves." She lifted out the first envelope. "People must learn the truth."

She closed her eyes—in prayer, perhaps, or simply gathering strength—then removed the letter. "I shall translate. You write."

"Give me a minute." Kerry opened her word processing program, then started the recorder app on her phone in case she missed anything. As soon as she was set, she nodded.

Mrs. Marino read the date and a few opening lines, then continued. "'God is with us, even here. He amazes me so with His goodness. Last night, we sang to Him and our hearts were lifted. Today Ivan'—that was one of his guards—'brought extra bread to me, enough to share with the others. God provided a feast! Keep Ivan in your prayers, my love. I believe the Lord will do a mighty work in him.'"

The letter continued with such praise. All the letters that followed contained similar things, much the same as what could be found in the apostle Paul's prison letters, with the same faith and optimism that made little sense.

In one letter, Andrei wrote, "I have lost another tooth. How thankful I am that we have only bread and porridge to eat. If we were given meat, I would starve."

And another: "My eyes are so swollen, I cannot see. All the better to imagine your beauty and God's glory."

With each letter, Mrs. Marino slumped more. Her voice became gravelly and her eyes red-rimmed. Hearing them was no easier on Kerry. The optimism, the constant glory to God, were underwritten with incredible horror. He reveled in the fact he didn't have to go far to relieve himself because the bones in his feet were broken. The authorities put him in isolation to prevent him from singing hymns with his cellmates, so he sang alone instead. "Everyone is a star when no one can hear them, so I was a star in my own little cell."

Kerry had given up trying to type and let the recorder do its work. Now, according to the phone battery, she had to either type or quit. From the looks of Mrs. Marino, quitting seemed the best option.

She turned off her recorder. "It's almost five. Maybe we should continue tomorrow?"

"Yes." Mrs. Marino looked exhausted, not at all like the vibrant woman who had greeted her this morning. "Perhaps that is for the best." She fell silent, distant. Still caressing the last letter she'd read.

Kerry repacked her computer bag and fished her keys from one of the pockets. She looked again at the crumpled woman in the bright yellow dress. "Mrs. Marino?"

The author focused on her, surprised to see her still there. "Yes?"

"Why me? Of all the agents at the museum—or any museum—why did you choose me to do this for you?"

She returned the letter to its box and stood. "Come."

She led the way to the staircase, opened the door to a small alcove underneath, and flipped on the light. The tiny room served as her office. It seemed stark, distraction free, save for a few reference books shelved on the right wall and a portrait-sized photo of Andrei over her desk.

She retrieved something from her desk and handed it to Kerry. A newspaper article from the day the boat capsized. The black-and-white image memorialized the moment she first learned she was a widow. She'd collapsed to her knees in the Coast Guard office, her lips twisted in a wail she still heard sometimes.

"You know what it is like," Mrs. Marino said. "You understand great loss."

Chapter 7

Kerry added an extra mile to her run, then dropped to the sand and wrapped her arms around Puddin, hugging him for a long moment. She could run another five miles and still not out-distance the images in her head. The letters didn't have to be graphic for her to imagine the scenes. And yet Andrei never once failed to praise his God and be thankful for His love.

Had God ever loved her? Her parents had raised her in the church. Before the boating accident, she'd been deeply involved in its activities. And God rewarded her by taking her high school sweetheart.

Quinn stepped up beside her. "Is this a private party?"

"Of course not." At this point, she'd welcome any diversion from her thoughts. "Pull up some sand and have a seat."

He settled next to her dog, who nudged his hand for a good rubbing. Quinn scrubbed his back with both hands, sending Puddin's hind leg to scratching. He rolled over for a belly rub, and again Quinn obliged.

"I think he likes you better than me."

"He just knows I'm a sucker for labs." He gave her dog a final pat. "So, how's the job going? Learning anything new and different about Mrs. Marino?"

"I learned that *Romanian Nights* is definitely autobiographical. She and Andrei were deeply in love." She told him about the letters, then recited the inscription she'd found in the earlier English edition.

"That's beautiful. It's from the King James version of Psalm Seventy-three. Verse twenty-five, if I remember correctly. The next verse is 'My flesh and my heart may fail, but God is the strength of my heart and my portion forever.'"

"They apparently lived by that second verse. Andrei frequently mentioned in his letters that God strengthened him, though evidence says otherwise."

"Does it? You're looking at the temporal, concentrating on their situation." He brushed Puddin's fur from his hands. "Do you wonder where he got the strength to endure as long as he did? Are you curious about the joy apparent in his letters despite his brutal circumstances? His sense of humor despite everything— where do you think all that came from?"

Nearby sandpipers skirted the waves and hunted tiny crustaceans, leaving tracks in the wet sand and drawing her attention away from questions she couldn't answer. The only sensible thing for Andrei to have done in the face of such cruelty was to denounce God, yet he hadn't. The others with him hadn't. Humans break. Given enough pain—excruciating pain, such as he'd experienced—humans would do anything to make it stop. Anything, apparently, but deny their God. If God had been as distant with Andrei and the others as He was with her, would the results have been the same?

"Either God was very real to him, very present with him," Quinn said, "or he was a lunatic. A masochistic lunatic who enjoyed the treatment he received. Did his letters give you that impression?"

"No, of course not."

"Then the other is true. God strengthened and encouraged him personally. He paid attention to an individual's life. Kinda blows the lid off deism, doesn't it?"

"Why did He let it happen to begin with?"

He held up his hands in surrender. "That's above my paygrade."

"Really? The man with a doctorate in theology can't venture a guess?"

"Oh, sure I can. History blended with prophecy gives an inkling. But until I can sit on the throne and view the great panorama of the world and understand its intricacies as well as God does, I'd just as soon leave the whys up to Him. He's God, I'm not. He has a plan, and He knows what He's doing."

"Some help you are."

"It's called faith," he said. "Unless you get to know Him and develop a personal relationship with Him, you'll never realize that He's worthy of your faith and trust."

*

By the time they'd finished going through all the letters the following day, Kerry was emotionally drained. How Mrs. Marino survived remained a mystery. At the end of the day, she resembled a pricked balloon. But Wednesday morning, she greeted Kerry with her amazing smile, then resumed humming the song Kerry could finally put a name to: "Great is Thy Faithfulness." She'd sung the song herself when she was younger. Didn't have much use for it now.

She needed to dig into her work before her foul mood rubbed off on her hostess.

Mrs. Marino left her alone until noon. Lunch consisted of tuna salad with plain chips and weak tea. They'd finished the leftovers from the creamed chicken the day before, and now Mrs. Marino would return to frugal simplicity.

Tomorrow, Kerry would surprise her with a casserole of her own, one that got better over time, to delay the inevitable shift from tuna to chicken salad.

Such a curiosity, this woman who served simple fare on china plates, who lived as if penniless in the largest house in town. Whose rooms were loaded with treasures, but whose clothes were dated by at least a decade.

And who had spent the previous week in the darkest gloom, but now was radiance itself.

"May I ask you something?"

Mrs. Marino set down her tea and folded her hands in her lap. "Of course."

"How did you … Did you …" Why was she so hesitant? She'd been digging around in the woman's past since the day she arrived, yet this question seemed more personal. "I'm sorry. I shouldn't pry."

"No, go ahead. Ask. That is why you are here, is it not?"

Was it? Was this why God brought her back to the coast, to glean some understanding of Him?

Okay, then.

"How did you know that God was with you during all that time? Andrei believed God was with him—"

"He was."

"How did he know that? How do you know that?"

"He promised He would be. He was." She shifted in her chair to face her more fully. "You know, do you not? You are not aware of His presence?"

"No. I've never felt Him with me. I have felt alone, abandoned, since—"

"This has nothing to do with feelings." Mrs. Marino squeezed her arm. "You know He is there because He said so. 'And lo, I will be with you always.' He cannot break His promise. He said it. Cling to it. His promise is true."

It couldn't be that simple. All that time of unanswered prayer. All those years of silence. Perhaps He'd been there for the Dinescus, but not for her. Maybe her suffering didn't weigh as heavily. Maybe it wasn't enough to warrant a confirmation of His love. It was nothing compared to what they'd been through.

Mrs. Marino studied her. "You do not have a firm foundation, do you?"

"I don't understand."

"Faith requires a firm foundation in God's Word. You have no faith because you have no foundation, and now you rely on feeling rather than knowing."

"That's not quite true. I was raised in the church."

"Yes, but were you raised in the Word? Did you spend time with God? Did you develop a relationship with Him?"

She'd read her Bible. She'd been in Sunday school and Bible studies all her life until the accident. "I thought I had."

"If you had, you would know."

"You mean, during all that time, that horrible time, you never doubted? Never questioned?"

"I wish I could say no." She bowed her head. "God forgive me, I failed Him often. I did not have the foundation Andrei had. But it was during those years that I built one. Those hard years were my proving ground. I learned to wrap myself in His Word."

Her face bore an expression of determination. Determined to make Kerry understand? She hoped so. She needed to understand, needed to receive whatever it was that gave this woman her joy.

"You heard the letters Andrei wrote," Mrs. Marino continued, "the evidence of his faith. If he would not turn his back on his Father, how could I? So I studied and I learned. I tasted and saw that the Lord is good, and I trusted Him despite our circumstances. And He blessed me."

"He separated you from your husband. He allowed Andrei to die a horrible death. How can you say He blessed you?"

"Andrei is not dead, child. The God who kept me safe when I escaped to Italy has my Andrei in the palm of His hand. I will see him again. Just as you will see your young man again."

"I can only hope."

"Build your foundation so you can know." She left the dining room for a moment and returned with a small book. "Here. Start in Hebrews."

The leather-bound New Testament fit in the palm of her hand and had fine, gilt-edged pages and tiny print. If she tried to read the letter to the Hebrews in this, she'd go blind. Much better to find a version on her Kindle or something. But the fact this amazing woman had given it to her made it priceless.

"Yes ma'am. Thank you."

*

After Kerry loaded the last bowl into the dishwasher—something she rarely needed since she lived alone—she dried her hands and flipped off the kitchen light. Preparing tomorrow's lunch had been an intensive labor of love, and she was ready to finally call it quits on the day.

She found a Bible app for her phone, set it to the New International Version, and searched for Hebrews. Though it had been years since she'd last read it, or anything in the Bible, many of the verses were familiar: *Today, if you hear his voice, do not harden your hearts; approach God's throne of grace with confidence; he is able to save completely those who come to God through him, because he always lives to intercede for them.*

Quinn had quoted that verse just recently. It was as if he and Mrs. Marino had ganged up on her. Was it possible God brought her here? She'd asked herself this before, and the question remained. Was this the real reason she'd had to return to the coast? Was He seeking to reconcile with her?

I will forgive their wickedness and will remember their sin no more.
Endure hardship as discipline ...

Discipline. He had taken her husband from her as discipline? For what? What had she done—what had *he* done that God would take him from her? What had either of them done to deserve it?

What had the Dinescus done to deserve to suffer so?

She turned off the app and clicked on the television.

Chapter 8

Next day, Mrs. Marino had left the door unlocked and a note taped to the coat hook. She'd be gone most of the morning but would return in time for lunch. Good. She wouldn't be around to watch Kerry yawn the hours away. She hadn't slept worth a flip.

She put the casserole in the refrigerator, then headed back to the Eastern Europe room. Though the letters were done and all the photographs had been identified and cataloged, she still had many things to work on. Monday, she'd begun the glassware collection with the urn. She would continue with it, then progress to the decorative spoons.

At eleven thirty, she quit long enough to put lunch in the oven. By the time Mrs. Marino returned, the kitchen smelled of a tomatoey-spiciness that promised a fulfilling meal.

The author clapped her hands, delighted as a child. "This smells like home."

"Close." Kerry pulled the casserole dish from the oven and uncovered it. "*Golabki*—cabbage rolls, just like my Polish grandmother used to make. I hope you like them."

"There is very little difference between *golabki* and *sarmale*. Romanians use sauerkraut for their cabbage rolls instead of boiled cabbage, and dill and different spices from what the Polish use. But I have had both and love both. You are too kind to do this for me."

"It was fun to cook for someone other than myself for a change."

They worked together quietly, setting the table and preparing the glasses. Mrs. Marino said nothing but the prayer, which was fine. Kerry wasn't ready to discuss Hebrews or the Bible or her lack of foundation. She'd gritted her teeth during the prayer.

Watching her hostess enjoy the meal proved to be the bright spot in her day. As the hours wore on, her computer became sluggish, slowing her progress and frustrating her beyond measure. The idea of shifting from one segment in the huge collection to another bit the dust when she had to shut down everything to run her computer through a backup and cleaning and virus search and yet another cleaning. After a reboot, she received an update alert.

She should've handled this the night before instead of wasting her time in Hebrews.

She slapped the lid shut and packed the computer back in its bag. By the time it updated, she wouldn't be able to concentrate anyway. Not that she could now. She slung the bag over her shoulder, and following an unsuccessful attempt to find Mrs. Marino to say good-bye, she left.

After kicking up such a fuss last week about cutting out of work early, she should've felt guilty about doing it today, but she didn't. It was only a couple of hours early, and Puddin would be happy to see her at home. But as she prepared to turn down the road to her neighborhood, she noticed the alarming position of the arrow on her gas gauge. The warning chime had broken years ago, and she'd never had the funds to get it repaired. Instead of turning toward home, she pulled a U-turn and headed back into town. The car gasped its last right outside the Community Bible Church.

Very funny.

Fortunately, there were vehicles in the parking lot, probably belonging to those who ran the after-school daycare advertised on the church sign. At least Quinn's truck wasn't among them. She strode through a side door and marched to the beat of "This Little Light of Mine" toward what appeared to be the office. She tapped on the frame of the open door, and Jeff Goodman looked up from his work.

"Well, if it isn't the lady who has me in hot water."

"Uh-oh. What did I do?"

"You got my kids to beggin' for a dog."

"Sorry about that. Puddin has that effect on people."

He laughed and rose from his desk. He wore jeans and a collared pullover and the shadow of whiskers she hadn't noticed Saturday. "Are you here to see Quinn?"

"No. I just need some help." His joyful expression shifted to concern, and she added quickly, "I ran out of gas."

"We can take care of that." He snagged his keys off his desk. "My truck's out this way."

As they drove to the station, he said, "We prayed for you this past Sunday."

"For me? Why?"

He shot her an odd look. Granted, most people probably would've said thank you, but she felt anything but thankful.

"Well, you know," he said, "you're new in town and all. Hope says she sees you out sometimes, you and Puddin, just watching the waves all by yourself. She thinks you might be lonely. She would've dropped in on you this week, but her mom's ill. She'll be gone a few days."

"Sorry to hear about her mother."

Was she lonely? She hadn't really thought about it, or maybe she'd grown accustomed to it. She'd been older than most everyone in college, so she didn't have many friends from her alma mater. She hadn't been working at the museum long enough to develop relationships there. And she'd lost touch with everyone from before …

Pathetic to think that her closest friends were a reclusive author and a shrimp-boat fisherman with a doctorate in the one subject she had little tolerance for.

"She'll probably have you over for supper when she gets back. Meanwhile, you're welcome to join us at the church tonight. Shrimp creole night. A fan favorite."

"I'm sure, but I brought some work home with me that I need to get done before tomorrow." Would she go to hell for lying to a preacher?

What was she thinking? According to God's rule book, she'd done far worse than lie to a preacher.

"Everybody's gotta eat. We'll have plenty. An hour away from work won't hurt."

"You make a tempting argument, but maybe next week."

He paid for a gallon of gas and refused reimbursement, which guaranteed she'd have to join them for dinner some night. She couldn't accept his gift, then refuse his hospitality. Not like she could refuse church attendance. Shrimp creole or not.

If she wanted it bad enough, she could make it herself.

*

Quinn knocked on her door that evening. If not for the fact he could see her through its glass panel, she would've ignored him. He offered a smile and a white Styrofoam takeout container. What was it with him and food?

She opened the door, not really intending to let him in, until he identified the takeout as shrimp creole from the church. She *could* make it herself, but she hadn't, settling instead for an apple.

"Thanks for feeding me again. But you do know I cook for myself, right?"

"I figured you weren't up here starving, but until you've had Phoebe's creole, you haven't had creole. I couldn't let you go through life deprived."

"Again, thank you. I appreciate your attention to my welfare. C'mon in."

He and Puddin went through their usual guy-pal greeting. "Heard you had a rough day."

"Who? Me or him?"

"You." He joined her in the kitchen. "Jeff said you ran out of gas."

"Yeah. I should've been watching. I don't think I've filled the tank since I got here." She put the creole in the refrigerator, then moved to the sofa and turned up the volume of the date-night romance she'd been watching. He could either watch the movie with her, or he could leave. She wasn't in the mood to answer his questions or get into any deep discussions tonight.

He sat on the other end of the couch. "I've seen this one. One of my favorites."

"You watch chick flicks?"

"Not often. Not on purpose. But on the rare occasion I have a date, it's usually to a movie."

"Don't get out much?"

His smile held a touch of irony. "When women say they want a good man, they don't mean a preacher."

"Rough life."

A shame, really. He was a good man. A little too inquisitive, but that shouldn't matter. Most women would be flattered that a guy as good-looking as he was would show such interest in them. She wasn't most women. And she *definitely* didn't want a preacher.

At a slow point in the movie, he said, "I saw Mrs. Marino in town this morning. She said she told you to read Hebrews."

She told him? Why would she tell him? How could something like that slip into a casual conversation? "Sounds like I was the center of everyone's conversation today."

"Small town."

"Small town, big noses." Couldn't everyone just leave her alone? "Jeff said the entire church prayed for me because Hope thinks I'm lonely. He told you about my empty gas tank. Mrs. Marino told you about our discussion yesterday. Is there anything you don't already know about me?"

"Like I said before, everyone knows pretty much everything about everyone else around here." He shrugged. "Small towns are like that."

Yes, but this was too weird. They seemed to have a tag-team match going. If Quinn wasn't digging at her, Mrs. Marino was. And now they were bringing Hope and Jeff into the act. Too suspicious. "Did you know I was coming? That Mrs. Marino requested me specifically? Did you research me like she did?"

"Whoa! Where's this coming from? Of course I didn't."

Right. Of course he didn't. Not even Mrs. Marino had known about her being on the outs with God until recently. It wasn't something that could be researched. "Sorry. It just feels like everyone is ganging up on me."

"I don't understand."

Neither did she. "It's nothing. Forget about it."

He studied her a moment, then shook his head. "No, I don't think so. This sounds serious. I'm here to listen if you want to talk."

On TV, the hero was kissing the heroine. Soon the credits would roll, and she'd have to flip through the channels to find something else. Not that she was likely to find anything.

Did God bring her here? Was this an invitation to reconcile with Him? What if she wasn't ready? After reading about discipline, she may never be ready.

"Tell me what's on your mind," he said. "It's obviously upsetting you."

She had his full attention—his full, compassionate attention—and if anyone could answer her questions, he probably could. She wanted to know where God had been all this time she needed Him. Where was He? Was He reaching out to her now? Was that the reason she was here, back on the coast, back where all the pain, separation, and hopelessness had started? She needed answers.

So she told him about Mark and the fight and the freak storm and the broken mast and the boat capsizing and the guilt—oh, the guilt! How could such venom have spewed from her mouth? And she'd never be able to take it back. Never be able to make it right.

But she couldn't bring herself to tell him about the baby. What she'd told him was enough to justify her anger. More than enough.

"And then I read that I should endure hardship as discipline. *Discipline*! Instead of taking my husband, why couldn't God have simply fixed our marriage? We still loved each other. Despite everything, I still loved him. I would have settled down eventually and seen that he was telling the truth. But God didn't give us a chance. He chose to punish me instead."

Quinn looked more stricken with every word she said, as if he could feel her pain as intensely as she did. Did he feel her anger? Did it make him angry too?

She wanted him to rail against God, shout against the injustices she'd suffered. Demand an explanation! But the righteous anger she needed from him wasn't evident in his eyes. Only sorrow and that blasted compassion that bordered on pity. She didn't want pity. She wanted fury.

"I can't speak for God," he said. "What you described would make anyone bitter and angry. It could shake just about anyone's faith. Problem is, without faith, it's impossible to please Him. If you're feeling disciplined now, it's probably not because of anything that happened back then, but what's happened since. You turned from Him."

"He turned from me. I needed Him, but He never seemed near. Never answered my prayers."

"He's always near, not even a whisper away. You may not have been ready to hear Him before, and subsequently you've forgotten how to listen for Him. To recognize Him in your life." He chuckled. "Seems to me He's got your attention now though, doesn't He? From the sounds of things, your being here is far too coincidental to be coincidental. He had a hand in it."

How could he find anything funny in this? "So … what? He's through punishing me now? He thinks it's time to make up? Doesn't that strike you as ludicrous?"

"Did you read the rest of that verse? The surrounding verses? What He does is for our good, to perfect us so we can share in His holiness. He's treating you as His child—you *are* His child. And as a father disciplines a child he loves, He has disciplined you. He has plans for you, and He hasn't let go of you just because you let go of Him. He loves you. That will never change."

He searched her face with a question in his eyes: Was he getting through?

She turned away. "Maybe you should leave."

He met her request with silence. Then he stood and walked to the door. "I'm sorry. I didn't mean to upset you."

His voice said it all. He felt like an utter failure. He couldn't know that the failure was totally hers. She had to be honest with herself. He'd nailed it. She couldn't hear God anymore, couldn't find evidence of Him in her life. She'd drowned Him out in the noise of her pain and didn't know how to reach Him. And in all honesty, she needed that more than her anger.

Chapter 9

Kerry had thought about calling in sick today. It had been an emotional week. No, it had been an emotional two weeks. An entire month. Ever since Alan told her about this assignment and hinged her career on her agreement to go, she'd been on a continuous mood swing. Two nights ago, her primary emotion had been anger. Anger was good. Anger kept her fueled.

But last night's sorrow had sucked every ounce of energy from her. She couldn't take this anymore.

After a fruitless morning, she joined Mrs. Marino for lunch. The woman prayed over their leftover cabbage rolls and dug in. "These are always better the second day."

"Yes, they are." Kerry picked at the cabbage, nudged a grain of rice around her plate.

Mrs. Marino chewed as she eyed her, then asked, "What is wrong? Are you ill?"

"No, I'm fine."

She reached across for Kerry's hand. "Then what is it, child? Do you have more questions? We are friends now. What have I to hide from you? If you have questions, ask."

"I do have questions," she said. Their joined hands seemed to give her the courage she needed. She took a breath and plunged ahead. "The other day, you said you'd failed God, that you didn't have the foundation Andrei had. Did you ever feel separated from the Lord? Like the entire ocean lay between you?"

"Oh, yes. Many times." She leaned back in her chair and studied a distant memory. "Whenever I heard of the pain my dear Andrei suffered, I would become full of hate and scream to God *why? Why!* I never understood. I still do not. And I would get so angry with Him."

"That's understandable."

"In the human realm, yes. But to let such feelings separate us from God—it is wrong. It is sin. How could I expect God to be with me when I was so consumed with hate? He is a God of love, and because He loves, He also promises justice. But that is not for me to do, this vengeance He promises. From me, He demands forgiveness. To forgive my enemies. And I could not."

"How could He even expect it of you? Those animals didn't deserve forgiveness for what they did."

"It was not for their benefit that He required it of me, but for mine. Hate, anger, and bitterness separated me from Him. How could I live? Where would I find joy without Him? I had to release it all, and the only way was to forgive." Her lips formed an angelic smile, and a look of pure joy brightened her eyes. "When I finally obeyed, it was as if a huge burden had been lifted from my shoulders. I felt lighter, happier, than I had in years. Despite everything, I knew joy again."

Kerry shook her head. "I've heard that huge-load-being-lifted thing before. It's almost cliché."

"You have heard it because there is no other way to describe it. When you are hungry, you eat. Then you are full. That is not cliché, that is truth. When you reunite with God, a burden is lifted. That too is not cliché, but truth."

Maybe so, but it was something she never hoped to experience. "My situation isn't the same as yours. There is no one to forgive for the loss of my husband."

"Yet you feel hate, anger, and bitterness, do you not?"

Not today. Today, she just felt tired. So tired of it all.

"Do you feel separated from God?"

"More than you know," she whispered.

"He is your Father, Kerry. Do you not think He hurts too? He misses you."

She twisted her napkin in her lap. Did He miss her? Maybe so. Maybe that was why He brought her here. Here, where two strangers could show her the way home again. "I don't know what to do. What to say."

"Finish your lunch." Mrs. Marino picked up her fork again. "Then go home. Tell Him you miss Him too and open your heart to Him. Regain His love and forgiveness. Then come back tomorrow and tell me about that huge-load-being-lifted thing."

*

While Puddin danced around her as if he wasn't through running yet, Kerry bent over with her hands on her knees. "I can't, God. You win. I can't be mad anymore. I'm tired of it."

She knelt in the sand and watched the gulls circle a fishing boat in the near distance. He would never tell her why it all happened. Why He'd taken her husband before she could forgive him, before they could reconcile. Why He deprived her of the baby that had been growing inside of her.

Thirty years had passed, and He'd never explained to Elena Marino why her husband had suffered so and died such a horrible death. Yet, she loved the One who could have prevented it.

Kerry glared into the sky. "You're not into this whole explaining thing, are You?"

Would it have mattered? If God had explained, would it have mattered?

"Yes! Yes, it would have mattered! I would have known. Maybe I would have understood." But she wouldn't have developed faith.

She hadn't anyway.

Mrs. Marino didn't have answers to her heartaches. But what she had was a joy and a certainty that she was loved. That God loved her.

"I want that, God." More than anything, her heart craved the peace Mrs. Marino evidently possessed. "Stop being silent with me! Aren't You there? Don't You love me? Please! Love me too!"

She doubled over, hugging herself against the ache in her heart. "Please, God. Love me too. I can't take this anymore."

For long moments, she stayed that way, rocking herself with her head almost touching the ground, ridding herself of every bitter thought, every angry emotion. So many years of emptiness and pain spilled into the sand to be carried away by the tide now lapping at her knees.

Finally, Puddin came and nudged her. She wiped her eyes and buried her cheek in his fur. A gull flew toward them, screeching for attention. He eyed her as he got closer, and she laughed.

"You sent Jesus a dove, and to me, You send a seagull."

The bird flew over them and beyond. He landed on her house and picked at something on the porch. Probably a morsel Puddin had dropped.

She sighed when he took off again. But her heart was lighter. The April sun warmed her shoulders. This was the warmest day they'd had this spring. Or maybe with the cleansing of her heart, she no longer felt cold. She smiled. God's mercies didn't come only in the morning.

Quinn called out, and Puddin galloped gleefully toward him. Unusual for Quinn to let his presence be known before he was standing over her. Or maybe she'd just never heard him before. Shame. She hadn't had the pleasure of watching him walk toward her.

She shaded her eyes as she looked up at him. "Why aren't you on the boat? Not working today?"

"It's in for maintenance." He grabbed an old stick and threw it for Puddin. "What about you? Mrs. Marino give you the afternoon off?"

"Yes. Again. At this rate, I'm never going to finish my work here."

"I'm good with that." He sat beside her and took a moment to study her eyes. "You look different."

She felt different. Happy and alive for the first time in years. And loved. "Let's just say I had a burden lifted from my shoulders."

"Good to know." He knew what she meant. It was written in his smile; it beamed from his eyes. He knew. "Does this mean you'll be in church Sunday?"

Church? She hadn't been in years. She'd already discovered she didn't know the music anymore. Her long-untouched Bible sat on a dusty shelf back home, and she'd likely embarrass herself trying to find a Scripture passage. But at this moment, nothing sounded more inviting than returning to His house—her childhood home. "I wouldn't miss it."

"Good," he said. "Does it also mean you'll let me take you out to dinner?"

"Like, a date?"

Puddin returned with the stick and dropped it in front of Quinn, pawing the air in a direct order to keep playing.

Quinn complied. "Yeah, like a date."

"Where is this coming from?"

"Oh, c'mon. You have to know I've been wanting to take you out since you got here. I don't special-deliver pizza and Phoebe's shrimp creole to just anyone."

"Right. I thought you just wanted access to my dog."

"He's icing on the cake." He threw the stick again.

"Okay, so what stopped you?"

"You would've said no."

True. She would have. "And you don't think I'll say no now?"

He grinned. "I think my charm has a better chance of penetrating your defenses now that you've made your peace with the One who really matters."

Did she even have defenses now? How liberating not to feel obligated to keep a wall around herself. "And does Mr. Doctor-of-Theology understand the magnitude of that peace?"

"Yes. I understand precisely."

The seriousness in his tone stole the smile from her lips.

"We're human, Kerry. We sin. Everyone sins and falls short of the glory of God. I'm no different." He swept her hair from her eyes and cupped her cheek. "I know what it's like. I recognize it. That's why I wanted to help you."

"You did. You and Mrs. Marino. You did what God put you in my life to do. I didn't know why He brought me here." The roar of the waves, the salt on her lips, the sight of pelicans skimming the water and plunging for their catch. The beach. She'd always loved it before, and now she could love it again without remorse, without pain. "Now I do. And I'm so thankful."

Lillie Beth in Summer

Eva Marie Everson

To

Lillie Elma Dubberly Purvis
1903 – 2000
The great storyteller.
The woman who unknowingly taught me that
if you know your character,
she will tell you her story.

Chapter One

Allensville, Georgia
Summer 1968

Lillie Beth

Granny always said God doesn't shut a door but what he doesn't open a window. Only when Granny said it, she said, "God don't never shut a door, child, but what he don't open a winda."

I smile every time I think of it. Because Granny was right. And because I can't help but remember her words, the cadence of her speech. The way she'd nod her head once to let me know she meant business.

Granny always meant business.

Elma Frances McCall was really my husband's grandmother, but in my heart, the minute David introduced me to her in the front room of their two-story farmhouse that smelled of bacon grease and Pine Sol, she became my own. She embodied the embrace of all the love I'd never known. Not once in my sixteen years.

I met David in 1965 when he was on leave from basic training and before he left for Vietnam. That same week, I'd heard about a hangout in Allensville where young people could listen to music and where cute boys bought the girls co-colas poured over crushed ice and served up in Dixie cups. My cousin Denise and I decided this was the place for us to be. But when I asked my daddy if I could go, he gave a flat no. I could tell Mama didn't agree, but Mama never put up a fight when it came to anything Daddy said. Or did. Mama even kept her feelings of love toward me at a safe distance, lest Daddy cut them down.

For the first time in my life, I went against one of Daddy's direct orders, not caring one whit if I got caught. Not caring what he'd do with a tree switch he'd force me to cut myself when he found out.

Sometimes a girl's just gotta do what she's gotta do.

I got lucky though. Daddy didn't mind when I casually mentioned I wanted to spend the weekend at Denise's, and he never suspected Aunt Loreen would give us permission to head on over to Allensville's little juke joint not thirty minutes after Uncle Melvin had gone to bed.

The dancing had been exhilarating and the co-colas had been cold, but meeting David made me sweat under my armpits from the pure desire he put in me. We both knew, right away, that one night of dancing would never suit. Somehow, I managed to head back to Allensville a couple of times, making up lies and excuses for the thirteen-mile trip, just so I could see David.

David managed to sneak into my neck of the woods too. Then, not two weeks after we met, he took me to where Granny and he lived, and introduced me as his bride. I quivered under the stress of not being accepted almost as much as I feared what would happen when Daddy got word of me and David running off like we did.

"Your gonna take care of her, right Granny?" he asked in that front room. "While I'm gone over there fightin' Charlie?" He drew me close. "She can help gather the eggs … and she already knows how to can vegetables."

She stood there—all five-foot-one of her—wearing an old house dress covered by a floral bib apron, and a pair of stained white sneakers with gnawed-through holes on the sides. The calluses of her pinky toes peeked out and I wondered if they hurt much. Or maybe, if in the hardness, she felt nothing at all.

Granny patted David on his face with both hands, then wrapped me in a hug like nothing I'd ever felt in my whole life. "Course I will, son. Course I will. And what she don't know, I'll teach her."

And she had. She'd been mother and grandmother and best friend from that night on. Even when Daddy got word and came beating on the front door, demanding that I "git yourself in tha truck and I mean right now," Granny stood between him and me and told him in no uncertain terms that I was a McCall now and he had no rights over me. "A married woman," she said, shaking a twig broom at him that she'd used to sweep the side yard. "What's more, she could be, right now, a-carrying my great-grandchild and the child of my David and I ain't about to let anything happen to nary one of 'em while he's off serving our country. So you git on now."

She shooed Daddy away like he was an insect and, for some reason, Daddy backed down like he knew who was now the boss of me.

Or maybe he was too drunk to care. Daddy could be like that from time to time. What worried me most though was that Mama would get the brunt of Daddy's anger once he got another pint in him, and I told Granny so.

"Yore mama is just go'n have to take it or she's go'n have to leave. Up to her."

"She'll never leave," I said, because I knew it was true. Mama had kowtowed to Daddy so long, she had lost whatever little bit of herself she'd brought to the marriage seventeen years earlier.

"Ain't no sense in it," Granny concluded. "A man acting like he can treat a woman like a punching bag."

Even with such a short courtship, Granny never questioned whether I loved her grandson or if I'd make him a good wife once he got back from Nam. "Gracious," she told me one afternoon while we sat out on the back screened porch and snapped beans into large bowls resting between our knees. "I hardly knew David's pappy a week 'fore I told Mama he was the one for me."

"How long were you married?" I asked.

She thought a moment, then raised a thin finger, gnarled from years of farm labor, toward the ceiling and said, "Not near long enough, my girl. Not near long enough."

Over the course of our time waiting for David to come home, Granny filled our evenings with stories about what life had been like for her. Growing up poor. Marrying poor. Living happy.

She'd come into this world, she told me one evening while we snapped peas in the living room, in "Nineteen-hundred-and-ten. My daddy was a sharecropper, just like my Carson started off to being. Mama worked just as hard beside him. Had seven kids—three died before the age of five, you know—and at some point they took in Mama's sister's young-uns after she passed."

"How many young-uns?"

Granny smiled. "Aint Petals left us another five mouths to feed." She held up a bean. "But we all worked, so that made up for it." She snapped off the ends, tossed them in the sack propped up on the floor between us, then popped the bean into three perfectly-sized pieces. "My whole life I've done this. Cain't remember a time when I didn't." She smiled. "But I'd rather do a week of snapping beans than a minute of shelling butterbeans, I'll tell you that much."

"Or cuttin' okra."

"Gracious, yes ..." Then Granny sighed. Looked around. "See this house," she said. "Carson worked hard, sometimes working more than one job to take care-a things. Saved his money. Bought this and the land that goes with it and even hired the sharecroppers what help us keep it going today." She shook her head. "But what with money being mostly tight and having to raise my son's boys without much help from their daddy, I couldn't do a whole lot with it."

I looked around at the simplicity of the room. The rag rugs, the little do-dads on the tables that David's daddy and mama had brought from their travels, and the sparse but serene artwork. Everything clean and put together. Compared to where I'd come from, Granny's house was a palace. "Looks all right to me," I said. "I got no complaints."

"I ain't got complaints either," Granny added. "But one of these days," she said, "I'm go'n stop putting things off, Lillie Beth. I'm go'n fix this place up a little. Put fresh paint on the wood. Some real carpets in the house. Maybe some wallpaper on the walls of the indoor bath." She looked at me. Winked. "Whatcha think?"

"I reckon so, Granny," I said with a laugh. "Whatever you say."

Chapter Two

Carson McCall was eleven years older than Granny, but she'd known him all her life. They'd gone to the same church. "But to Carson, I was just a little loud-mouthed child," she told me as she reveled in the story. Her eyes slid over to where I sat. "Till I turned fifteen and took on the shape of a woman." Granny sat back and sighed. Light from the sun slipping through the windows played with the salt-and-pepper pin curls that clung close to her head. "Oh, but he was good-looking." She resumed her bean snapping. "Then one day after church he comes up to me—we was having dinner on the grounds—and he started talking." Granny chuckled. "I will never forget the way he held his hat in his hand, running the brim of it over and over between his fingers. So nervous."

I laughed with her, all the while wishing I could have known the man David loved more than his own daddy.

"Then he started showing up at the house. Papa would set the courtin' candle on the table by the couch and say, 'Now when this here burns out, Carson, it'll be time for you to go on home.' And Carson and I would talk and the candle would burn and Mama would fret and then next thing I knew the candle was out and there went Carson into the yard and on his way to home."

"How long did Mr. Carson come over before you married?" I asked, wondering if they had me and David beat.

"A month. But I knew after a few days. He was my man right up till the good Lord took him away quick-like with lightning."

"Like Elijah," I said, marveling at the thought of walking among your crops one minute and being taken to Jesus in a bolt of lightning the next.

David's father—the only child Granny would have—was born a year after she and Mr. Carson married. Born breech too. "Nearly tore me to pieces," Granny said.

For this story, we sat on the back-porch steps shucking corn, the silks catching on the broken skin of my fingers and hanging like icicles from a tree in the dead of winter. Hard to shake off.

The bugs were out heavy that night too, so I blew the gnats and mosquitos away with my lower lip and tried to wipe the sweat from my brow with my upper arm so as not to interrupt the work. Hastening to get the job done so Granny and I could go inside, wash up, and find our places in the front room with a Mason jar full of sweet tea as reward. "Makes me never want to have a baby," I commented before I realized I'd spoken.

"Oh, you will," she told me. "My David will come home and you'll be anxious to give him a son." She nodded once before continuing with her memory. "Even as difficult a birth as it was, I wanted to give Carson a whole house full of children. But Doc told me I couldn't have any more. Told Carson in no uncertain terms that he'd best mind his P's and Q's, if you know what I mean."

I didn't, but I refrained from saying so. What I knew about the birds and the bees could be placed between our bedroom sheets one Friday night and David getting on a bus at the Allensville Bus Depot on Sunday. But I figured I had the whole rest of my life to find out once my husband came home.

"Course, Carson spoilt my boy something fierce. And maybe I did too. Wanting more for him than a life breaking your back on a farm." Shadows of sadness crossed the deep lines of her face. "I reckon I only have myself to blame for the way he turned out."

I'd heard all about David's daddy from David the second time we met up in Allensville. "He's a free-thinker," he told me. "Never could stay in one place long enough to plant roots." He grinned at me, his nearly-shaved head glistening in the moon's glow. Deep dimples cut into the sides of his narrow face as he said, "Gosh, you're pretty."

It took a while—words spoken between peppermint-flavored kisses—to hear the whole story. About how David's daddy had left home at eighteen to find his way in the world, all the while hiding from Uncle Sam during World War II. Two years later, he showed back up at the farm with a voluptuous woman with painted lips and eyes and a sleeping nine-month-old swaddled in a blue blanket. "That was me," he said, blushing.

After only two weeks back home, David's daddy and mama took off again, leaving little David with Granny and Mr. Carson, only to show up a year later with another son, this one who they called Nick.

"That Nick," Granny always said, as if she wasn't quite sure what to do with him. Of course, none of us did. Nick being ... *Nick*. Hard-headed. Mean as a snake trapped between a hoe and a shed door, especially when he'd had one too many—which was usually the case. And far too handsome for any woman's own good.

Any woman but me, that is. Whatever it was women in town saw in Nick McCall went right over my head. I could admit he was a fine-looking man—maybe even better looking than David. Although not by much. Still, what Nick had in facial features and muscles, David made up for with his kindness. His gentleness. His no-drinking policy and his love for Jesus.

And, of course, the way he smiled every time he looked at me.

Chapter Three

James Gillespie, M. D.

I tossed the leather-bound Bible that had been like an appendage since early childhood on the coffee table, grimacing as my mother's china tea set rattled under the assault.

"*James Warren Gillespie.*" My sister Julia glowered at me. She reached for the Holy Writ and gathered it to herself. "You do *not* throw God's Word around in such a manner."

I pushed against the pillows of the costly sofa my mother had purchased against my father's protests and crossed my arms. "What do I have to do with God? What did *He* have to do with me? Or with Cherilyn as she lay in that hospital bed fighting for her life?" I dared to widen my eyes at her. "Answer me that."

An arched brow rose a fraction as my sister's usually kind expression turned disciplinary. "Jim." She reached over and grabbed my hand, her voice softer than the warnings of her eyes. "Jim," she said again, her face now growing soft. "I know you're hurting. I do. And I understand your anger. But you have to be careful. You're angry at *God*." She shook her perfectly coiffed head. Not a hair moved. "I think that's not allowed. Especially in our circles."

Wondering if my sister's last words were an attempt at humor, I straightened, then reached into my coat pocket, pulled out a letter, and handed it to her without a word.

"What's this?"

"Read it."

She stared at the envelope. "Allensville, Georgia. Who do we know in Allensville?"

"*We* don't know a soul there."

"Then who is Dr. Lester Paul?"

I gestured to the envelope, still unopened between her fingers. "Read it."

I couldn't help but note her tremble as she removed the tri-folded piece of onionskin paper as if, somehow, she instinctively knew that whatever lay within would change things. Twins have a way of doing that, even fraternal twins. Such a thing—telepathic, she called it—had connected us since birth ... probably always would, especially if Julia had her way about it.

"Am I going to be happy about this?" she asked.

"Don't you know?" I challenged.

Julia opened the letter fully and, upon reading the first lines, gasped. "Jim."

"I'm taking the position."

Julia's eyes, a mesmerizing shade of gray, found mine. "Have you told Mother?"

I wanted to smile but refrained. Never mind telling our father. Our father rolled with every punch life offered. But our mother ... well, she was another story altogether. Everything to her was about "how it appeared." While Julia and I both tended to be like our father in character, Julia had the tiniest "smidgen"—as she put it—of Eugenia Gillespie's coursing through her blood.

I shook my head. "Not yet." I took the letter and re-read the words I'd nearly memorized. "I want you to go with me," I said. "Dr. Paul has already found us a house to rent—close to the office—"

"Go *with* you? Why would I—?"

I folded the letter and slid it back into the envelope. "Because you're my sister," I said. "And you know how to cook. I'm thinking that would work well for me. Besides, what's holding you here?" I glanced around the opulence of our parents' formal living room with its perfect order and modern style.

Julia smiled at me and I smiled back. "Mother, for one. And, of course, Daddy."

"Mother has her social clubs and the church and our father to contend with. You and I both know she'll be fine. Dad will—well, I believe Dad will want what's best for us. He always has." I stuffed the envelope back into my pocket.

"And you think leaving home and moving to this ... *Allensville* ... is what's best."

"I can't stay here so close to where I—to where we—I can't, Julia. I need to get away. Start over. See if I can make some sense of this world."

"But why—where is this place?"

"Near Savannah. Granted, I've never heard of it either, but from what Dr. Paul has told me, the town has a lot of charm."

"And outside of town?"

I pretended to straighten the tie I wasn't wearing. "Fine farm folk, according to the good doctor. The kind that pay you with a—and I quote—mess of peas or a plucked chicken, ready for the pan." I leaned over, my hands outstretched in a plea. "Look, Jules. What are you doing here but waiting for Evan to return from his duty to the good ole U.S. of A.? Hmm?"

My sister's eyes filled with tears and I immediately regretted mentioning her husband's absence. "I suppose."

I grabbed her hands again. "Besides. I'll need you to take care of me and, you know, cook those peas and fry that chicken."

Julia slid her hands from mine, then slapped at them. "Stop it." She blew a tiny breath from between pink-tinted lips. "All right. I'll go." She laughed hard then, as if something pent up had been released.

I felt it too. The start of something bigger than ourselves.

"When do we leave?"

"In a week. I told Dr. Paul we'd be there right after the Fourth's celebrations."

"Can't miss those."

"No."

"Mother would have an even bigger fit …"

Chapter Four

Lillie Beth

David never saw much of his mama and daddy. They breezed in whenever the tide turned. Whenever they needed some place to land, so to speak. And—as David told me in the quiet of our bedroom at the top of the stairs—when the tide turned and they left, they didn't bother giving a forwarding address.

"I'm not even sure *they* knew where they were heading." He laced our fingers together as we lay side by side on the sagging mattress, then held our hands up so we could see our union. "Not like us. Once I get back from that mess over there in Nam, Lillie Beth, I'll make a good life for the two of us." He raised our hands to his lips and kissed mine along the knuckles. "I promise."

But that promise would never be. Near 'bout a year after David left for his tour of duty, two men dressed in dark uniforms visited the house, asking for Mrs. David McCall. When I couldn't stop screaming, Granny came up behind me. Sensed what those men wanted. What they'd come to say standing out there on the front porch on the other side of the threshold to our home. They had taken their hats off, tucked them under their left arms, stared at me straightaway and asked again, "Are *you* Mrs. David McCall?"

Granny didn't give me a chance to answer. She demanded to know what this was all about. Instead of answering her question, they asked if she was Mrs. Carson McCall.

"Private David McCall's grandmother?" the taller of the two added.

Granny stifled a gasp, then squared her shoulders and said, "I reckon you men are here to tell me my boy has died over yonder."

"Yes, ma'am," he answered, his eyes holding neither sympathy nor the kind of cold that comes from telling folks their loved ones have died too many times.

We were given condolences and told that, soon, we'd receive information about David's body being flown back. And then, with a turn of the heel, the men walked off the porch and got into a car so shiny and long I thought, for one strange minute, that it must be some kind of wonderful to ride in something so luxurious.

Granny and I cried a lot that night. Granny cried because "David died in that awful jungle without his loved ones" and I cried mostly because Granny's grief seemed bigger than her. It seemed to take over the whole of her and, in doing so, the whole of me too.

Not that I didn't miss him something awful, especially as the days and weeks and months went on. How I could miss a man so much who I'd hardly known struck me as odd, but I did and that was a fact.

But that night, I had other things to concern myself with. Bigger things. I worried that Granny would send me back to Daddy and Mama's house—a place I hardly ever visited.

And that Daddy would finally get to cut that switch.

And then I prayed hard—prayed like I'd heard Granny pray in the mornings and at night before we went to bed and before we put a spoonful of food in our mouths. I even said "Sweet Lord Jesus" like she did. I prayed that Granny would see fit to let me stay with her. That her heart wouldn't stop loving me because my husband's heart had stopped beating.

The next morning, as if some little bird had flown three farms over and told Nick that death had come knocking on our door, he showed up to the house. Granny told him straight up that his big brother had died over in the war, serving our country. And for the first time since I'd known him, Nick looked like the wind had been knocked clean out of his lungs. He stumbled a step or two until his backside rested against Granny's spotless Formica counter. Then he rubbed his forehead and said, "Did they say where? Or what done happened?"

"No," Granny said. "And I didn't ask. Don't matter none no ways. He's gone and that's all there is to it."

I thought then to get a glass of iced tea for my brother-in-law. That it would be the Christian thing to do. But when I walked it from the counter to where he stood and said, "Here, Nick," real soft like, his head popped up and his eyes glared as though I'd brought him a sidewinder.

"What is *she* still doing here?" he asked Granny.

Granny sat at the old wood table that weighed more'n me and Granny put together. She slammed her hand down hard on it. "Don't you start this," she told him.

Nick straightened, shoved his hands in his pockets, and said, "She don't belong here. She's a nobody from nowhere. Just some little bumpkin David met at a dance and drug in and said, 'Take care of her till I come back.'" I gasped at the cruelty of his words, and he turned to me. "Well, now he ain't coming back, you hear?"

Granny slammed her hand on the table again, gaining Nick's attention while

I ran to the table and collapsed in the nearest chair. I buried my face in my hands and sobbed for all it was worth, scared out of my mind that all my fears would become a reality. "Now you listen, boy," Granny ordered. "I love you to the whole depth of my being, worthless though you may be right now. But this child is our family now. I won't have you talking *to* her or *about* her like she's white trash. She ain't. She's David's widda and this here is her proper place. You hear me?"

Nick didn't answer at first and I kept right on crying, having folded my arms and rested them on the table. Drool and snot ran from my mouth and nose like a child's, but I didn't make no nevermind about it. I didn't even care that Nick hated me so much he wanted to send me packing the minute he found out about David.

The only thing that meant anything to me right then was that Granny loved me and she didn't want me to go. That she had taken me in as her own. For good.

And so, two years went by. Me living right there with Granny. Me and her, keeping house side by side … until the hot summer morning in July when I had to go for the doctor.

Chapter Five

James Gillespie, M. D.

"Where's Dr. Paul?"

The young woman stared at me from under the dim front porch light, which cast an angelic shimmer to her white-blond hair. Her eyes—the clearest blue I'd ever seen—were wide with fear.

I pushed the screen toward her, my left hand still holding a cloth I'd used to dry my coffee cup only moments before. "I'm Dr. Gillespie. I work with Dr. Paul. Won't you come in?"

She took a tentative step before stopping a foot from me, giving me a chance to see her a tad more clearly. She wore a simple house dress—baby green in color—and flat black shoes, and her hands clutched the straps of a worn purse. Even in the half-light, I noticed a wedding band circling her left ring finger. "I need to see Dr. Paul," she said, her voice anxious. "Real quick-like."

"He should be here any minute now." I nodded at her. "Please. Won't you come in?"

"It's awful early, I know," the young woman said as she passed by me to enter the front door of the old house Dr. Paul both lived and worked in. I caught a whiff of cherry and almond, recognizing it immediately. My mother swore by Jergens, even when my father's bank account could afford costlier lotions. "I don't usually come to the front door like this," she said. "But I couldn't wait until Dr. Paul opened his back door for business."

She stood in the loveliness of Dr. Paul's living room—a room he had done little to nothing with, he told Julia and me after we arrived, since the passing of his wife more than a decade earlier. A room Julia had taken to right away, polishing the large pieces of furniture and dusting away cobwebs from china bric-a-brac and thick draperies. A room that now seemed to dwarf the woman-child standing three steps on the inside.

"I'm Dr. Gillespie," I said again, closing the heavy wood and beveled glass door shut. "And you are?"

The young woman tucked her chin in. "Name's Lillie Beth. Lillie Beth

McCall." Trembling fingers reached up to brush away an errant white-blond hair from her cheek.

"Lillie Beth," I said, keeping my voice calm as I urged her toward the sofa. "Tell me how I may be of assistance to you."

"Granny—my husband's grandmother—is real sick. Took to coughing bad again in the night." She clutched at her purse strap until I thought it would break. "I've tried everything I know to do, but nothing is helping this time. And Dr. Paul said that—"

I smiled at her, hoping she would respond in kind. Relax. But my efforts were without reward. "Dr. Paul went out for his morning walk," I said. "He likes to leave and get back early."

"Before the sun comes up good," she added.

"That's right." I glanced at my watch. "I'd say within fifteen minutes or so. I was about to pour myself some coffee." I held up the cup. "Can I make one for you too?"

"I wouldn't want to put you out any," Lillie Beth said, her voice whisper soft.

"It's not a bother at all." I smiled again for good measure, then stood. "I'll be right back."

"Oh." She stood. "I can help. I don't expect no one to wait on me."

We walked to Dr. Paul's living quarters where a large kitchen stretched across the back-left corner of the house. Lillie Beth placed her purse on the table before crossing over to the cabinet where Dr. Paul kept his odd collection of coffee cups. She opened it as if by habit, then turned toward where I stood, cup in hand. "You know this kitchen," I said more than asked.

Her naturally pink lips broke into a smile, showing a mouth slightly too full of teeth. "I come over and help Dr. Paul from time to time." She took the percolator in hand and poured first a cup for me and then one for herself.

"I've been here two weeks now," I said before taking a quick sip of the black brew. "Dr. Paul hasn't mentioned you, I'm afraid."

A natural blush kissed her cheeks, made pinker by the pale of her skin. "He wouldn't," she said simply. She brought the cup to her lips. Swallowed.

"Would you like cream?" I asked. "Sugar?"

She shook her head. "No. I take it black."

"Tell me," I encouraged as I pulled a chair from the table and lowered myself into it, my eyes never leaving her, "what you've done for your grandmother."

She sat opposite me. Took another sip of her coffee. "I started off giving her honey, but when it didn't seem to help much, I made her a cup of peppermint tea with ginger root."

In the time since I'd arrived in Allensville, I'd been exposed to a handful of home remedies, most of them explained to me by Dr. Paul. This one I recognized right away. "So her cough is productive..."

Lillie Beth pursed her lips and blinked. "I don't know what that means."

I smiled again, not wanting her to feel stupid in any way. "She's coughing up phlegm?"

"Yes," she said with a nod. "A lot of it. Some with blood in it."

I tried not to jerk at the mention of blood, but instincts being what they were... "Did the tea help?"

She nodded again. "But then around four o'clock it got worse."

"Fever?"

"Yes. Don't know how much, but she's shivering something fierce even though she's hot to the touch. I'm keeping her covered up, but—"

The door leading from the kitchen to a screened back porch opened and Dr. Paul stepped in, smiling. "Well," he drawled, placing his knotty walking stick next to the door. "My lovely Lillie Beth. I thought that was your bicycle I saw laying against the fence. To what do we owe this pleasure?"

It dawned on me then that I hadn't seen a car in the driveway earlier. But I hadn't seen a bicycle either. Lillie Beth obviously knew her way around more than Lester Paul's home and office.

She stood. "Dr. Paul," she nearly stammered. "I'm so glad you're here."

The good doctor—a man who took up nearly any room he graced with his robust presence—busied himself by preparing a cup of coffee. Lillie Beth walked to the Frigidaire, opened it, took out the bottle of milk I'd brought in from the back porch earlier, and handed it to him. "Miss Elma?" He poured a dollop of milk, then handed the bottle back to her.

"She's starting to talk to folks," she said. "Mr. Carson and her mama and daddy and even to David. I think it's the fever."

Dr. Paul nodded. "Hmmm..." He took a long swallow of his coffee before placing the cup on the counter. "Dr. Gillespie," he said to me. "I think it's time I introduced you to Mrs. Elma McCall."

I stood, glancing at my half-consumed coffee I knew I'd wish I'd finished before the morning was over. "Yes sir."

Dr. Paul gave a half smile to me and the woman-child. "I saw your car 'round back, Jim. What's say we take it out to the country a-ways."

Chapter Six

I grabbed my medical bag, hat, and jacket from the tiny closet of an office I'd been assigned, before meeting Dr. Paul and Lillie Beth in the back side yard where my employer insisted I park. "Gives more room for the patients," he'd told me. "You park in the back and they'll park over there under the shade trees."

After I'd skipped down the steps and onto the thick grass, I noticed that the good doctor and the young Mrs. McCall stood a good six feet away from the Lincoln I'd purchased shortly before moving to Allensville.

"Come on now, darlin'," Dr. Paul urged her. He opened a door and she slid in as though scared to death of being caught riding with two men. "Ain't a thing in this world to be afraid of," Dr. Paul said as he closed the door. He then threw his medical bag into the car before plopping himself in the front passenger's seat. I bit back a smile at the way my car rocked under his weight.

We drove through town in relative quiet with the front windows down, which let in a pleasant breeze. Occasionally Dr. Paul gave instructions like, "Turn right up there by the old Peterson place," which led to me reminding him that I didn't know the old Peterson place from any other place in town. "Oh, that's right," he said, as he always did. "Well, you'll learn."

I glanced in the rearview mirror a couple of times, especially as we drove farther into the country, past acres of farmland dotted with fat cows and dark green cornstalks stretching taller than a man. The aroma of hay and manure wafted through occasionally, and I wrinkled my nose against it, wondering how "farm folk," as Dr. Paul called them, ever accustomed themselves to the odor.

The car rolled on, and for the life of me, I couldn't imagine the young woman in my back seat riding her bike this far, and in a housedress, of all things. I tried to imagine Julia doing such a thing—even in the direst of situations—or Cherilyn, but couldn't. I also noticed the way Lillie Beth, whose hair had come partially undone from a loose chignon to tickle her cheeks, looked down as though she were admiring the seat, which led me to wonder if she'd ever been in a car at all.

Or, at the very most, one of this caliber.

Finally, Dr. Paul cleared this throat to speak but not before Lillie Beth slid up and pointed. "Right yonder. To the left there. That little dirt road."

The road was barely wide enough for my car—packed-hard Georgia red clay with deep ruts and a lone bike imprinted track. I figured all I had to do was follow the track, but Lillie Beth lingered now with her arms resting along the backrest of the front seat, the warmth of her breath blowing against my cheek. "One more left turn," she said. "Right up there. Past those railroad tracks."

My car bobbed and bounced along the ruts until we reached a clearing in the grassy foliage that stretched high enough to cut off nearly all sunlight. I turned left and followed my nose until we came to another clearing, this one expansive and sporting a white clapboard two-story farmhouse standing proudly beneath a canopy of oaks. Beyond it, over to the right, stood an unpainted barn and lean-to that looked as though it had seen better days. And beyond that, as far as my eyes could see, row upon row of vegetables stretched outward and upward, sporting glossy green leaves.

Lillie Beth jumped out of the back seat before I had time to shift the car to Park. "Hold on," Dr. Paul said to me.

"Sir?" I watched the young woman run up the front porch steps, then disappear into the house.

"First, let's roll these windows up if you don't want a car full of gnats when we get back in. Second, I want to warn you."

I instantly went to work turning the window crank and he did the same. "Warn me?"

"Elma McCall, I believe, is not too long for this world." His jaw went slack for a moment before he continued. "I've near about begged her to come into town and let me run some tests on her, but she won't hear of it."

"What is your diagnosis? Or guess at one?"

"Emphysema, perhaps. Cancer? Hard to say without the tests. But her lungs seem to be filling up right regular and she's losing weight. Loss of energy, although sometimes she does all right."

"She's quite elderly, then."

"She's not even sixty, if my calculations are right." Dr. Paul offered a weak smile. "Miss Elma never was one to tell her age, but I reckon I got at least a decade on her."

Sweat beaded along my neck and spilled down my back. "But you're her doc—"

Dr. Paul opened his car door. "Come on," he said, heaving himself out. I did the same to find him staring at me from across the car's roof, shining and baking already in the morning sun. "I have no idea what we're about to walk into, but I'll tell you this much … Miss Elma's had a hard life. Life like hers can wear a woman down before her time." He gave me a knowing look. "Something you wouldn't know anything about, son. Not me either, for that matter. At least not like this." He looked over his shoulder at the house, then back at me. "Way I see it is this—Miss Elma's holding on for something, and when that something comes, she's already got it set in her mind that she's going to give up the ghost and go on home to Jesus. Not a moment before and not a moment after." He slammed the door shut. "Our job is to make her comfortable until she does."

I hurried beside the man I'd come to admire, not only for his gentlemanly ways outside of the practice, but for his genuine caring for every patient, no matter their lot in life. "Dr. Paul," I said when I reached him. "Lillie Beth—the young Mrs. McCall—said something about her grandmother seeing folks?"

"The dead," he told me, his tone matter-of-fact. "That's why I'm thinking her time is closing in." He had lowered his voice as we climbed the steps. "I've seen it dozens and dozens of times." We stopped on the porch. "The dying start talking to those who have already departed before them. They *see* them, don't you know."

"No, I—"

"Ever lose a patient, Dr. Gillespie?"

"Of course, sir."

"Ever stay with the dying, right up to the end?"

Only one, I thought. But I said, "Well, no. I usually get called in just before— and typically not—" I had no idea how to say that I'd never met a soul in all my days who saw dead people and then died shortly after without sounding condescending.

Dr. Paul slapped my shoulder. "Come on, son. We need to get in to see our patient."

He reached for the bowing screen door's handle that may have, at one time, been brass. "Dr. Paul," I said, stopping him again. "One more thing, sir." I looked into the interior of the house—bright, clean, and sparsely furnished—then back at him. His bushy white brow had formed a peak in the center as he waited for my question. "Lillie Beth ... how old is *she*?"

"Eighteen, I 'spect." He shook his head. "And if she's anything like Miss Elma, don't expect her to answer if you ask."

If God had so much as sent a puff of His breath down on the little farmhouse in Allensville, it would have sent me over the edge of the porch. Eighteen years old. Married ...

I wouldn't have pegged her as being a day over sixteen.

Chapter Seven

Lillie Beth

Granny's bedroom set off from the kitchen. At one time, it was the dining room, but she'd turned it into her bedroom after Mr. Carson died. She told me she decided right away that she didn't want to climb the stairs alone at night only to sleep in a bed all by herself. Stepping out of the kitchen and into the dining room felt like camping out. I suppose she'd told me this over bean snapping or corn shucking. Or maybe over scrubbing the floors to keep them fit to walk on. Granny had always been proud of her floors.

"Granny," I said, kneeling at her bedside. "I'm back."

Granny opened her mouth to speak, but a fit took over and she coughed instead. After holding her up to keep her from strangling, I grabbed for a low stack of washcloths I'd left on the bedside table and wiped the phlegm from her mouth. "There now," I said as I eased onto the bed beside her and laid her head back onto a mound of flattened feather pillows. "Let me get one of these rags dipped into some cool water for you."

"What took you so long?" Her voice came out with a whispery croak.

I slid off the bed and back onto my knees. Drew her hand into mine. Felt the heat rise out of it. "I had to ride my bike, Granny," I reminded her. "It's a far piece. And then Dr. Paul wasn't home right away, but he has a new doctor—"

"Where is Dr. Paul, sweet child?"

"I'm right here, Miss Elma," Dr. Paul's voice sang out from the open doorway.

I peered over my shoulder. Dr. Gillespie stood directly behind Dr. Paul. I could see him clear as a bell, read the expression on his face, what with him being such a tall man. He had removed his hat, so I could see his eyes. See the concern in what looked to me like puppy-dog eyes. He knew what I suspected; what had hold of Granny was more than a bad summer cold.

"Lillie Beth, darlin'," Dr. Paul said. "Why don't you open up all the windows in the house? Let some of the summer breeze in."

I stood. "But Granny might get chilled," I said, crossing to him. "She shivered something fierce last night."

Dr. Paul patted my cheek with a callused hand. Granny always said a good doctor didn't need to have such rough hands, but Dr. Paul once told me how much he loved to garden, so I figured that was the cause of it. "I don't think we're in any danger," he said.

I showed him the washcloth in my hand. "I was going to wet this cloth—"

He took it from me. "I'll take care-a that." Then he stepped around me. "Now, Miss Elma, let me see how you're doing. Dr. Gillespie, why don't you help Lillie Beth with the window opening? Let's get a good cross breeze in the house."

Dr. Gillespie's puppy eyes met mine and I nodded. "Let's start here in the kitchen," I said before looking again at the frail figure lying on the bed. "I'll be right back, Granny."

Dr. Gillespie still held his doctoring bag in one hand, his suit coat and hat in the other. "You can put your bag on the table over yonder." I reached for his coat. "I'll hang this over one of the chairs so it don't get wrinkled."

"Then I guess I'll start with the windows over the sink," he said, almost as though he didn't know what else to say.

"And I'll go into the living room up front. Won't take two of us to open the windows in here."

A minute later he joined me. He'd loosened his tie and his white short-sleeved shirt didn't appear to be as neatly tucked into the waistband of his pants as it had earlier. I felt warmth cross my cheeks—not from the heat inside the house neither. This came from looking at a fine specimen of the opposite sex and noting things like shirtwaists and neck ties.

I didn't blame myself any. No, siree-bob. Dr. Gillespie was a mite older than me, no doubt. But I was a woman, fully growed, and my husband had been gone or dead for two years already. And besides, Granny kept saying it was time for me to start looking. To think about a husband and children of my own. We'd even fussed about it a time or two. Leaving her to find someone else didn't suit, I told her. But she told me she prayed about it every night, asking that the Lord would send me a man. A good man. Then she said she could see him in her spirit every time she prayed.

"I reckon it has gotten a tad balmy in here," I said as I heaved one of the windows up. Immediately a breeze shot through the screens and blew annoying curls away from my face.

Dr. Gillespie laughed a little as he raised one of the windows on the south side of the house. "I'd say so, yes." He puffed out a tiny breath of air, and I knew he felt the cool morning air as I had. Only he didn't have any undisciplined curls for it to muss.

"Should we open the windows upstairs too?" I asked as he took care of the other southside window.

"Heat rises," he said. "So I'd say yes."

I went straight for the staircase off the foyer, him right behind me. We reached my room first, which only had two windows and both facing west. The few evenings David and I had loved each other in this room had been spent in the glow of a setting sun. We'd watched it send its light over the fields, turning them first gold and then dark amber. Then, finally, gray to black.

"This here's my room," I said, walking straight for the farthest window. "If you'll get that one, I'll get this one."

Dr. Gillespie pushed back the sheers. "If you don't mind my asking," he said with a grunt as he pushed the window up, "where is your husband?"

From outside, I heard the chickens clucking, reminding me they were past ready to be turned out into the yard. I turned to face the man standing in my bedroom. "My husband?"

"You're married," he said, nodding toward my left hand.

"Oh." I held it out, almost as if I needed to see the evidence myself.

"Why didn't your husband come to get Dr. Paul? Leave you with his grandmother?" He splayed his own hands on narrow hips, as though he challenged my good sense.

"My husband is buried over yonder in the churchyard," I said, noting the direction of the church with a jerk of my head.

He blushed hard and swift, then looked at the floor where Granny and I had scattered the homemade rag rugs we'd made over the three years since I'd been living with her.

"I'm sorry," he said. "Truly." Then his eyes—gray like steel—returned to mine. "Do you mind, then, if I ask what happened?"

"Nam."

"I'm sorry," he said again.

I brushed past him, heading for the two other bedrooms. "Don't be," I told him. "Wasn't you who pulled the trigger."

Chapter Eight

James Gillespie, M. D.

For the second time in only a short while, I could have been knocked over by the mere utterance of words. These, not spoken unkindly. Or even with regret. More as if this was simply the way of it. She had been married. Her husband went to Vietnam. He was killed.

End of the story.

I followed the girl into the second bedroom—a room with only a twin bed, nightstand, and a dresser with freestanding mirror hanging overhead. Unlike Lillie Beth's room, which boasted framed embroidered pieces, these walls were nearly void of any kind of artwork. "I'm sorry," I said for the third time.

Lillie Beth had her back to me as she raised one of the two sheer-covered windows in the room. I immediately ambled over to the second one and slid the two-paned window up.

The woman-child crossed her arms as she looked at me. "No. I'm sorry. I don't know why I got sassy with you. I reckon—" She shook her head as though unsure what else to say.

"When did he die?" I asked. A light breeze billowed the sheer, startling me as it brushed across my arm.

"It's the angel's wings," she said, ignoring my question and focusing on the drapes instead. She nodded once toward the sheer, which had returned to lay in tranquil waves from the top of the window to the floor. "Whenever the sheers do like that, it's angel's wings." Another breeze brought the sheer out, then just as quickly eased it back. "See there," Lillie Beth said. "That was another angel coming in." She crossed over to me, slid her arm under the white sheer, and extended it. "The angel's wings catch the fabric here, and that's what causes it to puff out like it done. That's how God lets you know He's sent someone to watch over you."

I wanted to correct her. On so many levels, I wanted to correct her. There were no angels coming through the curtains, I wanted to say. And if they did, it wasn't God who sent them. Because why would He? The way I figured it,

God was too busy to care enough to send them or anyone else. Or perhaps too apathetic. Hadn't she learned that much from losing her husband?

I also wanted to correct her grammar, though I figured that to be a moot point. What difference did it make if she said "did" or "done"? What difference did it make, for that matter, if she believed in angels sent from God? After today, there was as good a chance I'd come only into rare contact with her as there was that I'd ever see her again at all.

Instead, I replied, "I see."

Her eyes became hooded. Knowing. "You don't believe that."

"No."

She tipped her head quizzically. "Do you believe in the Almighty?"

"Yes," I said. Because believing *in* Him was not the issue. *Believing* Him, however …

"Hmm," she said, then walked past me again, leaving me in a waft of Jergens-scented air.

Again, I followed her, this time into another bedroom, more like the one she slept in. She stood on the opposite side of an unpainted wrought-iron bed covered in a handmade quilt. A glance around the room showed a couple of inexpensive paintings—the kind some folks buy at a five-and-dime. But there was also a work of cross-stitch, which declared the marriage of a Gabe McCall to a woman named Arlene Butterfield.

I walked over to examine it—the dates, mostly—then said, "Anyone you know?"

Lillie Beth heaved the only window in the room up. "Not really. They're my husband's parents." She stepped over to a chest of drawers that looked like it went with the dresser in the other room and picked up a framed black-and-white photograph. "This here's them."

I met her there, took the photo from her, and studied it. They were a handsome couple—the man dark-haired and dimpled, the woman a tad too done-up to my liking. I'd always preferred a more natural look. No heavy lines in a woman's makeup or her dress. A woman such as my late wife had been—all sun-kissed and freckled and able to throw on a simple housedress and look as though she were about to have tea with the Queen of England. The only jewelry Cherilyn ever wore was a single strand of pearls with tiny studs and a bracelet that matched. A set her father had given her on her sixteenth birthday.

And, of course, the gold band I'd slipped on her finger the day of our wedding. "No engagement ring," she'd said adamantly when we'd begun to speak of forever. "I'm not an engagement ring kind of girl."

A swift glance at Lillie Beth's left hand told me she wasn't either. "They don't live here, I take it?" I asked, forcing myself away from the memory of my wife's look. Her voice.

Lillie Beth took the photo and placed it back on the dresser. "No. But when they come, this is their room." She shrugged one shoulder. "But they don't come often. I'm not even sure they know about David."

"David ..." The same name as one of the "folks" she'd said Mrs. McCall had "seen."

"My husband."

"Oh. How could they—" I stopped. This was none of my business. Which was true enough. Yet for some unexplainable reason, I wanted to know everything about this young woman. This child in grown-up clothes who sported the thinnest white-gold wedding band I'd ever seen.

"August the twenty-second, nineteen-hundred-and-sixty-six."

"What?"

"That's when my husband got killed over there by Charlie." She nodded once, then added, "I reckon we'd best get on downstairs and see what Dr. Paul has to say about Granny."

Dr. Paul met us at the foot of the stairs, and I wondered if he had been about to come up to see what caused us to linger. He placed his hands on Lillie Beth's shoulders, resting them there in a way I wondered if I ever could. "Now, darlin'," he said. "I want you to take in what I'm about to say to you."

Lillie Beth stood on the bottom step. Without a word, she stepped onto the landing, slid her arms around Dr. Paul, and laid her cheek against his barreled chest as though he were her grandfather instead of the old family doctor. Something I'd never seen before. Not in the sterile environment I'd both grown up in and had worked within. "She's not long for this world, is she?" Lillie Beth asked.

"No, darlin'. I'm afraid not. Now, I've given her something to help her rest and I've given her something to help with the fever." He squeezed her shoulders, then drew her back. "Lillie Beth, I'm going to need you to be strong. Both for me and for Miss Elma."

Lillie Beth nodded.

"Miss Elma is sicker than she's been lettin' on to you. I've given her something to help, but tonight you'll need to keep vigil. Before we go, I'll show you what you need to do."

She nodded again, this time sending pools of tears down her cheeks.

"And no crying. Crying time is later. Not right now. Miss Elma sees you crying, she won't meet her sweet Jesus in a jovial mood. And can you imagine Miss Elma seeing Jesus for the first time in a bad mood?"

Her lips trembled and she forced a wobbled smile. "No sir." Then she raised her chin. "I need to get my bicycle."

"Lillie Beth, I don't want you worrying about your bike, now." Dr. Paul cupped her chin. "We'll get it back to you later on, won't we, Dr. Gillespie?" I nodded dumbly as he looked at me, still three steps up on the staircase. "Son," he added, "I'll need you to take me back to the office. There are patients we've got to see. Then I'll have you run me back out here later to check on things."

I came on down the stairs and walked around them, my mind jumbled. Could I—*would* I—be able to speak words of the hereafter to these people after Dr. Paul retired? Could I say what I didn't believe in such a way as though I did? "Just let me get my things."

Minutes later, we left Lillie Beth standing on the front porch, hugging herself with feet planted a foot apart. She looked as lost as she did a part of something. "Dear Lord," I said as I started the car, a "mess of fresh butterbeans" in a bag between Dr. Paul and me.

Although I wasn't sure if the prayer was for her ... or for me.

Chapter Nine

Dr. Paul and I worked together until noon, seeing our patients under the watchful eye of Mrs. Bunny Kelly, a woman in her mid-fifties who wore her platinum hair as short as a man's. Bunny—whom Dr. Paul called "Miss Bunny"—stood tall and willowy behind the receptionist's counter, serving as greeter, scheduler, and occasional nurse when Dr. Paul needed her. She was no-nonsense. No one bucked her, least of all Dr. Paul. Or me. I felt fairly certain even her husband took orders from her. I also knew I could trust her.

I left for home as soon as we'd finished seeing our 11:45 patient—a four-year-old boy scheduled for a T & A the following week in Savannah. "See you after lunch," I told Bunny.

"Tell Julia I said hello," she replied in a clipped voice.

I told her I would.

When I arrived home, Julia had lunch—a bologna sandwich sliced diagonally, potato salad, and slice of apple pie—sitting on the kitchen table. "What do you want to drink?" she asked as soon as I ambled in and tossed my hat onto the yellow laminate countertop. Julia had every window open, allowing the heavy scent of gardenias to waft in and fill the room.

"Milk," I answered.

"Butter or sweet?"

"Sweet." My sister knew I hated buttermilk, but she felt inclined to ask anyway. Mostly to sweetly aggravate.

I draped my suit coat over the back of a sparkled-red puffy-vinyl and chrome chair, one of six tucked under a Formica matte white table, then pulled it out and dropped into it.

Julia set a glass of ice-cold milk in front of me. "We're having fried chicken tonight. Sound okay?" She took her place across the table.

"Yeah." I bit into the sandwich, tangy with yellow mustard. Just the way I liked it. I looked at my sister, who closed her eyes in silent prayer over a lunch identical to mine.

When she opened them again, she frowned at me. "What's wrong?" she asked.

I stabbed at the potato salad with a short-pronged fork. "What do you mean?"

"Jim ..."

"Ahhh," I groaned in early defeat. Because what was the point, really? Julia was the last person I could keep anything from. That telepathic communication she so believed in had passed between us once again. "I can't get this patient we saw this morning out of my mind. No. Not the patient. I hardly saw the patient. Her granddaughter-in-law is the one."

Julia held a triangular half of her sandwich loosely between her fingertips. "The patient's *granddaughter*-in-law?"

I spent the next few minutes telling Julia about Lillie Beth, sharing with her what little I knew about the woman-child I'd met earlier. Telling her that something about the girl had gotten under my skin. Deep under.

"What kind of something?"

"Something about her innocence. Her youth. She's a child, really, but ... I don't know—how can I explain this—it's like an old soul lives inside of her and it knows something deeper than—"

Julia's perfectly tweezed brows drew together as she took several sips of milk. She swallowed and smiled. "An *old soul* you say?" She laughed lightly. Teasingly. "Oh, if Mother were here right now ..."

"Dr. Paul and I will go back out there later," I said, ignoring her jab while at the same time imagining Lillie Beth in my mother's parlor. The thought brought both a smile as well as fear and trembling. "So, I may not be home in time for fried chicken."

She stared at me, waiting until she had something to say. Then, "How old *is* she, really? Logically, if she's a granddaughter-in-law and her husband died in Vietnam, she can't be a *child*, Jim."

"No. She can't." I bit into my sandwich again, then swallowed. "Eighteen."

The perfect brows lifted. "Ah." She smiled, a tad too sweetly for my liking.

"Don't be ridiculous," I said.

"Whatever do you mean?" Our mother's "innocent voice" gene leaked out between the words.

"You know full well ..." I pointed my fork at her. "I simply found her to be ... interesting." I shoveled the fork into the disappearing mound of potato salad. "Eighteen and already a widow, Jules. Who *are* these people?"

"Which people, Jim? The people of Allensville?" Julia started to take another bite of her sandwich, then thought better of it. "Or the country folk? Because I find them all quite lovely. In fact, I'm feeling quite at home here." Julia took the bite, chewed, and swallowed. "I'm thinking that when Evan gets home to the

States, I should insist we settle here."

The idea made me smile. My sister and her husband, in the same town as where I'd set up my new practice. A place I'd grown to appreciate myself. Perhaps Evan and I could go into practice together ... "That would be nice," I said. "Have you told Mother?"

She raised her glass of milk. "Touché."

For some reason, then, the idea of Lillie Beth folding into the mix came to mind once again. And, right after the trembling, that made me smile even more.

I returned to the practice around 1:30, fully expecting the usual—Dr. Paul in an upstairs bedroom taking his afternoon nap and Bunny bustling behind the counter, preparing for the 2:00 appointment. Instead, she met me at the back door. "Dr. Paul got called out to the Cambys'."

"The Cambys?" I walked into the waiting area.

"Noraleen and Irwin Camby. She's two weeks overdue and the baby's so big he's already been scholarshiped by the University of Georgia."

"Are they headed to the hospital?"

"Irwin Camby won't *hear* of his wife giving birth in a hospital. Says all they want is your money."

"My gosh ..." I clutched my medical bag a little tighter. "Do I need to—"

"Dr. Paul said for you to stay here, see the afternoon patients, and then head out to Miss Elma's." Bunny walked around the counter, picked up a chart, and handed it to me. "Here's your first one."

I glanced at the unrecognized name written across the top. "He wants me to drive out to Miss Elma's? Will he meet me there?"

"He said if he can make it, he will." She laughed lightly. "What's that look about?"

"I, uh—I'm just wondering if—if you think that ..."

"Miss Elma will make it through the night?"

In truth, yes. The notion of Miss Elma being my first at-home death sent a chill through me. How would it be, I wondered, being in the house without Dr. Paul, tending to a woman who spoke to dead people ...

And another who believed angels floated between window sheers?

Chapter Ten

Lillie Beth

Granny had been restless most of the day. Sleeping off and on. And when she wasn't, she whispered to the folks in the room. Souls she could see but that I could not.

I sat in her favorite bentwood rocker, right next to the bed, keeping watch. I talked to her, even when I wasn't sure she could hear me. And I prayed. I prayed a lot, asking the good Lord not to take Granny. To leave her here with me. "I'll stay with her until I die," I said. "I'll take care of her, like David would-a wanted me to."

The thought of David made my heart heavy, especially when Granny insisted he stood beside me. "Can you see him, child?" she asked. "He's right there …" She pointed and I turned my chin, lifting my eyes slowly. In some ways, wanting to see my beloved. In others, terrified if I did. Would he be the same handsome man who'd gotten on the bus in Allensville or the bloodied, bullet-riddled soldier who'd died on the battlefield?

But when I looked fully … nothing and no one stood beside me. But I answered Granny anyway with, "I see him, Granny. I do."

Near about five o'clock, after I'd given Granny more of the medicine Dr. Paul had left with me and she'd gone on back to sleep, I stepped into the kitchen, turned on the oscillating fan Granny and me kept on the counter near the sink window, then set about to prepare myself some dinner. Maybe a little something for Granny, if she would eat. I expected that soon enough Dr. Paul and maybe even his young doctor friend would show up. Figuring they'd be a mite hungry, I decided to put on some extra.

During the hot summer months, Granny and I ate mostly vegetables—sliced tomatoes and cukes fresh from the garden, some potato salad, and a sweet salad. Knowing how much Dr. Paul liked my fried crookneck squash, I set about to preparing it, even though I didn't cotton to the thought of how heating the grease would warm up the kitchen.

After I took the last of crunchy oval-shaped slices out of the grease, I placed it on a plate covered by a paper towel to drain. I'd just put ice in one of the

Mason jar glasses when a light knock came to the front door. I wiped my hands on my apron before taking quick steps in slippered feet to the front door. My expectations of seeing Dr. Paul fell away as soon as I spied the young doctor standing on the other side of the sagging screen in his shirtsleeves, looking as out of place as a dog in church, but I smiled just the same. "Good evening, Dr. Gillespie," I greeted as I unlatched the door and pushed it open.

Dr. Gillespie stepped in. "Good evening, Lillie Beth. How's Mrs. McCall doing this evening?"

I crossed my arms. "It's been a long day. Be a longer night, I'm sure. But I done like Dr. Paul said. Been giving her the medicine and keeping watch." I shrugged. "It's all I know to do."

"It's all you can do."

I gave a nod. "That and praying the good Lord will spare her."

His eyes clouded, much in the same way they had when I'd told him about the angels.

"You don't believe He will," I said, fear filling my airway.

"Sometimes God does what God wants to do no matter what we ask," he answered.

I lifted my chin. "God *always* does what He sees fit."

Dr. Gillespie raised his doctoring bag. "May I see her?"

I nodded, then led the way to Granny's room off the kitchen. I kept my distance at the door, watching him as he leaned over her tiny form. He laid a hand on Granny's forehead, then checked her pulse. Finally, he placed the bag next to her on the bed, opened it, and pulled out the heart-listening thing Dr. Paul had once told me what was called a stethoscope.

Granny slept through all his goings-on, never moving. When Dr. Gillespie was done and he walked toward me, I said, "She's deep in, ain't she?"

He nodded. "She's still a little feverish. But the fact that she's sleeping peacefully is good right now. When did you last give her—"

"Right before you got here."

He looked at his watch, recording the time in his mind I reckon, then glanced over his shoulder. Back at me with a smile. "Glad to see the window's still open. Helps keep your grandmother's body temp from becoming too warm."

I turned and walked out, him on my heels. "Would you like some sweet tea?"

"That'd be nice."

I retrieved the glass I'd prepared earlier from the counter, then opened the Frigidaire where a pitcher of tea stood tall on the top shelf. "Where's Dr. Paul?"

"He was called away. A delivery."

I poured the tea, felt the cold of it through the glass, then placed it on the table. "Sit," I said, and he did. "Noraleen Camby's baby?" He looked at the glass as though he'd never seen a Mason jar, then gulped the tea down in three swallows, nodding all the while. "You must have been thirsty, Doctor," I noted. Not that it took much noting.

His eyes met mine. "I was. It gets hot up in Atlanta, but the heat in Allenstown is quite something."

I reckoned that explained his lack of coat or hat. "It's the added humidity, living so close to the creeks and the coast."

"Mmm ..."

"How about more tea then?"

He held the glass up. "I'd appreciate that."

I poured his drink, then set the pitcher on the table. "Help yourself. There's plenty of ice in the trays if what you've got there has already melted too much for your liking."

He nodded again, something he seemed pretty good at doing. "Something sure smells good," he said, eyeing the plate of squash.

"Fried squash. Would you like—"

He shook his head. Held up a hand. "I wouldn't want to bother."

I stepped to the cabinet and pulled out a plate, thankful the one on top had no chips. Granny'd be mortified if I served a guest on a chipped plate, especially a fine-looking doctor who bore no wedding ring.

Ah, Granny ... I could hear what she'd say as plain as day, even over the whirring of the oscillating fan on the countertop: "He's a fine specimen of the male species, Lillie Beth. Your mourning time is far over, and I'm sure my David appreciates what you've done. Now go pinch your cheeks and remember to smile pretty ..."

"No bother," I said quickly. I removed a couple of tomatoes and two squatty cukes from the fridge, then walked to the sink and set the vegetables within the porcelain depth. "How long are you planning to stay?" I turned on the water and began to washing.

"Dr. Paul didn't say," he answered. "If I feel your grandmother's condition stables, I could go—"

I glanced over my shoulder as I turned off the water. "No," I said with a smile, then shook the water from the vegetables. "I mean how long are you staying here in Allenstown?"

The young doctor pinked, and I knew it wasn't from the heat in the kitchen. He took another swallow of tea, then added more to his glass. "Sorry," he stammered. "I'm Dr. Paul's replacement."

I turned fully, my hands full of vegetables, and water dripping to the floor.

"What do you mean?"

Dr. Gillespie loosened his tie. A line of sweat beaded along his brow. "I thought you knew. Dr. Paul is retiring."

"Retiring?" I placed the cukes and tomatoes on the table, then went in search of the cutting board and a sharp knife. "I didn't know doctors retired."

He chuckled. "What did you think? We work until we die?"

Now it was my turn to pink. I'd not wanted him to feel stupid, but here I was ... "I guess I never thought about it much. Dr. Paul's like a staple around here. Seems to me he's always been here, always looked just like he does now ..."

His eyes stayed on me as I sat at the other end of the table, cutting board in position. I sliced the ends of one of the cucumbers off, then slid the knife down easily to remove the rind. "Be careful with that," he cautioned.

I looked up. Smiled again. "I've been doing this since I was old enough to be taught," I said, holding up one hand. "Never lost a finger or cut my hand off yet." I raised my brow at him. "I take it you're not much in the kitchen, Dr. Gillespie."

Deep crow's feet formed around his eyes as he smiled. "No. Growing up ... well, my mother had help in the kitchen—"

"Like a maid?"

"Well, more like someone who took care of the cooking. I never really thought of Magnolia as a *maid*. She was just ... well, she took care of the kitchen. We had others over the years who came and took care of the cleaning, but only Magnolia was allowed in the kitchen."

"I help Dr. Paul sometimes. Sometimes in the kitchen."

His brow furrowed in question.

"Like, straightening up around the house. Washing, ironing ..."

"So that's how—"

"But only when *his* help needs me."

Dr. Gillespie waited until I set about to removing the skin from a tomato before he spoke again. "Then my wife took over the kitchen duties after we married and—"

I looked up. "You're married?" I blurted before I had a chance to stop myself.

His jaw twitched. "No. I'm—no—I was. I'm a widower."

Sadness, penetrating and deep, settled in my gut. "Like me," I whispered. "Only I'm a widow, Granny says."

Dr. Gillespie's eyes rested on mine long enough that we could offer each other our condolences without words. "Now," he said, leaning back in his chair, "my sister—Julia—takes care of me." He paused, as though weighing his next words. "She's with me while her husband serves in Vietnam."

Chapter Eleven

James Gillespie, M. D.

I hadn't been sure.

Telling a woman whose husband died halfway around the world in a jungle for reasons I still hadn't wrapped my brain around, that my brother-in-law was there now came with risks. I didn't want Lillie Beth's sorrow over the death of her grandmother—which I considered to be imminent—to be additionally burdened by the remembrance of her late husband.

But apparently Lillie Beth was as unpredictable as she was different from any woman I'd ever known. She looked up from her tomatoes and cucumbers and casually replied, "What's his name?"

"Evan." I reached for the tea pitcher, which I'd nearly emptied of its syrupy-sweet content by myself. "We're going to need more of this, I'm afraid."

She stood. Wiped her hands on her apron. "I'll set about to making it," she said, then walked to the stove and did just that—*set about* to making it. "Has he been a soldier over there for long?"

I blinked, embarrassed that I'd been so enthralled at watching her—a creature so lovely, so ethereal, and yet so young—that I'd forgotten the subject of our conversation. "Who?"

She looked at me as if I had three heads, then returned to the table for the vegetables. "Evan, you said." She stepped back to the counter next to the stove, a large, remarkably pristine Philco.

I shook my head to toss away the spiders that had no business spinning their cobwebs there. "He's a doctor. He—uh—felt he owed it to his country to go."

Her shoulders drew straight. "But not you?"

"No. I felt I could better serve my country by staying *in* it." I attempted a chuckle. "Evan has a wanderlust spirit though. He and Julia both …"

Lillie Beth brought a plate over filled with the squash, slices of the tomatoes and cucumbers, a boiled egg she'd pulled out of a bowl in the fridge, along with a fork and a paper towel I assumed was to serve as a napkin. "Salt and pepper's on the table," she said, pointing to the center where a Tupperware set nestled with a matching sugar bowl. "We don't eat much meat during the summer months," she explained. "Only on Sundays."

"This is fine," I said. And it was.

She sat again, across from me. For a moment I felt washed by a memory—Cherilyn and me, sitting at our kitchen table. Her telling me about her day with more drama than any one woman should have possessed, and then me telling her about mine in as few sentences as possible.

"Aren't you going to eat?" I asked, then once again pushed away a memory that had no business entering my thoughts.

"Later. I'm not real hungry right now."

I thought about it, wondering at the truth of her words. Was she hungry? Had I come in and taken what she would have eaten? "You should eat," I said. "You'll probably be up most of the night and you'll need your strength." She shook her head so faintly I almost missed it. I decided to take another tact. "I won't eat unless you do," I said. The same Julia had used on me after Cherilyn had died. After she no longer sat across from me at our kitchen table.

"All right." Lillie Beth stood, went to the cabinet for a plate, and then returned with her own prepared meal along with a fork and paper towel. "Will you say grace or should I?" she asked, stopping me as I went to slice into the fried squash I worried had grown too cold to enjoy.

I placed the fork next to the plate. "Perhaps you should."

She bowed her head while I continued to watch her, unwilling to close my eyes or lower my chin. "Precious Jesus," she said, "We thank you and our Father above for this good food. We thank you for wonderful doctors like Dr. Paul and Dr. Gillespie. And we thank you for Granny, asking that you give her strength to survive the night …" She paused. "Or show her mercy and bring her on home to you, to Mr. Carson, and to David." She looked up then, her eyes finding mine. "Amen," she said.

"Amen," I said without thinking.

"Tell me more about Julia," she said, picking up her fork.

I smiled easily at the thought of the one human being I'd been with longer than any other in my life. Other than my time away in medical school, she and I had spent scant hours apart. "She and I are twins, actually." I sliced the egg before salting it.

Lillie Beth cut into a slice of tomato as she slid the paper towel into her lap. "Who is the oldest?"

"Julia. By three and a half minutes. And don't think she ever lets me forget it." I bit into the squash, the grease exploding with flavor, and moaned. "Wow."

Lillie Beth smiled in appreciation. "David loved fried squash too," she said.

"The night before he left, Granny made him a big ole mess of it. Just for him."

I nodded as I stabbed another piece with my fork. "Did he eat it all?"

She gave a quick laugh—there and then gone. "Every bite." I looked at her, studying her as her eyes went somewhere else in the room, as her face turned reflective. "Said it would hold him till he got back." Her words were as whisper-soft as a mourning dove's coo.

"How did you meet?" I asked.

Lillie Beth's face flushed across her cheekbones. "At a juke joint near here. Me and my cousin Denise came over to dance and ... he was there. We danced and he bought me a co-cola and then we went outside ... sat on the tailgate of his friend's truck up under the oaks and the pines and ... we talked. A lot. He ... he really listened to me, you know?" Her breath caught in her throat. "Really listened."

"You weren't from here?" I asked from around a bite of food. "Hadn't met him before?"

"Oh, no. I'm from a community about a fifteen-minute drive up the road. West of here."

Having finished the egg, I reached for the salt and pepper again, then sprinkled the seasonings on the tomato and cucumber slices. "Brothers and sisters?"

"No," she said. "Just Mama and Daddy and me." She placed her fork on her plate and leaned back. "What about you? Do you have other sisters or a brother?"

I shook my head. "Mother was terrified after Julia and I were born that there'd be another set of twins." I took a swallow of tea. "Or worse. Triplets."

She laughed again, then sat up and reached for her fork. But before she could pick it up, a groan came from the bedroom. We both leapt out of our chairs, and even though I was nearer to the door, Lillie Beth beat me to it.

"Granny?" Lillie Beth knelt beside the failing woman. A woman I knew to be not yet sixty, but who appeared two decades older.

Mrs. McCall reached for her granddaughter's hand, then peered up at me as I stood behind her. "Who are you?" she asked.

I put my best bedside manner on display with a gentle smile. "I'm Dr. Gillespie, Mrs. McCall. I'm working with Dr. Paul now."

Lillie Beth looked up at me and shook her head, a notion I understood immediately. *Don't tell her Dr. Paul is retiring.*

Mrs. McCall offered her free hand and I took it. "My, my," she said. "You finally came."

Chapter Twelve

"I'm sorry," I said. "Were you expecting me?"

Mrs. McCall looked at her granddaughter. "It's about time," she whispered.

"Granny." Lillie Beth's tone sent a note of admonishment through the room, as though the walls and furnishings expected it, but left me in the dark. What was I missing here?

"Child," Mrs. McCall continued. "Go fetch the Bible and read it to me. I've got a hankering to hear God's Word."

Lillie Beth straightened. "Granny, wouldn't you like something to eat? I fried up some squash. Sliced some tomatoes and cukes. And I boiled some eggs earlier today. The girls were generous this morning."

The older woman shook her head. "Something to drink might be nice. Some tea. Bring me some tea and go fetch the Bible."

"Water would be bet—" I started, then stopped myself. What did it matter if the woman wanted thick-as-molasses tea when she should be drinking water?

Lillie Beth stood. Turned to me. "I'll go finish making the tea," she said, her shoulder against mine, her voice once again reminiscent of the dove's coo. A shiver attempted to rush up my spine, but I suppressed it, then wondered when Dr. Paul would make it to the house. Hoping it would be soon. In the little bit of time I'd been with Lillie Beth McCall, she'd managed to cast some form of spell over me and I'd fallen into it. Fallen into easy conversation with a woman no older than a child.

I cast a glance over my shoulder as she disappeared from the room.

"Come sit," the older woman said, and I did. I leaned in, elbows on my knees, waiting. For what, I was unsure, but waiting because I knew she had something to say. "You'll do," she said with a nod. "You'll do jes' fine."

"I'm afraid I don—"

"Lillie Beth," Mrs. McCall said. "Now she's a fine young thing."

"Yes—"

"But when I leave here, she'll be all alone. Nick—he's my other grandson—he'll try to kick her out of here. Try to bully her into leaving."

"Nick?"

"David's brother. He's a fiery one, that one is. Don't know how to love out of his heart. Devil's got his soul too. I pray. Ever' night I pray. But he—" She coughed, then choked. I lifted her shoulders, felt the heat radiating from her. She calmed, almost instantly.

"Here, Mrs. McCall," I said. "Don't try—"

But she pushed me away. Swallowed hard enough to be heard. I lowered her back to the stack of pillows, one with the perfect imprint of her small head. "Her daddy," she continued. "Meanest man you ever could meet."

"Whose?" I asked, wondering if the dead had come back into the room, then rebuking myself for such falderal.

"Lillie Beth. Sweet child. But that man ... he'd beat her over nothing. Don't you let him skeer you none."

"Why would I—"

"Mean to her mama too, but she won't leave. Best thing ever happened to my sweet girl is my grandson meeting her at the dance hall." She looked at me, eyes locking and showing mischief I didn't expect from someone her age. "She tell you about that?"

I smiled. "Yes ma'am."

"I 'spected she would."

Lillie Beth returned then, a Mason jar of iced tea in her hand and a look of concern etched across her face. "Granny?"

I helped my patient up as Lillie Beth sat next to her grandmother, then held the glass to her cracked lips. The older woman drank like a man parched from too much time in the desert, then pulled herself away, the weight of her falling against my left arm. "Now, darling," she said, "go and find Granny's Bible like I said to. I 'spect it's in the front room."

"Yes'm." Lillie Beth handed me the jar, then dashed out of the room.

"You've got your own wounds to bear," the old woman said, "to let God heal."

I looked at her, saw the gleam in her eye, and wondered how she could know this truth about me, especially when we'd hardly been introduced. "Ma'am?"

"Don't 'ma'am' me, son. You know. I know you do. Just don't you give up on life only 'cause you think life gave up on you."

I opened my mouth to protest—I had no idea why or what I would say—when Lillie Beth returned. I stood, the jar of tea still in my hand, and stepped back until I reached the painted shiplap wall. I attempted to take in a breath while the woman-child sat in the rocker, opened the Bible, and began to read aloud.

"*The Lord is my light and my salvation; whom shall I fear? The Lord is the strength of my life; of whom shall I be afraid?"*

I closed my eyes against the words. Words I knew well. The preacher had read them at Cherilyn's funeral. Why, of all the verses in the Bible, had he chosen those, I'd wondered then. Why, of all the verses in the Bible, had Lillie Beth chosen to read them now?

I glanced toward the still-open window. Beyond it, darkness had begun to close in around us. I looked down at my watch. Where had the time gone? And where, for the love of whatever was left of being sacred, was Dr. Paul?

"*One thing have I desired of the Lord,*" Lillie Beth continued, bringing my attention back to her. To the way the bedside light played on her hair. To the way her lips moved over the words she read, as though caressing each one. And her voice ... like one of those angels she said came in on the breeze.

If I believed angels could speak.

Even as I thought it, the sheers at the windows billowed. Lillie Beth caught the movement of them, then looked back at me, her eyes wide as a child's innocence, her smile faint. A brow raised, and without further ado, she turned back to the opened book on her lap. "*For in the time of trouble he shall hide me in his pavilion: in the secret of his tabernacle shall he hide me; he shall set me up upon a rock ...*"

"I'm a-going," Mrs. McCall said. "I'm going to that pavilion, Lillie Beth ... that tabernacle."

The young beauty leaned closer to her grandmother. "No, Granny," she begged, her voice now strained with fear. "It'll be a while."

The old woman's eyes found me, then returned to Lillie Beth. "Don't forget," she said. "The winda."

I shot a look across the room. The sheers had settled back into still folds. The world beyond was now completely dark.

But in that room, a light grew. I could feel it more than I could see it.

And I could see it plain as the day.

Chapter Thirteen

Lillie Beth

"Tell me about him," Dr. Gillespie said from where he sat, again at the kitchen table. Although this time he'd scooted the chair back and crossed his legs like a man who'd grown up with his feet under that same table.

I sighed. After Granny had done gone back to sleep, the young doctor and I had returned to the kitchen so she could rest better. I'd turned on the radio, keeping the volume low, and cleaned up the supper dishes, him watching the whole while. I felt his eyes on me, even when I wasn't looking. Just like with David back when he was here those few days before he left for Vietnam.

And sometimes, even after …

"About who?" I asked.

"Your husband."

"He was something else." I looked at him, testing him with my eyes as I returned to the table and sat across from him. "I only knowed him two weeks when we got married."

Sure enough, his eyes registered surprise. "Two weeks?"

"How long did you know your wife?"

"We dated four years before we married."

I nearly giggled. "I couldn't have waited that long." I took in a deep breath. Let it out. "David was more than husband. He was my savior."

Dr. Gillespie brought his hands together, lacing the fingers and resting them on the table. "In what way?"

"My daddy—was—is—nothing but an old drunk. Always beatin' up on my mama. On me. I never planned that David would be my way out, but he was. I knew it the minute I set eyes on him."

Pain pierced the doctor's eyes. "So you didn't love—"

"Oh, yes. I loved him something fierce. How can you not love someone who saves you from such misery?" I raised a brow. "Truth is, I didn't know I was all that miserable until he showed me something differ'nt. Something better. I thought all people lived like me and Mama did. Catering to a drunk's needs."

His hand flexed. Strong hands. Healing hands. "Did he ever—did he—*hurt* you in any way?"

"A whooping every time I turned around. Or at least it seemed that way. Never could do nothing right as far as Daddy was concerned."

"No. I mean—never mind. That's none of my—"

Understanding came. "You mean … did he ever try to do anything sinful with me?"

"Yes."

"No."

His shoulders sank. "Thank God for that."

I gave him a half smile. "Oh. So now we're *thanking* God?"

He smiled back. "You caught me." He rubbed his forehead, furrowed with thought lines, and said, "Why'd you read that particular Scripture in there? Earlier? From the psalms?"

"Number twenty-seven. It's Granny's favorite."

"Oh," he said, then nothing more until, "Tell me about the day you married David." One line that sure didn't seem to go with the other.

I sat back in the chair, crossing my arms. "We had to plan it ahead, you know. Had to get the license. David knew of this justice of the peace who'd marry you without the blood test, which I was real thankful for. I didn't think I could stand it if I had to give blood."

"You don't *much cotton* to that?" He looked proud of himself, like a baby who'd learned a new word.

"No sir, I do not." I reflected a moment on that afternoon which now felt like a lifetime ago. "So, I told Mama and Daddy I was going over to my cousin Denise's and they said 'fine.' I wore my dungarees and a pair of sneakers like we was going pea picking or something. But when I got to Denise's, she had me a pretty dress to wear—I got it still up in my closet—and a pair of her high-heel shoes what she always wore to church. And then my Aunt Loreen—she's my mama's sister—gave me a pair of pearl earrings for good luck."

His eyes met mine fully at the mention of the earrings. "Pearls?"

"Yes." I pointed up. "I still have them too. Would you like to see them?"

His breath caught. For a moment, I thought he'd say yes. I hoped he would, because for some reason, I wanted to share them with him. But he shook his head. "That's okay."

I watched him carefully. "So now it's your turn, Dr. Gillespie."

"To?"

"Tell me …"

"About what?"

"The pearls your wife used to wear."

His hands found each other and his fingers laced as he rested them in his lap. Long moments ticked by. Outside the wind whipped up a little while inside the Cowsills sang "The Rain, The Park, and Other Things" on the radio. "She loved pearls," he said, then he shrugged. "Well, she loved *one* set of pearls. Her father gave them to her on her sixteenth birthday." He pointed to his earlobes. "Earrings to match." His fingers touched his wrist, brushing it lightly, before weaving his fingers back together again.

"Bracelet too?"

He nodded. "We buried her in them. I wanted—I wanted to take them off before they closed the casket, but—but her father insisted. Said they would keep her warm …" His eyes moved quickly to the window over the sink as if someone stood on the other side and I turned. The curtains moved, then settled back down. When I looked again, he tilted his head as his jaw flexed. "Angels?"

"Angels." I breathed in slow. Steady. "Or maybe just one."

He looked at the window again before clearing his throat. "She died of brain cancer. Did I tell you that?"

I shook my head.

"Most awful thing I ever had to witness …" His eyes narrowed.

"And that's why you're mad at God?"

The jaw flexed again. "Who said I was—"

I nodded once. "You are."

"Yes." His fingers found his forehead and temple and he rubbed something fierce. "How can a loving God …" But he didn't finish. Finally, he looked up at me.

"What?" I asked. "Want His children to come home? Be with Him?" I waited for the words to register. "Did your wife love Jesus, Dr. Gillespie?"

He smiled a sad sort of smile, one brow up. "Yes ma'am, she did."

"You think He loved her any less?"

"I don't know …"

"Granny always says that long ago God loved us enough to send His Son to die for us. And that with that much love, He's not about to let us down none in our own days."

"Yeah, well … what about you? What about the way your daddy treated you? Losing your husband?"

I thought a moment. "I don't know if this is much of an answer, but Granny says that sometimes God closes—" I stopped at the sound of a truck—one I knew well—barreling up the driveway and coming to a stop in front of the house. "Nick," I said, standing. "Oh no."

Dr. Gillespie stood too. "Your brother-in-law?"

I didn't know how Dr. Gillespie knew Nick from Adam's house cat, and it hardly mattered right then. What did matter was that I couldn't allow him to come inside. He'd rile Granny up. Make her worse. "Come on," I said, then headed for the front door.

Chapter Fourteen

Nick was halfway to the front porch steps, arms swinging in a short-sleeved cotton shirt that stretched across his muscular chest. He took wide steps, his boots leaving a dusty imprint in the sand that scattered from the stoop. He stopped as soon as I flipped on the front porch light and Dr. Gillespie and I strolled out onto the porch.

"Who is that?" he demanded. He stood, feet braced apart, his jeans straining against his stance, and his jaw jutted toward the man standing behind me. "You got some man wallowing in your bed while my granny is downstairs dying?"

"Hey, now." Dr. Gillespie took a step around me, but I grabbed his wrist, hoping to stop him.

"Who says Granny is dying?" I asked as I released the doctor, sure now he wasn't going to challenge Nick to some fool-hearted duel. A fight he'd lose, I knew. Nick was strong as an ox and meaner than a bull kept back from a heifer in heat. The man standing beside me—this man raised by cooks who stayed in the kitchen and maids who took care of everything else—had probably never come into contact with someone such as my brother-in-law. But I sure had. I'd been dealing with men like Nick my whole life and all in the form of the one man who should have been my protector to start off with.

Nick crossed his arms. "You denying it?"

"I ain't saying yes and I ain't saying no, Nick McCall. Only God Himself determines when a soul releases from the body and when it stays put. Now, who says?"

"Ran into Gary Cooke at the feed store. He'd been out at the Camby place. Said Doc was out there tending to Irwin's wife. Said he'd been out here today and things are looking bad." He turned his attention again to Dr. Gillespie. "You that city doctor I heard tell was working with Doc Paul?"

"I'm Dr. Gillespie." He took a tentative step. "Would you like to sit down a while and talk about your grandmother?"

Nick pointed to me. "What I want is that piece of trash out of my house."

"This is Granny's house," I said. "And don't you worry none, Nick McCall. Soon as Granny dies, I'm gone. You can count on it."

Nick took two steps toward the house. Cocked his hip just so. Tilted his head a little. Squinted up at me through the wild bangs that fell over his eyes. "Then again, Miss Priss, maybe you and me can work something out … you looking awful *fine* in that apron and housedress. Ain't no telling …" He whistled between this teeth like a tomcat on the prowl.

Again Dr. Gillespie moved and again I stopped him. "It'll be a cold day in July, Nick McCall, before I let you touch me. I done told you that before and I'm telling you again." I spoke as boldly as I knew how, but Nick was bolder. Always had been. He made his way up the steps before Dr. Gillespie and I could catch our breaths, planted his nose so close to mine I could smell the whiskey what still lingered on his tongue. "I want you out of this house the minute that old woman catches sight of the Pearly Gates, you hear me?" He spoke through clenched teeth.

I blinked, but I didn't back away. Didn't take my eyes from his. "I hear you," I said.

Then he smiled, the dimples creating a cherub's face. But I knew better. Way better. "Now you be sure to give Granny my love, you hear." He puckered his lips and kissed the air near 'bout too close to my mouth. Then he looked at Dr. Gillespie. "Doc," he added before turning on his heel and strolling back to the truck as though this was a Sunday afternoon and he was returning home with a full belly.

Dr. Gillespie nor me, neither one moved as Nick hoisted himself into the truck, started it up, spun the wheels in the yard, and drove away. When his tail lights were out of sight, I took in a deep breath, then released it as slowly as I knew how. Mostly to keep from falling over. From collapsing right there on the front porch and hollering until there was nothing left in my lungs.

"Are you all right?" The doctor had turned to me, his arm nearly touching my shoulder.

I nodded. "Yeah," I lied. "But I need to go upstairs and pack, I reckon."

His eyes narrowed. "Where will you go? Back to your parents' home?"

Tears stung my eyes. Oh no … Not there. And wasn't that just the rub? I had nowhere to go, really. Aunt Loreen and Uncle Melvin had moved a year or so back after Denise married a soldier of her own from Fort Stewart. Denise being an only child, my aunt and uncle decided to go wherever she went. They sold the house, Uncle Melvin quit his job, and off they went. Said there wasn't much left for them here anyhow.

For a while Denise and I wrote a few letters back and forth … If I could find her, then maybe … "I don't know," I said finally, aware that the man beside me waited for an answer.

We returned inside, checked in on Granny who slept on, then stepped back into the kitchen. "You don't have to stay," I said, ashamed for what Dr. Gillespie had witnessed out there on the front porch. Knowing he'd never been around such as Nick McCall ... or the kind of woman who'd married the first man to ever kiss her. To tell her he loved her.

To offer her a way out.

I reached for the radio, to turn it off, just as The Association's "Never, My Love" began to play.

But then Dr. Gillespie's hand touched mine, stopping me from ending the song before it got going good. Without a word, he turned me into his arms, his right hand cupping mine, and his left sliding across the small of my back, pulling me to him. "Dance with me," he whispered. "One song."

I didn't have to think to step closer to him. Within a breath of time, we swayed to the gentle beat. To the hushed harmony of the voices. I inhaled through my nose, afraid if I opened my mouth some stupid word would slip out and the magic would be broken. I closed my eyes, pressed my forehead against his shoulder, the shuffling of our feet on Granny's spotless linoleum becoming one with the song on the radio.

And for a moment, I imagined David holding me again. I allowed myself to feel safe in a man's arms, even if only for the time it took for a single song to play.

Chapter Fifteen

James Gillespie, M. D.

I had lost my mind.
No two ways about it. I had stepped over the imaginary boundary I'd created for myself with my patients or their family members and I'd set something in motion neither Lillie Beth nor I were prepared to look in the face of.

Yet, for the briefest of moments, I closed my eyes, remembering the way Cherilyn had felt in my arms. The firm muscles of her petite body. But as my hand flexed at the base of Lillie Beth's spine, I felt the soft flesh and I knew …

I knew exactly who I held.

What I didn't know was why.

Only a short time earlier I had prayed for Dr. Paul to get on with the birthing of a baby fated to be a linebacker, and to hurry to the McCall farm. But now… now I hoped he never came. I prayed—if I could call it a prayer—that he'd leave us be until …

Until what?

Until the song ended? Until the older woman died? Or until I figured out what power this beauty I held in my arms held over me. Why she made me feel things I'd thought I'd never feel again.

The song ended, but we continued swaying as if it had not. No more than a minute ticked by, and yet it felt like forever.

Or more like a second. "Lillie Beth," I whispered.

She raised her head from my shoulder, her blue eyes misty with tears, her lips pursed like the petals of a rose ready to bloom. "Lillie Beth," I said again, and then—God help me—I pressed my lips against hers with an anguish I couldn't understand. Didn't *want* to understand. But one that had haunted me since the day I'd watched my wife take her final breath. Had listened as it repleted the room with life … and then death.

"Deliver me," I half whispered, half begged the woman-child whose life-filled body I crushed against my own.

And then Lillie Beth kissed me back. Kissed me like a drowning woman hungry for the air that hung just above the water's surface. Kissed me until she slowly drew her head back and the atmosphere around us crackled.

She threw her hands over her face and sobbed.

"No," I said forcibly, reaching for her fingers to pull her hands away. "No."

"I'm sorry," she whimpered. She kept her eyes to the floor, ashamed—I knew—to look at me.

"No," I repeated. "*I'm* sorry." I stepped back. Rubbed my forehead. "What am I saying?" I asked out loud, shocked by my own voice.

She looked at me fully then.

"I lied," I said. "I'm *not* sorry."

Tears spilled from her eyes, trailed down her cheeks.

"I'm not ..." I rested my hands on my hips. Hung my head like an old dog. "You—you've made me feel what I haven't felt in—good Lord, Lillie Beth."

Her arms came around my neck then, her fingernails clawed at my shoulders. "You must think me awful," she whispered against my ear, then kissed the lobe. "Please forgive—"

I squeezed her waist, my fingers digging into the soft flesh, then stepped away, aware that if she kissed me again, I'd lose my mind. And probably more than that. "I don't think you're awful."

"Don't worry," she said quickly. "I'm not thinking—I don't expect you to save me—not like—" She stopped suddenly at the groaning that emanated from the adjoining room. "*Granny.*" Lillie Beth hurried toward the bedroom, me right behind her.

The older woman's eyes were open. Wide and expectant. Wide and expectant and turned toward the window. "There you are," she said, but not to us. Even I—a doubter—could see she wasn't looking at us.

"Who, Granny?" Lillie Beth asked, once again dropping to her knees. The housedress she'd worn all day pooled along the floorboards in soft puddles. The tips of her flat shoes peeked out from beneath them.

"Oh, Carson," the woman said. "My love ... my love ..."

"Granny," Lillie Beth grabbed for the woman's hand, pulled it to her breast, and held tight, then look up at me. Fresh tears spilled over dry trails. "If she's seeing Mr. Carson—" She looked again at her grandmother. "What about David? Is David with Mr. Carson?"

Mrs. McCall blinked once. Twice. "David? My David. Ah, yes ... he's smiling, Lillie Beth ... he's so happy now ... he can rest ... knowing you're go'n be all right."

Ridiculously, I looked in the direction of the woman's gaze. Saw nothing. Then, on cue, the curtains billowed, as if a strong gust of wind had set them in motion. Yet, outside, the air was as still and heavy as a headstone. A chill ran through me, too preposterous to give in to. Still, I crossed my arms, raised my shoulders, and stared into the picture the window made. I willed David to appear. To give me permission to love his wife. To take care of her after his grandmother died. Or to scream at me across the chasm of life and death and tell me to back away.

Which is what I should do. What I would have done, if I were any kind of decent man at all, which I clearly was not. Decency and I had parted company the day I raised my fist at God and told Him what He could do with Himself. With His promises. With His life-and-death decisions.

Yet, apparently, as much as I wanted to be done with Him, He had not finished with me, because here I was, wrestling with the things I could not control. Life and death ...

... and Lillie Beth McCall.

More than that, I found myself willing Cherilyn to pass though the sheers hanging pristine on both sides of the window. To stand like an apparition in front of me. To tell me I *could* love again. To chastise me for my anger at God. To frown at me and tell me she'd seen my moment of wrestling with the Almighty and she was not pleased. And then to smile at me one more time with that perfect smile, her teeth the color of her pearls.

Instead, the curtains fell still again. The woman beneath the mussed and wrinkled sheets stirred, and I instinctively took a step closer to her bed. I was a doctor, for pity's sake. Not a clairvoyant at the county fair. I had a job to do.

"Child," she said to Lillie Beth. "I'm ready now. *You're* ready now."

"Granny," Lillie Beth all but begged. "It's too soon. You're still young. There's still so much we need to do ... the autumn harvest ..."

"Age got nothing to do with this." She saw me then, standing behind her granddaughter. "Do it, Doc?"

"No ma'am," I said, my voice a frog's croak, my thoughts remaining with the twenty-nine-year-old I'd laid to rest only a few years before.

"What's your Christian name, son?" she asked me, the words coming slow. Deliberate.

"James—Jim. My family calls me Jim."

She looked again at Lillie Beth. "Jim will take fine care of you, darling girl."

"Granny, don't *die*—"

"Don't you worry none, child," she said to her granddaughter. "I ain't go'n die." She attempted a smile, coughed instead. I took a step toward the bed, but the cough subsided with her next breath. "Don't you know I'm go'n live forever?"

"Granny ..."

"That's right ... that's right. I'm go'n live forever. It's just my address that's changin' ..."

"Then take me with you," Lillie Beth said, startling me. I knelt beside her and slipped my arm around her waist once more as if to hold her by my own power and emotion. Before that day, I would swear on the Bible I'd stopped reading that I didn't believe the dying could take the living with them. But after what I'd experienced in the last twelve hours, I just might accept any far-flung bits of folklore as truth. Any myth as a fact.

"Not this time, Lillie Beth," she said. "You'll be staying with Jim here." The watery eyes slid within deep sockets to focus on mine. "You'll do that for an old woman, won't you, son?"

"Yes ma'am," I said without any need to think it through. Although what did occur to me was how I'd explain all this to Julia.

Mrs. McCall closed her eyes then.

"Not yet," Lillie Beth pleaded.

"No," she answered. "Not yet." The old woman swallowed. "But soon enough."

Then, as her breath wheezed from between her lips, she said, "Sell the farm if need be, Lillie Beth."

"Ma'am?" Confusion rose from the question.

"Sell the farm, darling girl... and climb through the winda ..."

Allensville, Georgia
Summer 1970

Lillie Beth

I needn't have packed a bag that night. For one, Granny lived on another few days, her body weakening with every hour, but her spirit determined not to leave the house until "my Carson comes to get me for the final time."

As Jim said, "In many ways, she's already gone, Lillie Beth. She just hasn't left yet."

Three days after Jim and I danced in the kitchen and Noraleen Camby brought a nine-pound, eight-ounce baby boy into the world, the sun rose over the white clapboard farmhouse and the wakening fields of our little corner of the world as it always had and always would. As the coffee brewed in the percolator, and near-bout fifteen minutes after Dr. Paul and Jim had stopped by to "check in on their patient," Granny called out as she'd been doing a lot over the last hours. But this time, clear as a bell, she hollered, "He's here," in a voice triumphant. "He's here," she said again, "and he's brought the good Lord with 'im!"

We leapt from the comfort of the kitchen table—the three of us—leaving behind half-consumed cups of coffee and the crumbling remains of breakfast biscuits I'd made long before daylight. As we rounded the doorway, Granny's eyes—vibrant and green—fixed on the open window. She gasped, smiled, and without so much as a wave to the three of us, the life of her blew out. As surely as the Holy Spirit of God had blown life into her at birth, He took it back on that hot summer morning.

While Dr. Paul took care of what needed taking care of with the body, Jim carried me to the front room where he held me as I clutched at the front of his shirt and wailed. All the while breathing in the scent of him—fresh soap and woodsy cologne. When my tears finally hiccupped to submission, he whispered that I shouldn't worry. "I won't let anyone," he said, "not Nick, not your daddy, not anyone drive you away from this house until you're ready to go."

I shook my head. "Nick won't allow me to stay another minute once he finds out Granny's gone," I said.

Where I thought I'd end up right then I don't know, and right then it didn't matter. It also didn't matter that Granny had asked Jim to take care of me, because—as good and kind as he had been since he'd made the promise—he surely didn't owe me nothing. One kiss and one dance didn't add up to the sum of a marriage proposal. Least ways, not twice in my life. Those kinds of stories only happen once.

"You'll come home with me," Jim said then. He kept his voice low, I figured so as not to alert Dr. Paul to any words exchanged between him and Granny … or him and me. "My sister will welcome you with open arms."

I shook my head. "That wouldn't set right …"

"With who?" he asked, tilting his head. "Who do you have to worry about?"

I looked him straight on. His brow had scrunched so, he looked more boy than man. "Folks," I said. "Them that live in town in the fancy houses like what y'all live in." I nodded once. "I don't belong there, Jim. Never have. Never will." I looked at his hands holding mine. Took in the perfectly trimmed nails and uncallused palms. "And you *sure* don't belong here."

His eyes searched mine. Then he leaned in, kissed my cheek, his lips lingering a long, sweet time. "All I know, Lillie Beth, is that we belong together. I don't understand it … but I know it."

I raised my eyes to his and smiled. "I reckon that's what you call faith."

"Yes ma'am," he said, smiling back. This time, he pressed his lips to my temple. "We'll work it out," he said. "I promise."

And we did.

As it turned out, Granny had gotten herself a good lawyer when the rest of us hadn't been paying attention. Turned out, she had left me the house, the farm, and all that went with it. Much to everyone's surprise, she'd left Nick only a scant handful of things—the photo of his parents and the framed cross-stitch sampler declaring their love for each other, and a hundred dollars. And that was it.

Nick fought Granny's Last Will and Testament, of course, but ended up losing "in a reasonable court of law," as Jim put it. When our hearing was over and we met up on the courthouse steps, he threatened to burn down the house and everything in it. Granny always said his temper would get the better of him one day, and I reckon that day arrived, because the next thing Nick knew he was being arrested by Sheriff Marsden, who happened to be standing not ten feet away when Nick made his untimely threat.

At least untimely for him.

I managed to wait until Jim and I got into his boat-sized car before I let myself go enough to laugh. Jim laughed too … and then he slid me across that long front seat, wrapped his arms around me, and kissed me for all the world to see. Or at least the part of world called Allenstown.

We courted long enough to appear respectable. By the time we married in the little church Granny and I liked to go to, Jim had made his peace with God. Said he reckoned God must surely love him because He'd been plenty patient with His wayward son.

Julia's husband returned from the war soon after. With Dr. Paul's retirement and Jim's increased acceptance in the community, he and Evan went into practice together. With Evan back, Jim and I moved out to the farmhouse, leaving Evan and Julia to enjoy the rented house in town. A house they eventually bought outright.

Just like Granny had done, Jim managed the farm and the sharecroppers when he wasn't doctoring. I helped him, same as I'd done for Granny, but mostly I enjoyed fixing the place up in the manner Granny and I had spoke of from time to time.

Paint here. Carpets there. Maybe some new wallpaper.

Two years to the day after Granny went to be with the Lord—and nearly to the exact minute—Jim and I welcomed a baby girl into our family. Elma Frances Gillespie—Francie—came in at six pounds, three ounces ... a tiny bundle of pink and wrinkled skin, dark wisps of curls swirling on her head, and startling green eyes that still peer at us as if they hold wisdom we'll never know.

After she was born—after they'd cleaned her up good—Jim brought her to me and laid her in my arms, kissing first her tiny forehead and then mine. "I love you," he whispered.

All I could do was nod. Once. Just like Granny when she meant business. After a few minutes of counting fingers and toes, I asked Jim if he'd mind going to get me some orange juice. "I'll buzz for the nurse," he said, reaching for the call button.

"No," I said, then smiled sweetly. "I want to be alone with my daughter for a minute." I gave him the look I'd learned got me my way every time. "Go get it for me?"

He smiled back. "Yes ma'am," he said. "Whatever my darling girl wants."

When the wide hospital door had closed behind him, I took my chance to say a mother's first words of wisdom to her daughter. I'd thought about them for months, rehearsed them for weeks. Them words she'd hold on to for the rest of her life.

"Always remember, little one," I said, "that God don't never shut a door but what he don't open a winda."

And then I smiled. Fact is, I smile every time I repeat those words to her, even now ...

Because Granny was right.

Through an Autumn Window

Claire Fullerton

DEDICATION

For Weetie and Shirley
Incomparable Southern queens.

Chapter One
October 2017

There's only one downside to being a transplanted Southerner living in Pacific Grove, California—to fly home (which is what I'll always call Memphis), I have to leave the Monterey Peninsula and either drive seventy-five miles to San Jose, or one hundred and five to San Francisco. Either way, it's a hassle, especially when the trip is unplanned.

I was on automatic pilot as I followed my husband through what seemed like blind paces from San Francisco to a layover in Charlotte, where we got in another plane and landed in Memphis. One foot in front of the other into Memphis International Airport, and I realized I was walking into the valley of the shadow of death because my mother wasn't waiting at the gate to catch me. It was the first time in my life when she hadn't been at the arrival gate, jockeying for position to spot me, jumpy as a golden retriever to have me back home.

Daphne Goodwyn had a knack for creating indelible memories in the most mundane of affairs. Airports were a big deal to my mother, whether I was coming or going. She'd suit up her size-eight figure in loud colors, as if needing something eye-catching to draw attention to herself, which, of course, she didn't.

The good Lord saw to that when He colored all five feet seven of my mother with ivory skin, deep auburn hair, and green oval eyes. She had an hourglass shape, a stallion stride, and walked with her chin in the air. She had a gregarious personality, a memorable laugh, and a manner that never meant maybe. I was just fifteen, flying alone for the first time on my way to a friend's vacation home in Florida, when I realized the full extent of my mother's attraction. Rushing through the Delta terminal to the departure gate with her hand on my wrist, she clipped through the crowd with such purpose that strangers got out of our way. Hurtling toward us from the opposing direction, an airport employee driving a six-wheel baggage cart sported a nametag embroidered "William." One look at the sprinting, high-heeled Daphne packed into her Lilly Pulitzer, and he screeched to a halt, angled a U-turn, and offered us a lift. The long and the short of it is my mother's crowd-parting looks were traffic-stopping, and I happen to know she knew it. I, on the other hand, am small boned, dark haired, and flat chested. Whereas my mother cornered the universe, through most of my stumbling childhood you had to look twice to notice I was in the room.

I feel a little guilty saying this: my mother cast a shadow I had difficulty getting out from under. I don't think it was intentional. She loved me dearly, but in some ways, she made me feel eclipsed. I was conflicted throughout adolescence, but it was a subtle unease, rich with subtext, deep below the surface. I rationalized my discomfort by subscribing to the notion that I am artistic in nature, introspective in a way so different from my sparkling mother that my fear was I'd never measure up to her.

I spent years at variance with how I was wired, but my tug-of-war was an internal one. My mother's aspiration had been to turn me into her replica, but I wanted to forge a different life, a life of my own beyond the confines of Memphis. Because I never wanted to create discord between us, I blended seamlessly in my mother's world until I grew up and moved away. The truth is, I'm a terrific actress. I am Daphne Goodwyn's daughter. I'm Southern to the core, after all.

My best friend from childhood was gifted at birth with the name Margaret Ambrose. She waited curbside in her navy Ford Explorer, when the sliding glass doors by baggage claim swished open. Although illegally parked, she got out of her car and gave me a hug. "Cate, I'm so sorry about your mother."

My husband, Eric, who hails from Boston, hauled both our suitcases into the hatchback, then unzipped his own to retrieve his leather jacket. "I thought you said it doesn't get cold down here," he said, his voice baffled. Though Eric and I had been married four years, he'd only been down to Memphis once, and that was in the summer.

"It's anybody's guess how it'll be in the fall," I explained. "That's why I suggested you bring two coats down here. What I meant was for you to pack two different weights so you could be prepared for anything. Sorry about that, Eric, I should have clarified. At this time of year in Memphis, you have to play it day by day."

"More like minute by minute," Margaret said. "Y'all just missed a big storm. The lights are all out in East Memphis. It's supposed to rain off and on all week."

I've never minded the rain. Autumn has always been my favorite time of year in the South. I've missed its stark changes since I moved to California. I still wait for it with fevered expectancy. In California, I look for any hint of fall in the air, and almost will it into being. The temperature drops, and that's me in the slightest of breeze, putting on a knee-length coat and wearing autumn colors in shades of khaki, maroon, and green. Californians look at me as if I've lost my mind, but I don't care. I'm a forty-year-old Southerner, I have carte blanche to be as off-beat as I want.

But I don't have to wait for the fall in Memphis. It creeps up slowly and gives me a sense of anticipation, knowing, as I do, that Halloween dangles like a carrot before a horse at the end of October. I'm more compatible with the fall than any other season. I look forward to Halloween more than any other date on the calendar. Everything about the fall offers something to intrigue me: wind and mist and all things unseen. I've always liked the idea of that which lies beneath the surface. Even my way of God-fearing has a sense of mystical magic. There's something about fall's hesitant introspection that speaks to the core of my being, when everything on earth takes a big exhale before winter comes barreling through to freeze it. I'm not saying there's a good time of year to bury your mother, but if I were given the choice, I'd want to do it in the fall, for something about the bleak, languishing season is compatible with pending change.

I looked out the car window as we drove from the airport in mid-October's seven o'clock hour, and thought how fitting it was: the trees burnt rust, the sun down low, rings like halos over the tops of streetlamps, everything sullen and quiet and still. There was scarcely any traffic out Union Extended Avenue. We were on our way to "view" my mother. Margaret had called Griffin Funeral Home earlier, for such is the personal wiring of Memphis that you can call a place like Griffin Funeral Home and ask them to keep the doors open even after they close.

"I told them you'd just flown in and wanted to see your mother." Margaret met my eyes in the rearview mirror. From the backseat, I saw her forehead crease beneath her dark curls, her brown eyes darting askance. "You still want to do this, right?"

"I guess so," I answered. "I've always heard you should for closure. I might be sorry I didn't later. I don't know. I'm on the fence."

Eric turned around from the passenger seat. "I'll support whatever you want to do, Cate, but if it were me, I wouldn't want to live with that vision in my head. You might want to remember your mother the way she was."

"The way she was?" I said without thinking, "My mother was so larger than life, I don't believe she's dead."

Margaret rerouted the moment. "What do y'all want to do afterward? Aren't y'all staying at the house?"

"Absolutely not," I said. "We're staying at the club. I wouldn't put myself in the position of staying in the house with Dr. Purvis, without my mother as a buffer. We wouldn't know what to say to each other, we never have. It's bad enough Lincoln will be there. He's already being snippy. You should have heard him this morning on the phone."

My older brother, Lincoln, didn't bother asking to speak to me when Eric answered his call at six that morning. He preferred to divulge the full Monty to Eric, while I sat up in bed and waited interminably to hear what was wrong. One bout of sensitivity would have told my brother I couldn't have been anywhere but in the room at that early hour, but then deep-seated hostility sometimes comes out sideways. Lincoln has always taken any opportunity to show me my place in the hierarchy of his resentment.

Eric met my eyes across the bedroom, but didn't relinquish the phone. The look on his face was so hangdog despondent, I knew right away something was wrong. He put his hand over the mouthpiece and whispered, "Cate, your mother passed last night," and I knew right then my brother was still talking, engaged in his favorite role as the bearer of news I didn't know. As I watched Eric, the following minutes unfurled as if in a seven-second delay, the way radio stations operate so they can edit out any live infractions.

Sometimes I think it's too bad life doesn't work this way because in that moment, the earth slammed to a stop and shifted to slow motion, recalibrating itself so I could get my mind around the implacable news and jump to the phone.

"Lincoln, tell me," I prompted, and in thirty seconds I had the abbreviated story; my mother had been rushed to the hospital in a lung cancer-induced fit of pleurisy, and exited this world through the portal of Baptist East Hospital. In some ways, it wasn't a complete surprise. That she had been diagnosed with lung cancer at age seventy and died within seven months was exemplary of my mother's style. She was demonstrative, but never one to carry on unnecessarily. Though I couldn't picture her dead, neither could I summon a vision of her as a tottering old woman. She wouldn't have done it well. Old age just wouldn't have suited her.

"You want me to come in with you?" Margaret asked, parking the car beneath a mature oak in front of Griffin Funeral Home. Overhead, the wind tore through flourishing branches heavy with drama, sending raindrops airborne from the recent downpour. Fall leaves the size of a giant's hand fluttered down in burnt gold and brown, their wrinkled veins raised and jutting like old broken bones.

"Y'all both come with me." I slid out of the car. Gathering my cashmere pashmina tighter, I closed the car door and walked through grass so damp and spongy that my rubber-soled T-straps were soaked to the ankle by the time I walked through the front door.

There was nobody around when we entered Griffin Funeral Home's vacuous foyer. I turned to Margaret and sent her a *what do we do now?* kind of look. Margaret was raised the same way as I was. All either of us ever aspired to is doing the right thing.

Taciturn and self-possessed, Margaret shrugged her shoulders then walked across the foyer, picked up the pen from the lectern, and signed the leather-bound guest book. Eric, hip to our unspoken agreement of communicating in semaphores, snapped into take-charge action. He raised a hand as if to say give me a minute, then set off down the hall because he's that kind of guy.

None of us said a word in this dismal setting. Death down the hall stills the loosest of tongues. My eyes reviewed the breadth of the black-and-gray tiled foyer. Up ahead, a living room spread with a seating arrangement of brown leather club chairs facing a fireplace. My feet fell to a muted cadence as I walked onto the living room's burgundy area rug. The gas-burning logs in the fireplace were turned flickering and low, casting a shimmering blue corona upon the floor.

The first thing I thought as I looked around the room was now I know I'm in Memphis. The Memphis I know is coiffed but understated to an elegant degree. It is tasteful without being flashy. Homespun without being down-home. On the mahogany credenza beneath a still life of peonies by Memphis's Charles Inzer, a trio of Royal Crown Derby plates were displayed on wooden stands. In the face of where I was and why I was there, it was funny to catch myself wondering where the plates were procured, whether they came from Gift and Art, Robert Crump's House, or perhaps Sister's Antiques. Because the thing of it is, the Memphis I know is tightly woven. It's a web of connections in an old family milieu, and it's the rare one, such as me, that ever strays outside it. That everyone knows everybody seems to be the draw.

Margaret crept up behind me. She put her hand on my shoulder and said, "Eric just found someone. He's coming."

Into the twilight of my life's darkest hour slinked Kevin Griffin. I use the word *slinked* here because that's just what he did. He slinked instead of walked. I had to check to see if he wore shoes, because I hadn't heard him coming. There'd been no hint from the foyer that anything human this way approached. The irony of it was, I knew Kevin from high school. Margaret did too, but she hadn't tipped me off. Everyone liked Kevin in high school, he was a nice guy, but there was no pretending his family's line of work didn't give everyone the heebie-jeebies.

I looked over Kevin's shoulder as he extended his hand and discovered Margaret suppressing a smile. Eric had a bewildered look on his face, trying to piece together the humor.

"Miss Goodwyn—" Kevin began as he steadied himself in his black suit, white shirt, and sober tie. "Pardon me, I'm sorry. What is it now?"

"Barton," I said. "You can skip the formality. Don't you remember me as Cate? I believe you've met my husband, Eric."

"I have," Kevin said. "I was just on the phone. Forgive me for not meeting you at the door. I did know you were coming."

"Thank you for staying open," I said. "I appreciate you understanding that I just flew in."

"I'm happy to accommodate you. I was so sorry to hear about your mother. Lovely woman. If there's anything I can do …"

"Thank you. You've done it already," I said. "It's nice to see you, Kevin. It's been a long time."

"Last time I saw you, you were in your Memphis University School cheerleading dress," he said, giving me a wink.

"And you were out on the football field," I added. "I thought I heard you were in Knoxville. Didn't you play ball for UT?"

Kevin glanced down at his knee. "I did for a while. I was injured in my junior year. I've been here at the family business ever since." Kevin pushed his graying brown hair off his forehead, and as he did, the keys he held in his other hand rattled and chimed. I looked at Margaret, who indicated with a movement of her head that it was time to get things moving along.

"Don't let me hold you up," I said, suggesting closure.

"Oh yes, of course," Kevin said. "Come right this way."

Margaret sidled up beside me. "He still creeps me out," she whispered, and inappropriate as it was, I started giggling as we followed Kevin down the hall.

"Shhh, don't make me laugh. I can't take you anywhere," I said. "Eric's going to think we're irreverent and disrespectful."

Behind us, Eric whispered, "I married her for her inappropriate sense of humor," and in that moment, I suddenly knew it was the perfect way to walk into the room that held my mother, flanked and supported by my husband and my best friend, carrying on in a way that reminded me that we were still young and alive and laughing.

Because death will do that to a person. It gives you laser perception. Suddenly, the veil between worlds is released and floats off somewhere up in the cosmos, and you're left squinting at what is through the lens of clear perspective. There was a part of me that almost couldn't let in the immutable gravity, that my life was still on while my mother's was off. In one fell swoop that landed with a hard thud, I was inexplicably aware of my own body as I looked at hers lying inanimate, and a voice in my head cried out *how could this be?*

Because there was no life force, and everything about my mother was all life force. Everything about everybody is all life force. There in the ivory, satin-lined casket my mother's show-stopping looks were nothing without the flair of her sparkling spirit, which was canted to such a pitch that therein lay her beauty. Turning my head away and reaching for the eyes of Margaret, I knew in that instant it's this way with each of us. And it's not as if I didn't know this, I just don't go around thinking about it. Glancing back at my lifeless mother, I made it out of the room thinking that would probably change from here on out. Sometimes it takes a visual to bring things home, when it should have been there all along.

Chapter Two

"The house is on Club Walk, isn't it?" Margaret asked.

"Yes," I said, "it's right there on Southern Avenue by the club."

"Keep your eye out for the entrance. I don't want to miss it," she said. "I still can't get used to y'all not being in that house on Mud Island."

Because my mother had moved seven months before she died, it was the second time I'd visited her house in Memphis. I'd only been there once since her diagnosis, but she'd flown out to California to see me twice. Dr. Purvis, her husband of twelve years, had wanted to separate my mother from her former life. He never got comfortable with living on my family's turf, though he managed to do it for eleven years.

My father, Tom Goodwyn, designed the house I grew up in. He was an architect, neat of manner and spare of gesture, and every inch of who he was appeared in its angles and planes. An amateur astronomer, my father designed the Frank Lloyd Wright-inspired house with an octagonal ceiling in the living room, and twelve feet of its roof was domed with a skylight to let in the stars. It was a modern house, ahead of the times for 1987, the kind of house that defines a family and bestows it with an unusual reputation. We lived in what is now called Harbor Town, on Mud Island in the middle of the Mississippi River, before the rest of the city got on board with the idea that it was chic. We were the first family to live out there before it was convenient, but in my father's antisocial mind, that was exactly the plan.

My mother lived in the house after my father unexpectedly died of a brain aneurism in 1998. It was a five-bedroom house, more room than she needed after Lincoln and I moved out. She hadn't the heart to leave it, but neither could Lincoln nor I bear the thought of her letting it go. When she married Dr. Purvis, he moved into the house with little more than his stethoscope. It sounded to me like he spent the following years begging my mother to move, but she wouldn't. He must have doubled up on his efforts the moment my mother was diagnosed because in the same telephone call she made to tell me about her cancer, she told me the foundation of my childhood had been sold.

"It's a smaller place. It's just going to be easier," my mother had said in an attempt at cushioning the blow. "I simply cannot rattle around that house forever. I'm fine now, but there's no way of knowing how long it will be so." Up until her final hour, my mother never admitted to a moment of discomfort. She was a Southern belle through and through. Because she wouldn't allow herself unseemly behavior, she acted as if her cancer was little more than the flu.

The house on Club Walk was a zero-lot line, which is realtor-speak for saying it didn't have much of a front yard. Set in an enclave of eight sand-colored traditional houses, it was tasteful and sophisticated, close in proximity to the Memphis Country Club. Cars were parked nose to end on either side of the gated community's street.

Margaret leaned out the window and announced to the guard, "We're going to the doctor's house." Rolling her window back up and pulling forward, she glanced at Eric. "The whole world's going to be here," she said.

And in that instant, I knew she was right. I don't know why I hadn't thought of it earlier, but in the walk of Memphis I grew up in, everything is done in a pack the size of an evangelist revival. Once through the front door, I was bombarded. At least a hundred and fifty people were packed into the house. They spilled from the foyer, perched in the den, socialized in the living room, hovered in the dining room, smoked cigarettes in the backyard, and chattered in the halls. Two full bars were set up, one in the kitchen, and even though it was windy and cold out, the other on the flagstone patio in the elm-lined backyard. Everyone held a drink in their hand, damp with condensation on a monogrammed cocktail napkin.

To look around the first floor of the house, you would have thought it was any other party, instead of a gathering in mourning. Though people in Memphis show up for every occasion, they have an implied, collective knack for the fine art of social discretion. The worst tragedy in the world could happen, and you could count on them all to never fully let on.

I was pounced upon the moment I set foot in the foyer, as Daphne's prodigal daughter, newly arrived. Lincoln's hazel eyes glowered at me from the den because my arrival had stolen his thunder. He stood smack in the middle of his superiority complex, six privileged feet tall in his austere black suit, and I thought for a second I should go to him, but an uncharacteristic sense of familial duty must have seized him, for he weaved his way to the door.

"There you are," he said, his tone impatient and directorial, then holding out his hand to Eric, he said smoothly, "Nice to see you, Eric. Come on in." One after another, I was set upon as my mother's coiffed friends came gliding on high heels to kiss me. "I'm so sorry, you know how much I loved her," seemed to be scripted, and I stood captive in the foyer for the better part of an hour.

Presently, I saw Dr. Purvis standing in the living room. His name was

Purvis Engle, but no one ever used his surname, including my mother, who never bothered to take it when they married. I never thought of him as my stepfather. He was plainly and obtusely my mother's husband, implacably and squarely *there.* Now that the common glue that bound us was gone, I knew with a certainty there'd be no future pretense of us being family. We would simply and irretrievably disband. My mother loved Dr. Purvis, but I couldn't fathom why. I couldn't see my way around his glasses-wearing, featureless demeanor to find the attraction; he seemed little more to me than a background fixture to my mother's spot-lit glow.

Standing beside Dr. Purvis was his balding, soft and spongy son. People called him "Young Purv," though he was in his mid-fifties. He was every bit as generic as his father. They both had a calm detachment that verged on boredom. A doctor himself, Young Purv was chief of staff at a hospital in Joplin, Missouri. To tell you all you need to know about Young Purv, he and his family, out of every place they could have lived in Jasper County, Missouri, chose to live an uninspired, sedentary life outside Joplin, in the sticks of a self-fulfilling named town called Stark, population 139.

In my mind, neither doctor had an attribute to recommend him. I had little to say to either, but as my mother's daughter, I was expected to fake it, which I did, but it wasn't easy, for what idle banter can possibly be made with a dripping, lackluster personality? There was nothing to go on, no point on which to connect, and I can say without doubt neither knew what to make of me. What with Lincoln under the roof and my mother in heaven, I suddenly realized I had no patronage at all in this house.

I reached out my hand for Eric's and whispered, "I just met eyes with Dr. Purvis. We have to go speak now or it'll be rude. Whatever you do, don't leave my side."

The doctors stood shoulder to shoulder, in serious suits and boring ties. Young Purv's thirteen-year-old albino-lashed, red-haired daughter clung to her father. She didn't so much as look at me to offer a challenging glare. For some unknown reason, she was the apple of her grandfather's eye, but I found her petty and cloying and spoiled. My mother hadn't cared for her at all, though she always pretended she was charmed. The two of us had laughed endlessly at her unfortunate name, which my mother said had all the panache of a sneeze. Her name was Winifred, and she was known as Winnie. When she turned thirteen, Dr. Purvis took the guesswork out of which of his three grandchildren he favored by buying Winne a gold watch, earrings, and a horse.

"Winnie," I gushed falsely, "thank you for coming down with your father. My mother would have been so touched."

"Granddaddy always said Grandmother Daphne loved me so much," Winnie said. "I think she loved me more than you."

I took my nails off the chalkboard and shook Dr. Purvis's hand, as was our way of greeting. Eric, ever the one to catch a fumble, stepped up and shook the doctor's hand, man-to-man style.

"I'm so glad you brought Cate down here safely," Dr. Purvis said, as if I couldn't find my way on my own. "Tough times. It was all so very sudden. I don't know how to say it another way, I'm completely in shock."

"I know," I said, "me too. I thought she was doing so well."

"She had a couple of bad bouts with pleurisy in seventy-two hours, dear thing. They drained her lungs the first time, but when it recurred, I knew she was so weakened, I suspected. Did Lincoln tell you your mother asked him to call you?"

"No, when was this?"

"On our way to the hospital. God bless her. I think she knew intuitively that it was the end."

"Lincoln didn't mention it," I said, seething. I knew I had to park my anger, but I'd get back to it later.

"Oh, before I forget," Dr. Purvis said, "your room is ready at the club. You must be exhausted, what with all this and your long trip. Any time you want me to run y'all over there, just say the word."

Young Purv clapped an awkward paw on my shoulder and left it there longer than he should have. "Sissy said to give you her love," he said, then looking at Eric, "My wife is at home with the other children. We thought better than to take them all out of school."

"Of course, I understand," I said. "But Winnie being here helps with their absence."

Eric looked at me for a stunned second, then said, "Cate, can I get you a drink?"

"Yes, please. I'd love something. See if there's some white wine."

"But you don't drink alcohol," Eric reminded.

"Well, I know that, Eric, but I'm going to now."

Margaret cut a path through the living room on her way to come find me. In an act of sheer telepathy, she handed me a stem of white wine. "Here," she said, her tone uncompromising. "It's getting late. I'm going to run on."

"I'll walk you to the door," I said, grateful for the excuse to go elsewhere. "Eric, I'll be right back."

Margaret and I made for the front door, but to get there it took forty minutes. So many people were in the house, so many I hadn't seen in years stopped me to talk that there was no expedient way to the door. When you grow up with a mother like mine, a product of the old South, in a Southern city that feels more like a small town, as Memphis does, there's a pitch and roll to the milieu, a living, breathing way of acting in the scrum of a collective of people so integral to your makeup that no move to California or anywhere else on the planet will ever effect. It's a sense of belonging that goes beyond the idea of tribal concerns. It's a membership that stretches long and reaches wide, and regardless of how far or how long you've wandered, you are utterly and perpetually one of their own.

"I have to say it," one of my mother's friends said to me. "It was exemplary of Daphne. As much as I can't take it in that she's gone, I will say she left the party while she was still having fun, so to speak."

Another of my mother's friends put her hand on her heart when she saw me. "Cate, you startled me for a second," she breathlessly said. "The older you get, the more you look like your mother."

And maybe I did, though I couldn't be objective. But age does level the playing field between a mother and daughter, this much I knew. I'd noticed that many of my girlfriends had unwittingly grown into replicas of their mothers. Whether by repetition of manner or the inevitability of maturity, when it comes to mothers and daughters and the passage of time, there's no pretending the apple didn't fall from the tree.

Margaret and I stepped outside and stood beneath the portico as the rain poured from the eaves like sheets of metal, the wind whipping cold and ceaseless. "How you doing?" she asked, drawing the hood of her raincoat over her head.

"Fine," I said perfunctorily.

"No, really," she pressed.

"Apart from the fact that I didn't think to bring a raincoat, I'm in a daze, thank you for asking. I just can't believe she's gone. I hate this. I'd say it's as bad as when my father died. At least my mother was there for that. To top it off, I feel like I have to be *on*. All I want to do is take to my bed and stay there."

"You can't take to your bed. You have to step up. You're the only daughter, which means you're the hostess. And I realize this will sound macabre, but you could borrow one of your mother's raincoats."

"Borrow?" I repeated.

"Who's going to miss it?" Then, as Margaret and I have always done in the direst of circumstances, we both started laughing. We were oscillating between guilt and full tilt, when the front door opened behind us and Eric stepped out and handed me another glass of wine.

"I've been looking for you," he said. "I don't want to rush you, but Dr. Purvis asked if we were about ready for him to run us over to the club. I think it's a good idea. It's past ten, and we've got a long day tomorrow. Let's get over there and check in."

"You're right. I think we've got a long three days ahead of us," I said, and turning to Margaret, I gave her a hug. "Thank you so much for everything. It means the world to me that you're here."

"I'll see y'all tomorrow," Margaret said. "Call me in the morning and tell me where to be. And listen, I want to help in any way I can. I'll be happy to drive y'all around while you're here. Whatever you need, okay?"

"Okay. Thank you, I'll call you in the morning."

With that, Margaret secured her hood over her dark curls and ran to her car.

"Give me a second," I said to Eric when we entered the foyer. "I'll just be a minute. If you want to go get Dr. Purvis, I'll meet y'all by the garage door in the kitchen. I'm just going down the hall."

In my mother's room, worlds collided. I could hear the howling wind thrashing the elm branches against the window panes of the well-appointed bedroom she shared with Dr. Purvis, and my stomach dropped low when I entered to discover her absence. I was five years old in that moment. I wore a green jumper dress with a drum and two drumsticks crossed on the front and new saddle shoes for my first day of kindergarten. My mother and I had had a time of it that morning. It was my fault. I'd been in a pout at the prospect of leaving her for too much of the day and was despondent. I'd pleaded and bargained and gone to great extents of creativity to dissuade the inevitable. Being separated from Daphne would be such an insufferable episode, I'd even promised to clean my room.

But my mother had done as she did so magically—she filled the air with her silver-bell laughter. Lowering herself, she'd put her slender hands on my shoulders and looked unblinkingly into my green eyes, eyes that matched hers in intensity, eyes she'd bestowed upon me as if by explicit design. "Catherine, you're growing up," she had said. "I'm so excited for you that you get to go to school. I can't wait to hear all about it. I want you to go, and then come back to tell me who was there and what they were wearing. I bet there won't be one girl at school who is as pretty as you are. Do me a favor, will you?" she asked, her whispering voice conspiratorial. "I want you to look around carefully, don't let anybody know what you're doing, but pick out a little girl to make friends with, and this weekend, I'll call her mother and we'll have her over to play. Can you do that?" I'd nodded agreeably, my pout beginning to lift. "The trick to making new friends is to make eye contact," my mother continued. "Keep a smile on your face, and let your new friend do the talking. This way you can appear interested. People always like those that do." In no uncertain terms, in that indelible instant,

I learned the game rules of Southern society to see me through the rest of my life.

I crossed the floor and entered my mother's dressing room. The white slat double doors across from her vanity table were closed, and I opened them to the wafting of florid perfume. My mother wore perfume that preceded her, and one good hug in her slender arms meant I'd be doing the same. Perfume was yet another example of her endless femininity. She was bestowed at birth with every bell and whistle the fairer sex could ever aspire to, and those that she lacked, she acquired.

I reached into her closet and found a series of raincoats, one in every primary color, none with a hood, for she zipped up the hair she had tended at the beauty parlor every Friday in a helmet of thick clear plastic. It took more than rain to stop my mother from being perfectly turned out. Shrugging into a water-resistant Anne Taylor, I buttoned it in front of my mother's vanity mirror, and caught sight of her red-lacquered jewelry box laying upon the table's mirrored top.

I was not overcome with memory until I walked back into her bedroom.

The last time I'd been to Memphis, the air was freighted with unspoken implications. It was not my mother's way to come out and state the obvious, when doing so would bring her distressing condition to the fore. She preferred to skirt issues, make light of tragedy, so in lieu of an overt conversation about her cancer, she'd taken the covert route by carrying her jewelry box into the bedroom as I sat on the edge of the four-poster bed.

In a gesture performed as if a matter of course, as if she'd been long in the habit, she'd carried her twenty-four-inch jewelry box in from her dressing room and placed it on the coral-colored duvet, then perched beside me and lifted its lid. It was then she told me the story of her life in emblematic totems, lifting each treasure within and placing it in my hands. A twenty-four-carat gold-link charm bracelet held the codes to her twenty-year marriage with my father. It began with a charm of the Eiffel Tower, and ended twenty charms later with a charm of the Bible.

My mother and I sat on her bed for more than an hour, inspecting pieces passed down from Catherine, her Southern mother whom she named me after and whom she adored. A baroque solid-gold charm hung regally from a box-chain. My grandmother had received it from her mother. With its opaque-amber embossed carnelian end, it was once used to stamp wax in a monogrammed signatory seal. I'd seen it many times around my mother's neck, and had heard the story of its Hampstead, England, origin. Without saying more, my mother stood and clasped the chain behind my neck, saying, "Take it, Cate, now it's yours." And I knew as she did she was gently passing a torch symbolically down my family's generational line of women. I started to be demure, wanted to deflect in an attempt at staving off the implication. Some things really are better off left unsaid, especially when saying something you don't want to admit makes it real.

Shaking off the memory before I broke down and cried, I put my fingers to my neck and touched the carnelian seal I'd thought to wear as I packed for my trip. For some reason beyond the realm of self-government, I walked back to my mother's dressing room. As I opened her jewelry box, my eyes reviewed its partitioned contents, then I selected a ring to put on my right hand. It was a meaningful gesture, an attempt to connect with the woman I wanted beside me. I picked up my purse, headed out to the hallway, and there blocking my path was a scowling Winnie.

"Granddaddy said nobody's supposed to be back here," she snipped, and it was all I could do to resist the urge to slap her.

"I'm borrowing a raincoat," I said, brushing by her, then I walked down the hallway laughing.

Chapter Three

The night shivered with finality and sinking grief, as Dr. Purvis drove Eric and me around the corner to the Memphis Country Club, our suitcases in the back of my mother's four-door white Lexus. It had been a series of inconsequential things that poured salt into the wound of her absence. The daily accoutrements of her life scattered about as if she'd walk in the room any minute: her toothbrush by the sink in her dressing room, her handwritten grocery list by the kitchen telephone, her leather handbag on the bedroom's toile-slipcovered chair. All the little articles that gave testimony to her life, all the unique variables of the way she lived left out in the open waiting to be resumed in the small gestures of living.

Even the drive to the Memphis Country Club chaffed my soul like sandpaper. I'd never had reason to go to the club unless my mother was there lunching in the red room, or perhaps throwing a party, or attending one. And the thing about grief is it's bottomless. Just when you think you're low, you fall lower. The rain came down sideways in thrashing, unremitting sheets as Eric finagled our luggage from the trunk, and I made a mad dash up the red-carpeted stairs under the porte cochere. The last time I'd ascended these stairs, my mother was beside me, and after I'd whisked the heavy door open to the club's tiled entrance and stood waiting for Eric, a series of memories scrolled across my mind in flashes of other times I'd stood in this same place at my mother's behest, and I quickly focused on the last time Eric and I stayed at the club.

By my mother's decree, Eric and I had been summoned to Memphis, six weeks after we'd married in Pebble Beach, California. My mother insisted on throwing us a proper Memphis party, since our wedding had been outside the reach of her endless group of friends.

"Y'all simply must come down here," she'd said to me over the telephone. "No daughter of mine sneaks off to be married. People will think I didn't raise you well."

"Mom, you were at the wedding," I reminded her. "Eric and I didn't sneak off. You were right there with us on the beach."

"Well, I know that," she'd said. "But you have to bring Eric down here to meet all your friends."

"Those closest to me have already met him," I said. "What you're really saying is you want *your* friends to meet Eric. Go on, tell the truth."

"All right. My friends. There are just some things you should do, and this is one of them."

My mother's party for Eric and me took place in two ground-floor rooms of the Memphis Country Club. The setting could best be likened to a beehive of my mother's Southern-to-the-bone, over-the-top friends. Many of my friends were there that night, and it was gratifying to have so many of them assembled in one place at one time to meet Eric. All, of course, loved meeting my husband, but my mother's friends set upon Eric like queen bees upon honey. To this day, I'm not convinced Eric's fully recovered from his forced indoctrination into my mother's gregarious side of the South.

Because, you see, being born to my mother's Memphis, I was bestowed with a particular walk of life, and along it my mother's friends flit like fireflies carrying keys to the kingdom. In the lounge overlooking the south side of the Memphis Country Club's golf course, Eric and I didn't move from our stationary positions in front of the heavy mahogany bar for three hours because we couldn't. We stood side by side like statues at the head of a receiving line as one after another my mother's spectacular friends floated up to the jangle of jewelry, wearing stockings and heels and clouds of perfume, wanting a good look at the outsider who had married Daphne's daughter.

"Now tell me, where is it you're from?" one of them asked, gushing with *I'm so thrilled to meet you* enthusiasm that verged on the flirtatious. "I'm from Boston," Eric said, then fifteen minutes later, as the line flowed like river rapids, another glittering woman stepped forward, her ecstatic face an inspecting inch before Eric's startled eyes. Grabbing Eric's hands, she exclaimed, "I understand you're a Yankee from Boston!"

It went on this way for the entirety of the party and gave Eric a good dose of the fact that he hadn't just married me, he'd married into a network spurred by the engine of Southern social graces, where everyone had to have the facts on everybody. The night was so overwhelming, we all but crawled to the guest room my mother reserved for us down a long hallway on the second floor of the Memphis Country Club. We fell through the door of the symmetrical, stately room, where matching ivory duvets lay folded on identical beds set on either side of an English console, its porcelain lamp casting a hushed, dim glow upon the hunter-green carpeting.

It was going to happen, sooner or later. I suppose it was inevitable that when we least expected it, a culture clash would arise between Eric and me, with all its untidy ramifications. We'd skirted three years of courtship without the salient difference in our background becoming a point worth seriously discussing, but when it came up, it came up fast and disillusioning, in the late hours of the night after my mother's party.

Eric, you see, is a Yankee born and bred, which fundamentally means we come from two different cultures and had two different kinds of parents. Eric's mother is a Midwesterner, born and reared on a farm in southeastern Wisconsin. She was the God-fearing, domesticated sort who raised five boys, sent them to Catholic school, baked bread, and knew her way around a Singer sewing machine. The only domestic gift my mother ever had was an aptitude for interior decorating, at which she excelled, knowing, as she did, about fine art and antiques. But she couldn't boil water without something cataclysmic happening. For all her abilities in every other quadrant of her life, her ineptitude in a kitchen reached stratospheric proportion. And our fathers couldn't have been more different if you'd searched the world over looking for opposites.

Eric's father was with the Boston Police Department. He was a big, burly man, rugged, brass tacked, and fearless. My father was a gentleman in every sense of the word. He was painfully thin, detail oriented, scientific of mind, and a bit of a dreamer. Suffice it to say, regarding general influences, I grew up in a gentle, courtly environment verging on the impractical, while Eric grew up with his nose to the grindstone, preparing to navigate the salt of the earth. We'd managed to keep a nice balance between us, and our friends often remarked on our complementary traits.

And yet, that the Memphis Country Club's bartender and waiters, whom I'd known since I was very young, addressed me as Miss Cate all night and answered me with a deferential, "*Yes ma'am,*" seemed to take Eric aback. He'd never been exposed to the formalities of the South, and, he divulged, he thought it rang disharmonious notes of a time and history no longer appropriate to the current day and age. Our late-night conversation had turned into an exhaustive vortex, in which I also told him about making my debut during the Christmas season, the year I turned eighteen.

"Your debut? You're a debutant?" Eric had asked, his voice riddled with suspicion. "How come you never mentioned it?"

"I don't know, Eric, it's not a big deal. It's not like it's a source of self-identification. How was I supposed to work it into a conversation? I'm not a debutant now, since you asked, but at the time, I guess you could have called me one. It was only for a little more than a week."

"A week? I thought it was for one night."

"It was for one night, but there were parties leading up to it."

"For what?" he asked. "I'm not completely ignorant. Girls on the East Coast make their debut too, but I'm curious to hear your explanation."

"It'll sound like rationale no matter what I say, but summarily, it's a long-held tradition."

I'd said there really wasn't much more to it than age-old Southern custom, that as my mother's daughter, this was part and parcel to the parameters of what I'd been born to. It had been this way for all my friends. We'd agreed to the yearly traditional party because none of us ever thought to defy our mothers. Because Eric made such a big deal questioning this, I'd never tell him that, in her day, my mother was voted Queen of the Memphis Cotton Carnival, a Memphis city-wide tradition staged every June since 1931, with its secret societies, series of parties, and festivities to rival Mardi Gras.

"I had no idea I married a debutant, Miss Cate," Eric laughed, and I, not in the mood for humor, quit trying to explain the way it has always been, for how do you explain long-held social mores to someone with a dubious vantage point, without sounding as if you're defensive? But truth be told, in some hidden corridor within me, I, too, was uncomfortable with the address that now came to me. It's one thing to be called Miss Cate when you're a child. When you're young, it's somehow placating, but the "Miss" had a different spin on it now. It was smoothed to a "Miz" now that I was grown and married, and it tacitly catapulted me into my mother's echelon, when I didn't, in the least, identify with the strata. I'd always assumed "Miz" was reserved for a certain age, though I couldn't pinpoint exactly what that age should be.

After Eric and I had gone through endless rounds that night, trying to find the bridge between our cultural gap, I'd stayed awake for hours, convinced that from here on out, I would be misunderstood by my husband. I'd constructed every self-defeating thought imaginable until the wee hours of morning. Although I can't recall where the roiling thoughts began, I can vividly recall wondering, before I finally drifted to sleep, if I should have brought him down South before we were married. After all, how can one get a firm grasp of whom someone is, without having a good understanding of where they come from? I awoke the following morning worse for wear, but Eric had diffused any residual tension by taking me in his arms and laughing, "I guess I'm in it now, Miss Cate, but I have to say I'll never regret it."

I was shaking off my mother's raincoat when Eric walked into the foyer wheeling both of our wet suitcases behind him. "Dr. Purvis just said the rain's going to quit tomorrow, thank God. Also, he gave me the room key and asked us to call him in the morning. He offered to come get us tomorrow afternoon for the visitation, but I told him I was pretty sure we'd be getting a ride with

Margaret."

"I have to give it to him, he's accommodating. It must be hard for him without Mom here. She's always been the one to take care of everything. Anyway, I'm glad you said we're going with Margaret. I'll call him in the morning to check in."

Chapter Four

Upon the high-ceilinged antique ivory walls of the Memphis Country Club, a gallery of past club presidents stared at me as I made my way down the hall to the kitchen looking for coffee. It was eight o'clock in the morning, and just as I decided to peek in through the kitchen's swinging doors to see who was about, they flew apart, and Justine bustled through in her white-collared, black-skirted uniform, carrying a carafe of steaming coffee, its rich chicory scent fully waking me up.

"There you are, Miz Cate," Justine said. "I'm bringing this in to your brother. You about ready for a cup?"

"Lincoln's here?" I asked, startled.

"He sure is. He's in the red room," Justine said. "Listen, honey, I'm so sorry to hear about Miz Daphne. They just don't come any finer. We're all so sorry, but we're glad to see you home. You let me know if there's anything I can do for you while you're here."

"Thank you, Justine," I said, touched by her sincerity. "And yes, I'd love a cup. By the way, how's your daughter?"

"Second year of medical school. She's doing just fine up in Chicago."

"I'm glad to hear it," I said. "When you can, please tell Stella I said hello."

"I sure will do that," Justine said, walking beside me to the red room, then peeling off to the sideboard to get me a cup and saucer.

Lincoln sat at a linen-draped four-top by the window overlooking the shrub-lined gravel pathway before the golf course. Outside, the warm autumn light filtered in soft and golden, now that the rain had quit. There was always something lounging about Lincoln's nonchalant demeanor. Wherever he was, he exuded a proprietary slouch, a cool entitlement, and he got to his feet when I walked in the room as if he'd been expecting me in his personal jurisdiction.

"You're up and about early," I said in greeting.

"Yes, I am. I need to talk to you," he said as Justine placed china cups and MCC monogrammed menus before us.

"Thank you, Justine," I said, looking up at her, grateful for the distraction. Whatever it was Lincoln wanted to talk about, I had a feeling it wouldn't be good. After Justine filled our cups and said to let her know when we were ready to order, I leaned back in my leather chair and said, "Talk to me about what?"

"Mother's trust," he fired. "Dr. Purvis wants to go over it while you're down here."

"What, you mean read it to us? When?"

"He wants to do it after the funeral. I don't know if you want Eric there with us or not."

"Of course I want him there. Why wouldn't I? I don't have anything to hide."

"You never were discreet, I figured. Dr. Purvis and I are co-trustees of the estate, so I thought I'd ask."

"Co-trustees? What's Dr. Purvis doing in the picture? I just assumed after Mom died, he'd want to wash his hands of both of us and get on with his life."

Lincoln gave a derisive snort. "From what I hear, he's just about done that already."

"Meaning what?" I asked, taken aback.

"Meaning he wasted no time in filling Mother's shoes. And I can tell you exactly who he has his eye on."

"What in the world are you talking about?" I said, stung. "Are you trying to suggest he's been having an affair?"

"No, not an affair, but the man is a planner. He's pushing eighty. He's too old to be alone. Men like him don't know how."

I couldn't take in what Lincoln suggested, though I knew he had an uncanny aptitude for keeping his ear attuned to the Memphis grapevine, which had always been a few short steps away from incestuous. If any tidbit of gossip swirled around Memphis, Lincoln was firmly footed in his black-tassel loafers at its epicenter. He loved knowing who was doing what and passing judgment. Gossiping was Lincoln's favorite sport. "So, who does Dr. Purvis have his eye on?" I had to ask, subscribing to the drama of it now, for how could I not? I was already halfway informed, and although I have an aversion to back-biting petty talk, which is clearly what this was, it was too tempting not to continue.

"Camila Thurman," Lincoln divulged. "She lives across the street on Club Walk."

A vision came to me then of a woman with flaming-red hair, thin and tall and stately, with an obsequious manner. "Please tell me you're making this up," I said. "Wasn't she a friend of Mom's?"

Lincoln waved his left hand dismissively, the hand that bore my father's gold oval insignia ring, and the movement couldn't have been more timely in calling to mind my resentment for my father's replacement. Dr. Purvis had been a thorn in my side for too long. He never could hold a candle to my father, and now here was evidence of his perfidy. "Camila wasn't a close friend of Mother's," Lincoln said. "She wasn't part of her group. At one time, she worked in a flower shop. An upscale shop, mind you, but still, she worked. She just isn't our kind, but she raised herself up when she married rich at age sixty. It was her first marriage. She's only been widowed a year."

I couldn't stop thinking about how insulting this all seemed. My mother's death should have had much more of a devastating effect on Dr. Purvis. I'd assumed it would take forever for him to get back up. Instead, he wasn't even dusting himself off before he switched horses. "I don't know how I'll be able to look him in the eye after hearing this," I said. "Do you know if Camila will be at the funeral?"

"Of course she'll be at the funeral. Even though most people know what's going on, they'll carry on as if they don't. This is the South. You've obviously forgotten how the game is played. You very deliberately moved too far away."

"I haven't forgotten, Lincoln," I said, sensing a burr beneath the saddle of his comment. "And I haven't been too far away. I've always kept current."

"Well, you broke Mother's heart by moving to California. She wanted you to turn out differently. She wanted you to stay here, get married to someone whose family she knew, and have children. Mother wanted to be a grandmother." Lincoln gave a big, dramatic sigh. "But you've always done whatever you wanted."

"Yes, I have," I snapped. "It has no bearing whatsoever on how much I loved Mom. I won't apologize for not doing as you did by staying tethered to her apron strings. And by the way, I don't see you in any semblance of a stable relationship, much less with any babies, but of course, you're incapable of looking at yourself. Why are you always so nasty? You didn't even bother to tell me Mom asked you to call me moments before she died." I rose to my feet and stormed out of the red room.

"You need to be at Griffin Funeral Home this afternoon at three-thirty," Lincoln called from behind me. "Be on time, or you'll make us all look bad."

In the upstairs hallway before our room's door, I paced back and forth for ten minutes before I put my key in the door to face Eric. Eric didn't understand my contentious relationship with my brother. He had no frame of reference because he got along so well with his four brothers.

Eric took an assessing look at me when I closed the door behind me. "What?" he asked. "What's wrong?"

"I hate him." I said.

"Who?"

"Lincoln. He always manages to push my buttons."

"He's a momma's boy," Eric said summarily. "Don't let him bother you."

I started a rebuttal, then realized that what had just transpired between Lincoln and me included a jab at Eric. He was the someone I'd married who wasn't from Memphis. I decided to shut my mouth and drop it.

"I'm going to call Margaret and ask her to come get us a little after three," I said. "Do you feel like taking a walk with me to Chickasaw Gardens? Now that it's not raining, we have perfect fall weather."

In midtown Memphis, an historic neighborhood called Chickasaw Gardens lies like a testimony to classic Southern architecture, between Central Avenue and Poplar. Many of my friends grew up in columned homes beneath its canopies of mature oaks and elms, where the neat streetscapes are so head turning, nobody balks at the fifteen-miles-per-hour speed limit. At Chickasaw Gardens' center is a wooded man-made lake, where all of us gathered throughout high school, for all its verdantly secluded park-like atmosphere.

From the Memphis Country Club, it is a lovely, leisurely walk down Goodwyn Street, so named after one of my civic-leading forebears, and worth every breathtaking step at any time of the year, but, to me, Goodwyn is at its best in the fall. Both sides of the residential street were resplendent with towering trees in various degrees of decline. They reached, stoic limbed and regal, for a last deep breath before winter's slumber. I knew every impressive house down Goodwyn's hushed corridor. Many are set back from the street by an acre or two of manicured lawns appointed with flourishing gardens.

Since Eric and I were unscheduled until early afternoon, we took our time strolling in air so crisp and clear, it seemed the rain had washed away the glare from Memphis's incessant humidity. I brought my childhood with me as we ambled along, saying this house once belonged to the president of the Coca-Cola Bottling Company, and that one over there, to the head of Schlitz Brewery. My heart glowed with adolescent memories along the twenty-five-minute walk to Chickasaw Gardens. I took Eric's hand and spoke my thoughts. "I've always thought if you really want to feel the soul of a place, it's best to see it on foot."

From the corner of Goodwyn and Central, we dodged both directions of traffic to enter the enclave of Chickasaw Gardens. "There on the left," I said softly, "a murder took place in that house." Switching tempo, my voice rang out with unbridled excitement. "And look just ahead, there's the house of my mother's best friend."

When the memory came to me, the ground heaved and I fell to my sinking knees.

The last time I saw my mother, we drove to Chickasaw Gardens and dropped in on her best friend, Amelia Bondurant. Mom and Melia, as she was known, had known each other since they were four. It was my mother who gave Melia her nickname, for her four-year-old tongue couldn't handle the logistics of three syllables. Melia and my mother were birds of a feather, cut from the same cloth, who went to the same school, literally and figuratively. They were so emotionally and psychically connected, I never believed it was coincidence they each gave birth to a son on the same day, in the same Memphis hospital, within an hour of each other. They had that kind of a friendship.

Although our visit to Melia was unplanned, she answered the door as if expecting us. I'd never seen anyone caught unawares so thrilled to receive anybody. She was much like my mother in this way, which is to say her manners were so lovely, you would have thought she spent her days sitting on ready to receive company. Both women were Southern ladies to the manner born, who arose each morning and dressed impeccably, even if there was no plan to leave the house. I'd once asked my mother why she never relaxed, why she took such deliberation in pulling herself so tightly together, and without skipping a beat, as if her reply was the most obvious one in the world, she'd answered, "Well, Cate, I do it for myself, of course. Why ever in the world do you ask? I know I taught you it's just how you do."

Melia's golden hair was perfectly flipped under, two inches above her delicate collarbone. She wore a navy pantsuit, lipstick, and an effervescent smile on her heart-shaped face as she opened her front door. The late-July humidity felt like an inferno as my mother and I stood smiling on the Bondurants' doorstep, but I had the foresight to bring a cardigan, knowing from experience the central air-conditioning in the house would be on full blast.

"Daphne, so good to see you," Melia sang, "and oh, you've brought Cate. I'm so tickled. Y'all come on in."

At the end of the Bondurants' long front hallway, a tile-floored solarium spread elegantly, its bay-window view of the shaded backyard rioting in rich colors from dahlias, azaleas, geraniums, and hydrangea, patterned beneath mature elms from which birds sang in staccato rounds. "Y'all sit down. I'll be just a minute," Melia said, and when she returned, her white-uniformed maid was behind her carrying ice tea on a black-lacquered tray. After small courtesies were delivered of thanks and gratitude, Melia's help retreated and I watched these two seraphic women settle upon scrolled wrought-iron, slipcovered in large floral print, and knew I was privy to a scene they'd performed a million times throughout their lives, yet, in this instance, it was in a distressing context. For what is there to say with the full knowledge that your best friend has cancer, and how is one to possibly know if this visit might be the last? And I, fraught and weighted with inevitability, did as I always had. I deferred to these two gracious women to take the lead.

"Cate, I don't know how you keep your little figure. You look the same as you always have. I don't know how you do it," Melia gushed.

"It helps that she hasn't had any children," my mother said, to which Melia waved a slender hand.

"She's still young, Daphne. Girls wait longer in this day and age. You and I went rushing off to have children before we even grew up."

"Well, I thought I should go on and do it," my mother laughed. "I didn't know I'd live this long. How was I supposed to know I'd be an old lady?"

"Mom, you're not an old lady," I said. "You're only seventy."

"Seventy is old when you're used to being young and cute. I still think of myself as thirty."

"I do too," Melia chimed. "If I were to pick any age to be forever, I'd choose thirty."

"I might choose twenty," my mother said, musing. "At thirty, I was saddled with two children."

"Thanks a lot, Mom," I said, laughing. "I never meant to weigh you down."

"Daphne, don't pretend for a minute we ever aspired to anything else," Melia chided.

"We didn't, but I still wanted to keep having fun."

Melia lowered her chin and looked at my mother. "Now Daphne, you've had plenty of fun."

"Well, I'm not having fun now," my mother said with a hand to her custom-made auburn wig. This was the full extent to which reference was made to her cancer, because Melia changed course by changing the subject.

"I saw Lincoln playing tennis at the club yesterday. Cate, I know he's happy to have you home," Melia said liltingly.

I exchanged a look with Mom that spoke volumes, and was surprised to hear her laugh before I could.

Melia looked from Mom to me. "What in the world is so funny?"

"This will sound terrible," I said, looking at Melia. "Lincoln looks forward to having me home with all the enthusiasm of bad news. Let's just say he's not my biggest fan."

Melia nodded, and I knew Mom had told her a little something about how it was between me and Lincoln. "I will say y'all are nothing alike, but that's not so unusual in siblings. Y'all are five years apart in age, which probably has a little something to do with it."

"His five-year jump on me just made it more of a threat when I came along and stole Mom from him," I said. "Before my unfortunate birth, he had Mom all to himself."

"He is unusually tied to me," Mom agreed, which, in my opinion, put it mildly.

"He's not as independent as Cate, is he?" Melia added. "Ah well, it's little more than a territorial game. It won't be this way forever. Relationships do go through phases."

"They do, but it'd be so convenient if this little phase of theirs could end soon. I'm not going to say anything more," Mom said, uncrossing then re-crossing her slender knees, as if shifting to another position signaled a shift of topic.

"No, let's not say another word more," Melia agreed, and as I sat observing Mom and Melia, I gathered a great sense of how they kept their lives so evenly keeled. They simply never discussed anything potentially upsetting. I believed both had been raised this way by their Southern mothers, and herein lay the key to the house of Southern civility, presided over and passed down by women such as Melia and my mother. Sometimes I think the world is sadly bereft of their equal. They were the way-showers who taught by the power of feminine example. They were role models who kept Southern culture beautiful by keeping everything light and pleasant.

Eric looked alarmingly at my blanched face, seconds after I pointed out Melia Bondurant's ivy covered Tudor-style house. When he spoke, it was with urgency. "Cate, are you all right?"

Because I was schooled in the tactics of pleasantry by two of the finest women to ever grace the earth, I didn't let on to my husband. "I will be in just a minute," I answered. "I hope you won't mind if we head back."

Chapter Five

Winnie stood beady-eyed and sentry outside the front door of Griffin Funeral Home. Three-thirty on the dot, and the cool autumn breeze blew her red hair in tangles over her elfin face.

"You're late," she sniffed. "I told Granddaddy you would be."

"Winnie, we're not late, honey, it's three-thirty now. I see you're wearing your watch. You can see for yourself."

Winnie didn't glance at her watch. "I know what time it is, but you were supposed to be here before three-thirty because it starts at three-thirty. The family was supposed to be ready to receive, and you're just walking in the door."

I locked eyes with Margaret, until she rolled hers and put her hand to her forehead as if she already had a headache.

"It'll be fine, Winnie," I said, taking Eric's hand and mounting the concrete stairs. "This is Memphis. Everyone will be fashionably late."

Nobody was in the funeral home's foyer, save for Lincoln and both doctors. Young Purv idled about looking uncomfortable, and Dr. Purvis stood reading one of the many ostentatious floral arrangements' cards.

Sometimes, too much really can be too much, in the way of flower overkill. One second inside Griffin's lugubrious hall, and my eyes torrentially watered. I looked at Eric, who has an olfactory system as sensitive as a dog's, and saw him wince. I was on the verge of mentioning that I was overwhelmed by the stifling funeral scent, when Lincoln derailed me.

"The Canales sent these," Lincoln pontificated. "And Gretchen and Speeds Worthington sent the gladiolas from Le Fleur. I haven't seen anything from the Harrises, but the Phillips's are over there. They sent from Mason's, of course. They were delivered here late yesterday." One after another, Lincoln put his hand to spray after stand after vase, while I stood dumbfounded. "Dr. Purvis, who sent those over there on the desk?" Lincoln asked, and when he turned, his eyes met mine. Pausing, he sighed and said, "Well, I don't know what you're looking at."

"For heaven's sake, Lincoln. What does it matter who sent what? This isn't a popularity contest."

"It will be if we don't get our family acknowledgments out on time. Believe me, people will talk, and I'm not going to fall out of favor just because you don't think anything matters. By the way, I ordered the cards. They're monogrammed. I didn't think you'd think to do it."

"That's what I suspected," I snapped. "You've done everything else without including me."

"Now stop this, the two of you," Dr. Purvis interrupted. "This isn't the time or place. Your mother wouldn't have wanted this. Can't y'all just get along? Could you possibly wait until after your mother's funeral tomorrow?" On that note, Dr. Purvis completely fell apart. He covered his lowered face with his hands, shoulders trembling, then reached in his breast pocket for a handkerchief.

Kevin Griffin padded, cat-footed, from the back hall as if on telepathic cue. He draped a firm consoling arm around Dr. Purvis's shoulder and shepherded him to a chair before the low-burning fire in the living room.

"There's not any alcohol here, is there?" Margaret said to me under her breath, and I knew she meant to diffuse the moment.

"No, but hang on. Everyone will be swimming in it on Club Walk after this. Southern visitations are always scheduled to end in time for the cocktail hour. We just have to get from here to there."

Young Purv rambled up to me. I couldn't decide if the tight look on his face was shame or appropriately funereal. "You'll have to excuse my father," he said. "This has been hard on him. He loved your mother so. He'll be lost without her."

Lost until he picks up with the woman across the street, I thought. "I understand," I said. "It's to be expected. We're all on edge."

"Yes. He hasn't been sleeping these past few nights. He's a quiet man, not used to having so many people in his house. He's never been the social kind. He's always left that to your outgoing mother. You know, this is the second wife my father has buried."

Wait a minute. It's my mother who died. Why is this about him? "Of course, that explains it. Bad luck," I said.

Young Purv stepped in closer, having found me a willing confidant. "The one stroke of good fortune is that your mother finally agreed to move out of that house they were living in on Mud Island. He always felt too removed from things down there, too isolated. The timing of their move was perfect. I wouldn't want him living down there alone now."

Perfect timing? He tried to get my mother out of that house because she owned it. The second my mother was diagnosed, he probably thought he'd better move or he'd be out on the street. He plotted the move in case she left the house to her children. Lincoln was right in saying the guy is a planner. I wonder what else he knows about her trust.

The doors opened behind us, and within the half hour, Griffin Funeral Home had the ambience of Grand Central Station. The two and a half hours allotted for visitation were but a formality, a prelude to the service and burial tomorrow, and I knew tonight there'd be a party tantamount to an Irish wake, that my mother's legion of friends would take over Club Walk in one last gesture of poignant assembly, then reappear at Independent Presbyterian Church tomorrow for the service. They'd caravan to Elmwood Cemetery to lay my mother in final rest, but I knew the customary swing. After that, they'd leave us alone.

I just had to get through what was essentially any other extended party. My mother's friends had a knack for turning everything into a soiree. But I needed to get my head on straight. I wanted a reprieve to get used to walking this world without my mother, and for that, I wanted space. And it may be the whirlwind wrought by well-meaning people is designed as a distraction for the bereaved family, as a way of commiseration and support, but I was annoyed with what seemed like the inconsequential logistics, which Lincoln seemed caught up in concerning who came when, wearing what, and what was said inappropriately or otherwise. Lincoln would maintain a running commentary on things I didn't care about, but the one thing I knew from my history with Southern funerals is all you have to do is wait for it because something always goes wrong.

In the middle of the living room of the house on Club Walk, I stood beside Eric holding a glass of white wine in my right hand, thinking I now understand why so many people like to drink something that loosens their brain, gets them out of themselves, and mutes the glare of reality to a warm, gauzy haze. I felt lighter, less grounded in corporeal sensibility, congealed in an environment suddenly relieved of my usual self-conscious, me-versus-them demeanor. Because I've always experienced the world from the outside looking in. In this way, I have never been at all like my mother, who was in and of all environments with a custodial belonging that made everyone else look like an outsider.

I could just picture her in the room. If she were here, she'd be the center of attention. She'd be presiding over this house like a queen holding court, setting the tone for the rest of us from the sonorous gift of her melodic laughter. The air was vacuous with her absence. I looked around the room, and my mother's friends seemed conspicuously without context. Melia Bondurant made her graceful way toward me, and I watched her gliding forward, thinking we are, all of us, one Southern belle less.

Kissing my cheek, Melia laid a hand on my shoulder and said, "Your mother was so proud of you," and in that moment, I saw the three of us laughing in Melia's solarium, inclusively in such a way as to stage Melia and me as equals in an indelible memory crafted so very recently. In Melia's eyes, I saw the schoolgirl she once was, part and parcel of my mother's coming of age, and I could almost feel my mother standing beside her in a phantom aura.

"Thank you, Melia," I said. "She loved you so much. You were more than her best friend, y'all were like sisters."

"We were closer than that, Cate. I say this because there never was a time when we didn't get along," Melia confided. The gravity of the moment was suddenly lifted as Melia looked at my right hand and said, "Oh, you're wearing that ring she always hated. Did your mother ever tell you about that?"

"I never heard anything about it, other than it was a gift from Dr. Purvis. I did see her wearing it a few times."

"Well." Melia looked over her shoulder, then lowered her voice to a whisper. "She had to wear it. Poor Dr. Purvis wanted to surprise your mother for her birthday, for the first time ever. You know how men are, they never know what to do when they need to get their wives a present. It irritated your mother to no end when, year after year, Dr. Purvis asked her what she wanted for her birthday. It took the surprise out of everything, and you know your mother liked to be surprised. But I told her those who can't tell their husband what they want for their birthday don't get anything. Anyway, for some weird reason, Dr. Purvis decided to go out and buy your mother that ring, without her involvement. It taught her a lesson, believe me. She hated the ring. You can look at the circle of diamonds and sapphires and see it just isn't her taste. She had to break down every so often and wear it. She pretended she was thrilled so she wouldn't hurt his feelings. I'm so glad you're wearing it, Cate. She would love that," Melia said, taking my hand and lifting it for a closer look at the ring. "You know, I really don't think it's all that bad."

Lincoln came up behind me. He took one look at my raised hand and said, "You're not supposed to be wearing anything of Mother's until her estate is appraised."

"Lincoln, who cares?" Melia scoffed. "No one will miss this." Looking me in the eyes, she leaned in close and whispered, "Cate, you go on and take that ring."

"Dr. Purvis has already laid down the law. Nothing goes out of this house until every scrap is appraised," Lincoln continued.

"Well, don't tell him," Melia said. "That will take care of that."

In the front hall, I heard a commotion. It took me a few disconcerting moments to synthesize that the woman trying to steady herself against the wall was blatantly drunk.

"Oh, for heaven's sake," Melia said, watching across the way. "It's always something. Let me go see about this." And with that, I watched her walk toward the front door and take matters in hand, in what I knew to be the stead of my mother.

"Is the woman ill?" Eric asked me. "What's going on over there?"

"She's been overserved," Lincoln said with no alarm to his voice.

"Eric's parents don't drink," I informed. "He didn't grow up in a crowd like this. He's not used to this kind of thing."

"They don't drink?" Lincoln asked, his tone completely baffled. "Then what do they do?"

"Eric, I tried to tell you people down here drink like fish. Maybe now you'll believe me," I said.

"I can't just stand here," Eric announced. "Let me go see if I can help." And as he hustled to the front door, it flew fully open, and I could see the woman just beyond the porch light, weaving as if boneless in the front yard.

The shame of it was, I quickly discovered that the woman's husband was also well into his cups. I saw this immediately, when I followed Eric to the door. In the damp night air, the pair seemed to be making their way to their car. Intervention sprang instantly, for those I grew up with in Memphis are well versed in such a scene. There was nothing whatsoever new happening here.

Dr. Purvis materialized from the kitchen, alarmed and poised to dial the cell phone he held in his hand. Young Purv stood aghast and feckless on the doorstep, with a smug Winnie holding his hand as a voice rang out joltingly, "Now hold on there, Doctor, no point in making a call." It was the tenor of my mother's friend, Frank Harwood, come booming from behind me. He bolted to the front yard, swooped the drunken woman up in his arms and threw her over his shoulder like a sack of potatoes, with a jaunty, "Good thing I drove my truck." In short order, a crowd of spectators stood in the front yard and I saw draperies part from across the street, for all the racket being made.

"She's my wife, and I'm driving her home," the drunk woman's husband bellowed.

"You get in the car and kill yourself," Frank Harwood retorted. "I'm not letting you kill your wife. I'll be driving her home."

It was all over in a matter of minutes, and when it was, everyone simply filtered back inside. You'd think a scene such as this might have broken up the party, but as it was, it served only as the beginning of winding it down.

Melia assumed a position between me and Eric. "Your mother always did say a party's no fun until someone gets drunk. God love her, she's looking down from heaven right now and laughing."

"I don't know the couple," I said to Melia. "Who are they?"

"Nobody you need to concern yourself with, honey," Melia said.

"I bet they'll be mortified in the morning," Eric said.

"Oh no, they won't, Eric. I'll tell you right now, when they show up tomorrow to retrieve that poor woman's purse, which is over there on that chair," Melia said, gesturing with her hand, "they won't say a word, and nobody beneath this roof will either. It'll be as if it never happened. Dr. Purvis will simply hand back the purse, and that'll be that."

Chapter Six

In the anteroom of Independent Presbyterian Church, Eric and I stood whispering in emotionally charged tones at this inappropriate time, in this inappropriate place. Any second now, the door to the church would open, and we'd file to the front row to sit with our backs to the capacity-filled congregation. It seemed every person I ever met in Memphis was in this holy house of worship, which had been built by my mother's father and his three brothers, who'd taken it upon themselves to spearhead the construction of the spare church on tree-lined Walnut Grove Road in East Memphis.

Driving us to my mother's eleven o'clock service, Margaret clamped her mouth shut, after she had asked how it came to be that my mother's family built the unadorned colonial style church. That my mother's family were Scottish descendants with a Presbyterian aversion to any suggestion of symbolism was an explanation Margaret's Catholic faith and good Southern manners wouldn't let her further explore. So Margaret switched the subject, and when she did, it opened a can of worms I should have thought about earlier, yet, in my travel-weary, disoriented grief, I hadn't.

"Cate, are you nervous?" Margaret asked. "I shake at the thought of standing up and speaking in front of people. What are you going to say? Knowing you, I bet you'll read a poem."

"The service hasn't been discussed among us," I said. "Lincoln has been so busy barking orders about where to be and what to do, I didn't think to ask about a eulogy. You know I can't even say hello to him without something blowing up. Our relationship is that contentious. I only know he planned every minute before I even arrived in Memphis."

Margaret had all but swerved off the road at the thought of it. "You mean you're not going to say anything at your mother's service? Cate, this just can't be. You'll have to live with it for the rest of your life. You have to sort this out with Lincoln before it starts."

"Good luck," Eric said. "It's twenty minutes until eleven, but Margaret's right. And now I feel bad about something. I should have said something to you last night, but that scene in the front yard derailed me."

"What?" I fired at Eric.

"I don't know, Cate. I hate to say this because he's your brother, but Lincoln's off his rocker. He gave me a long sappy speech last night about how he's the most distraught over your mother's death because they were so close. He said he was really her best friend, that she loved him the best of her children because she never did understand you."

"What? He said that?"

"Yes, and not to just me. There were a couple of other people standing there. I don't know who they were, but they seemed to take him seriously."

"Oh, for Pete's sake," Margaret said. "This is typical. This is all you need, Cate, sibling competition at your mother's funeral."

"I'm not competing with Lincoln," I said. "He can think whatever he wants. I know the truth. Mom didn't favor one of us over the other. She loved us each for who we are, which happens to be polar opposites from each other. Anyway, I'm not feeding into his nonsense. Anyone listening to his mouth is bound to figure out that's all it is. No sane person goes around slandering his sister in public."

"Well, he did. What are you going to do?" Margaret sounded incredulous.

I took a minute to weigh my options. "To quote David Bowie, 'get me to the church on time,'" I said.

Margaret stepped on the gas pedal and made stealth maneuvers through changing traffic lights all the way out Walnut Grove Road. Rounding the car to the side of the church, she screeched to a stop and said, "Y'all jump out. I'll be behind you in the church."

"You should be thinking of what you're going to say," Eric said, opening the door to the anteroom, and when the door opened, I saw a small assembly of relatives I hadn't seen since I'd been home. In the confusion, it was as if I were being passed from one effusive character to another, where I was hugged, cooed over, and repeatedly given handkerchiefs in cotton and linen. Maddeningly, Lincoln was nowhere around.

"Go speak to Dr. Purvis," Eric whispered. "Ask him what the plan is."

"Believe me, Eric, he's clueless. He's not the man to talk to," I whispered back. "You can see him over there crying. Just look at him, he's beside himself." Then I did a double take with my disbelieving eyes. "Wait a minute," I said, "I need to take that back. He's not beside himself because look who is."

Camila Thurman stood with her consoling hand on Dr. Purvis's shoulder, while Young Purv and Winnie hovered nearby.

Eric looked from them to me and whispered, "Isn't that the woman you told me about from across the street? Dr. Purvis took a date to your mother's funeral?"

The door from the church swept open, and into the anteroom swooped Reverend Sartell in his black cassock. He held a Bible in one hand and held out his other in a gesture directing us into the church. Just then, the outside door of the anteroom blew open, and Lincoln sauntered in behind us like an actor taking center stage. Without acknowledging anyone in the room, he bellied up to Reverend Sartell and entered the church ahead of the rest of us to the organ strains of J. Pachelbel's Canon in D. Filing behind Young Purv and Winnie, I managed to locate Margaret sitting six rows behind the front pew. She raised her eyebrows over her intense, questioning eyes, but all I could do in this queue of formality was gently shrug my shoulders.

I was sandwiched within seconds between Winnie and Eric, when Reverend Sartell began the service. Winnie chose that moment to let loose with sobbing histrionics, so I thrust one of the linen handkerchiefs into her palm. Bible passages having been read and hymns sung drolly, Winnie threw her revolting handkerchief in my lap and stood. I gave Eric a *what's she doing now?* look as she made her way up the three steps to the lectern, and in response, Eric narrowed his eyes.

"Grandmama Daphne loved me so much," she began, with all eyes in the church riveted on her. Young Purv and Dr. Purvis glowed beatific, while I slumped in my seat, squeezing the life out of Eric's hand and wishing I could disappear. Winnie rattled on forever, in a whining, meandering monologue that hit all the high notes of why she was so special. Just when I thought I couldn't take it anymore, Lincoln flounced up, gave her a hug, and replaced her at the lectern.

You would have thought Lincoln was my mother's husband instead of the phlegmatic Dr. Purvis. In a speech that defied all rules of decency, my brother told anecdote after allegory of his extraordinary, exclusive standing with my mother, as if he and only he had a relationship with her and I wasn't on the planet. In my wildest imagination, I'd never heard anything like it. Lincoln postured and swayed between humorous stories and tasteless indiscretion about my mother's relationship with my father. I couldn't even look at Lincoln, when he finally finished his self-aggrandizing oration, but I knew I wouldn't stay mute forever. I'd make my sentiments clear eventually, but it would be after we buried my mother in Elmwood Cemetery.

It's an eight-mile drive from Independent Presbyterian Church to Elmwood Cemetery. I didn't say a word to Lincoln on the way there, other than to say I wasn't speaking to him. Eric sat beside me in the black Town Car, while the doctors and Winnie rode in the car behind us, and an assortment of cousins rode at the front of the procession of cars, in a caravan comprised of eighty or more.

Over a large span bridge, listed in the National Register of Historic places, Elmwood Cemetery rolls over eighty acres, shaded by fifteen hundred trees. Four sections of graves are marked by granite and limestone, bronze and marble. It's a beautiful hodgepodge of weathered archangels, cherubs, vaults, and mausoleums stretching over lawn like a chronicle of Memphis's history.

My father and both sets of grandparents were buried in the breathtaking parkland, and as we drove over the bridge, I thought of my mother once saying, rather off-handedly, that the day would come when I'd take her there. We'd driven to Elmwood to see my father's grave, and at the time, I couldn't fathom the day of her funeral. I'd also thought it uncharacteristic of my mother to mention something so morbid, but despite her aversion to the unpleasant, she took her maternal teacher position seriously. Her aim had not been to scare me, it had been to prepare me. "Listen to me, Cate, since we're on the subject," she'd said. "When the time comes, I don't want you carrying on. I'll not have my only daughter making a scene in public. I won't have you boo-hooing and throwing yourself prostrate on my casket. I want you to do as my mother told me. I want you to comport yourself with dignity."

I looked at Lincoln, who sat flush against my mother's casket, while the mourners gathered behind the immediate family—graveside. He wept openly and kept tapping on the casket's lid repeatedly.

Eric watched Lincoln, then finally whispered in my ear, "You have any idea in the slightest what he's doing rapping on the casket?"

"Yes," I whispered back," he's tapping out *I know you loved me best* in Morse code."

Eric's suppression of laughter started his shoulders shaking. I looked off to my left at Margaret, who mouthed a questioning *what?* so I put my index and middle fingers on my forehead and tapped them rhythmically, and one intuitive glance at Lincoln set Margaret off. Once she figured out what was so funny, she couldn't even look at me. With her full hand shading her lowered head, Margaret turned and stepped away from the group to collect herself.

Reverend Sartell closed the service with the twenty-third psalm, and, as if in tacit agreement, the mourners disbanded, drifting away from the site onto the autumn ochre parkland to stand in small huddles beneath languid trees granting a respectable berth for the immediate family. I stood looking at my mother's casket in the midst of a sinking finality, feeling hollow and disoriented in this surreal moment. I'd been so long following my mother's lead, I felt rudderless.

I glanced behind me at the congregation, many of them speaking in low, reverential tones, each of them in my life by my mother's design. Because my mother populated her world by deliberate appointment. She'd constructed her life by deciding who she would become and arranging a complimentary fraternity around her of friends who shared a sense of belonging in this beautiful corner of Southern culture. In an unpredictable world, she'd secured her parameters with safety in congruent numbers, and I knew that this was her intentional gift to me. Yet without her stabilizing presence, I would be stepping into my own. I now belonged to this gracious, well-mannered domain in a different context, and it came to me with confliction that no woman truly discovers who she is until the day she buries her mother, when she is left to walk this earth alone.

Margaret caught up with me on the way to the car. "Cate, it's been so wonderful seeing you. God bless your mother. I'm glad I could be here for you. I know y'all are going back to the house now, then leaving in the morning," she said, holding both of my hands.

"Yes," I confirmed. "We'll fly out at ten. Thank you so much, Margaret. I can't express how much I appreciate you standing beside me."

"Give me a call next week to tell me how you're doing, okay? And I hope you don't mind if I say this. Y'all are an unusual family, but you're a lot of fun. This has been the best time I've ever had at a funeral."

Chapter Seven

My mother had an armchair designated as hers alone. It sat slipcovered in chintz, conspicuous and venerated in her absence, for none of us could bring ourselves to occupy it, as Lincoln, Dr. Purvis, Eric, and I sat in the living room of the house on Club Walk, the amber late-afternoon sunlight filtering through the rustling trees in desultory prisms through the bay window. Having passed each of us a hefty copy of my mother's trust, Dr. Purvis sat imperious and weighty on the sofa, settling into the spotlight, conducting the flow. I was surprised at the unwieldy heft of the document for one reason. After my father died, my mother had had a streamlined four-page will, constructed by a family-friend lawyer, that simply divided her money and assets between Lincoln and me, which I'd seen because she'd shown me.

Dr. Purvis appeared to be making a production of the come-to-Jesus moment. It was so rare that Lincoln and I gave him our undivided attention, but here we sat now in this mandatory meeting, focused on going over my mother's trust. In that moment, Dr. Purvis had facts the rest of us did not. I could tell by the timbre of his voice that the contents of my mother's trust were no surprise to him, for he read it as if by rote, in a listless tone that rambled over painstaking minutia so tedious and categorical, it made my eyes glaze over.

I didn't snap out of my stupor until Dr. Purvis divulged with emphasis that Lincoln and I would receive nothing until each of us were aged sixty-two, and, should we not live to see that advanced age, everything in my mother's trust would be passed to Young Purv and his three children. "Also," Dr. Purvis amended, "your mother and I shared title to this house. I want to own it outright, so I'll be buying her half, and the money will go directly into the trust. Lastly, to avoid taxes, your mother and I had a handshake agreement stipulating that her monetary remains be released to y'all after I signed a waiver relinquishing my marital claim to her money. Which brings me to your mother's jewelry, Cate," he said, looking at me. "As I gave your mother valuable jewelry throughout our marriage, I won't sign the marital waiver releasing her money unless you forfeit all your mother's jewelry to Winnie. Winnie is my blood, and you're not."

"Excuse me?" I said.

"Now hold on there, Dr. Purvis," Lincoln said. "Our mother had an arsenal of her mother's and her grandmother's jewelry. She wanted Cate to inherit all of it. Since you've mentioned blood, Cate is blood, and Winnie is not."

Dr. Purvis clamped his weak jaw. "These are my terms," he retorted.

Lincoln, on his feet now, erupted. "You're holding my sister at emotional gunpoint, and what's this age sixty-two business? Our mother would never come up with that. Not in a million years." It was the first I'd ever heard Lincoln use the words *our mother,* as opposed to acting as if he was an only child and I didn't exist.

I looked at Eric, who sat up straight, as if expecting the roof to blow off the house any minute.

"I've given you my non-negotiable terms," Dr. Purvis said, closing his copy of the trust and standing abruptly. "Think about what you want to do, Cate, and let me know," he snapped, then clipped out of the room.

Eric stood and looked from me to Lincoln. The three of us were speechless until Eric said, "I think you two should discuss this among yourselves. I'll go for a walk and give you a little space." He walked to where I sat, leaned down, and kissed my cheek. "I have my cellphone on me," he said. "Call me at any time."

When the front door closed, I walked over to the bar and poured a glass of wine. "I feel like I just got socked in the stomach," I said.

"It's because you *were* just socked in the stomach," Lincoln said. "This is wrong. I had a feeling Dr. Purvis was up to something. He only told me I'm a co-trustee, but I had no idea what was in the trust until now. His paw prints are all over this. My suspicion is he had everything drawn up to his advantage, and Mother didn't fully comprehend what she signed. He, no doubt, had the age sixty-two put in there, thinking our family dies young, which they do. We'll never know. But anyway, everything Mom had came from her family and Dad. It was to go to us after she died. This is totally messed up."

"Now we know why Dr. Purvis pushed so hard to get Mom out of the house on Mud Island," I said. "That should have been the first warning sign."

Lincoln walked to the bar and poured himself a stiff scotch in a tumbler. Walking across the room, he lowered himself into the chair across from me. "I think you should stand your ground on the jewelry, Cate. I don't care if I never see a cent of Mom's money. You're her daughter. That you have the jewelry is more important. Tell the son-of-a-gun no dice, is what I suggest."

I couldn't wrap my mind around this new version of Lincoln. *Who is this person squarely in my camp?* I thought.

"I wouldn't do that to you, Lincoln. I don't want you to be disadvantaged over that. It's only jewelry."

"I won't be disadvantaged if we put both doctors and that wretched Winnie in their place. And the jewelry means something, Cate. Don't pretend it doesn't. There are three generations of women represented in Mom's jewelry box. I say take that ugly ring Mom hated off your finger now and go throw it at him. Tell him that's all Winnie will ever see."

The thought of the gesture struck me as funny. "I think I will, and I'll be sure to say, 'Give this to Winnie, and I hope she chokes on it.' Could be worse, Lincoln. At least we'll be shed of them."

"Yes, we will, praise God," Lincoln sniffed.

"Can I just mention that I like hearing you say *we*?" I said. "Allow me to point out the obvious—this is a first from you."

"I know, I know. I'm sorry, Cate," Lincoln said, sounding exhausted, as if he'd set down a burden. "I've been terrible to you, haven't I?"

"Yes," I said. "What I'd like to know is why."

Lincoln took a deep drink, then balanced his tumbler on his knee. He didn't look me in the eye, but I didn't require it. What I wanted was for him to finally come clean. "I suppose it's been jealousy," Lincoln said.

"Over what?" I said, not able to imagine.

"You've always followed the beat of your own drum, which is something I could never do. You're like Dad in this way. I think I take more after Mom. I like things unchallenged, if you know what I mean. I could have never upped and moved away like you did. Mom never knew where you got your gumption, but she admired it. I guess I always felt, when she'd sing your praises, that what was unsung was me. I've resented you, that's the only way I can explain it, other than to say the more I invested in it, the more of a habit it became."

I knew in that moment, I had a choice. It was remarkably clear that the cards were now on my table. I could do as Lincoln confessed by further investing in the acrimony between us—hold onto the soul-killing nonsense through sheer force of habit, but it would only become like an ongoing lawsuit with a counter suit, and there would be no liberation. I knew a crossroads when I saw one. If one wants to end a dynamic, one has to quit participating in it.

"Well, Lincoln, Mom's gone now, and we have to stick together. We're all we've got."

"Well, you've got Eric," he said.

"True, but I need you too."

When Eric returned from his walk, he walked into a scene that must have tossed him sideways. There in my mother's living room, my brother Lincoln and I hugged and cried on each other's shoulders.

"What's all this?' Eric queried. "What'd I miss?"

"You haven't missed anything," I said. "You're standing in witness."

"Of what?" Eric said.

I took a step back from Lincoln and gathered myself. Turning, I listened to the autumn wind howling outside, drawing my attention to swaying limbs, swirling leaves, and the beginning of quicksilver rain as the moon kept its bargain in its cyclic appointment. In the backyard, an ode to autumn played in symphonic sounds. Turning back to Eric, I took Lincoln's hand and met Eric's waiting eyes.

"What you're witnessing is one door closed and a window opened."

Epilogue

October 2018

The freestanding full-length mirror framed in blond oak threw prisms of California morning light through the bedroom window as Eric stood laughing at me. I turned left, then right before it, trying to decide if I could pull off the dress. Ultimately, I arrived at the conclusion that Lincoln's reaction would be well worth the effort, incongruous as the dress was to everything about me.

"Really?" Eric narrowed his eyes. "You're going to wear that," he said in more of a statement than a question.

"Definitely," I answered. "I know how Lincoln thinks. He'll see it as an homage."

"It's a bit loud, don't you think?" Eric continued in what I knew to be a veiled attempt at dissuasion.

"Well, that's the entire point," I explained.

"Meaning what, exactly? Give me a hint."

For feigned dramatic effect, I affected a loud sigh. "Do they not teach Boston Yankees anything about women's aspirations? If a woman wants to draw attention to herself, she has to dress loudly. My mother told me so."

"Suffice it to say you'll draw attention to yourself, but don't you think the dress is a bit off-season? I mean, this is October. You look like you're dressed for the dead of summer."

"This is California, Eric. Anything goes. I've seen women wearing that tacky stretch-velvet in April. Out here people don't even know the deadline for summer dress is a hard September first. Trust me, in California, it flat doesn't matter."

"Okay, fine, but I've never seen that before. It's not like anything I've ever seen you wear. Where did you get it?"

"Oh, this little ol' thing?" I said, looking down as if it were nothing, as if I hadn't moved heaven and earth for the very moment I'd zip it carefully up my back, all for the thrill of surprising Lincoln. "It was my mother's. I took it from her closet when Dr. Purvis wasn't looking. It's a Lilly Pulitzer, an emblem of the South. Because my mother maintained her perfect size-eight figure, she had a Lilly Pulitzer collection. Lillys never go out of style, you know. They just become classic."

"But you're a size two, Cate," Eric reminded.

"I know that. I had it altered after I invited Lincoln out here to visit."

"You altered the dress and everything else around here. You've practically redecorated our house. I've never seen you as excited over anything as you've been over your brother's arrival. I guess you're not kidding. You really are going to wear that dress in public," Eric deduced.

"Yes, I am." I looked at my wristwatch. "I better leave for the airport now. Lincoln's plane lands in an hour and a half. I don't want to be late."

But I ran late anyway. I knew as I pulled into the Delta terminal's parking lot and looked at the dashboard clock of my black BMW that the nine a.m. traffic jam on the 101 North had caused my delay. With frenetic energy, I leapt from the car, heart pounding with excitement, and bolted through the airport's sliding glass doors. I clipped my high-heeled way through the throng of travelers, searching for the escalators, at the bottom of which I'd arranged to meet Lincoln. Uncertain of which way to proceed, my confusion must have shown on my face, for in short order, a man driving a wheeled baggage cart angled a U-turn and offered his assistance.

"Can you point me the way to the escalators?" I asked.

"Just my bad luck," he said, smiling. "They're right in front of you. I was hoping to give you a lift somewhere."

Laughing, I thanked the man and positioned myself at the bottom of the escalator, jumpy as a golden retriever, calling forth the diaphanous image of Daphne Goodwyn, ready to catch my brother, Lincoln.

A Magnolia Blooms in Winter

Ane Mulligan

Dedication

To my grandniece, Anna Kunz.
Always remember to keep God in the center of those stars in your eyes.
Then, my darling girl, bloom.

Author's Note

I took liberties with my sweet hometown, Sugar Hill, for this story. Sugar Hill is a little over seventy-five years old, but never had a proper downtown, just a city hall. Thanks to our mayor and city council, we are currently building and will soon finish the first phase of our downtown. I'm tickled pink to have a performing arts theatre as part of that first phase. I'm also blessed to be on the steering committee for future growth. Imagine that—they actually want to hear my thoughts!

Chapter 1

"Morgan? Is that you?"

"Who else would be answering my phone, Mama?"

A siren—police or ambulance?—filtered through my window, an ever-present part of New York City. Trapping my cell phone between my shoulder and ear, I entered ninety seconds on the microwave's digital pad. After a sniff of the leftover Chinese takeout for edibility, I slid in my supper. Mama's laughter wrapped around me like a warm hug from home as the plate spun around.

"You've lost most of your drawl, sugar. I hardly recognize your voice anymore. For a second, I thought it was Lisa or Michelle."

I'd heard that lament several times. My roommates were from California, and I'd worked long and hard to adopt their accent. I'd never play a convincing Silicon Valley housewife with a Southern drawl.

"How are you, Mama? Is Daddy still treating you like a queen?" I leaned against the two-foot-long kitchen counter. Affordable Manhattan apartments were miniscule compared to ... anywhere, but especially to home.

"He's a keeper, that's for sure."

I heard a "but" in her voice.

"Sweetie, I called for a reason."

Yep, there it was.

"Are you between roles now? Can you come home?"

Between roles? Uh, yeah. Way between. I hadn't played so much as a walk-on since September and it was now November. I actually had to take a second job to pay my rent, which was due in—I flipped a calendar page on my tiny fridge—two days. I stifled a groan so Mama wouldn't hear.

"I might be able to, but I just had two different auditions. Rehearsals start in a few weeks for one and six weeks for the other." I didn't really feel I was right for the part that started soon. But the other? Oh, I was born to play the lead in *Bloom!* "Why? Is something wrong?"

"Sugar Hill Community Church needs you, darlin'. I don't know if I told you, but we hired Andy Wayfield as our worship pastor six months ago."

"Andy?" My heart did a little flutter. How long had it been? Over four years, and his name could still send my pulse to racing. "No, you didn't tell me. I wouldn't have forgotten something like that. Wait a minute. Did he leave the band?" Another thought hit me like a wrecking ball. "Did he get married?" I swallowed my heart as I waited for her answer.

"Yes and no. Left the band, not married."

That last bit of news zipped a delicious shiver down my spine. Andy. My college leading man. He always encouraged me to reach for the stars, telling me God had gifted me and I should use that gift for His glory. At the time, I sort of hoped he'd ask me to stay—and I would have.

Three years to make it to the top. That's what I thought. How could I tell him that even stretching on my tippy toes, my touch never reached a single star?

I opened the microwave, checked the temperature of my supper, then added another minute to the timer. "I'm sure he's had plenty of girlfriends by now. The last time I saw him was when his band, Night Star, played a New Year's Eve gig at Brooklyn Tabernacle." They had topped the Christian charts, while I had yet to land a decent role. I remained on needles and pins until he went home, certain he'd discover my failure. "So, how's he doing as the worship pastor? I'll bet he really brought the music up to date."

"Oh, he's raised a few eyebrows, not to mention some blood pressures, but he's a good boy and everyone loves him."

"He's hardly a boy, Mama."

"Well, that's beside the point, sugar, because right now he needs you."

I bounced on my toes and held the phone close. "Me? I don't understand."

The microwave beeped. I pulled out my plate, sniffed the whatever-it-was and took a tentative nibble. The noodles were slightly rubbery, but it tasted okay. I doused it with lite soy sauce.

"Remember that wonderful Christmas play you wrote, *Three Men and the Baby*? Andy resurrected it and is—or was—producing it."

"Was?" I took my supper to the living room, which was only two steps from the kitchen, dropped onto the sofa—the end where the springs weren't broken—and set my plate on my lap.

"Oh, Morgan, it was awful."

"My play? Why was it awful?"

"No, your play is wonderful. Everyone is excited to do it again. The accident was awful."

"What accident? Mama, start at the beginning."

"I ... well, that's why Andy needs you. I ..."

I could have screamed in frustration. "Mama, what did you do?"

"I sort of ... squashed him."

I bolted up from the sofa, flipping my plate off my lap and to the floor. A glob of noodles landed on my pants leg. "Sort of *what*? Is he … is he … alive?"

"Well, of course, silly. It wouldn't make a lick of sense for him to need you if he wasn't."

I beat my fist against my thigh, smashing a hot noodle in the process. "Mama. What. Happened. To. Andy?" I shook off the mess stuck to my fingers.

"I broke his foot."

"You broke his foot?" I paced my apartment. Ten paces north to the faux fireplace, eight along the west wall to my desk.

"I'm afraid so. In several places."

I retraced my steps back to the dilapidated sofa. It didn't help. I was still confused. "Is Daddy there? Put him on the phone."

"Of course he is. Where else would he be?"

"With Pastor, seeing Andy. He's still on the visitation team, isn't he?" I dropped back onto the couch. This conversation was exhausting.

"Well, yes, and he did go see him this morning when he got out of surgery."

"Why was Daddy in surgery? Is he all right?" I had to slow my breathing before I hyperventilated. This was getting worse. "You didn't squash him too, did you?"

"No, silly. *Andy* had the surgery to put pins in his foot. The thing is, he'll be laid up and can't direct the play, and since you wrote it, you're the perfect person to do it. So, can you come? Please? I'd feel ever so much better if you did, sugar."

My thoughts flashed to the latest flicker of hope in my vanishing career. I couldn't think of any reason for me not to get the part. I was perfect for it. *Please, God?*

"Mama, I'll come, but I auditioned for the lead in a new musical. If I get a call back, I'll have to run up here. But we can probably work out the schedule."

"Of course we can, darlin', and thank you. You've made your mama feel a lot better."

"I'm glad. Now, how did you manage to squash Andy? What were you doing?"

"I was helping your daddy change the lights in the fellowship hall."

"Changing lights squashed him?" Why was Daddy changing the lights when that was the job of the facilities manager?

"Not the lights, the cherry picker."

"The cherry—Mama, you're not hurt too, are you?"

"Just a fractured wrist. But I didn't need surgery. The doctor said mine was a clean break."

She sounded so proud of herself. "But how—? No, never mind. I'll get

Daddy to explain it when I get home. I'll—oh." My gaze drifted to the mini calendar.

"What's wrong?"

"I, um, I don't have enough money for a plane ticket right now, Mama."

"No problem. Call me back with the flight information and I'll book it for you. Just choose one that will get you here fast. And I hope you can stay through Christmas."

"If I get the part in *Bloom!*, I'll have to go back to New York before then. Maybe we can have an early Christmas while I'm home."

"That could work. Oh, and the church is paying you." A smacking sound filled my ear. "Muwah!"

I returned Mama's phone-kiss and said goodbye, then touched the "end" circle on my iPhone. I was happy about getting paid, but poor Andy. I picked off the noodles still clinging to my pants and used my napkin to dab at the soy sauce stain. Paper towels quickly took care of the mess my supper made on the floor. After I tossed the towels into the trash, the first order of business was something to replace my spilled supper.

A quick check of my bank account verified there was enough to pay my part of the light bill and buy a sandwich from the deli downstairs, but not much more. The cash in my tip jar from waiting tables at Barney's would have to carry me until payday. Hopefully, my roommates would give me grace for a week. Mama didn't mention how much the church would pay. I supposed if it wasn't enough, I could tap Daddy, my biggest fan, for a short-term loan.

I trudged down the stairs to the deli. While I waited for Nate to make my sub, I pulled Andy from a hidden pocket in my memory. His dark blond hair, streaked by the Georgia summer sun, made an enticing frame for his golden brown eyes. And his smile. It always made my knees weak. What would it be like to see him again after all this time?

A young couple entered the deli, bringing a blast of frigid air in with them. The husband—I assumed they were married—held the door open with his back, never letting go of his very pregnant wife's hand as he guided her inside. How lovely to be cared for like that. Like Daddy cared for Mama. I'd dated a lot of men, from actors to Wall Street wizards. Every single one was full of himself. Not a one cared about me, really—only what I could do for them.

Except for Andy. He'd be like that husband.

"Here you go, beautiful." Nate handed me the Italian sub in a nest of butcher paper.

My mouth watered from its aroma. "Thanks, Nate. You sure I can't get you to adopt me?"

His ample belly jiggled as he chuckled.

I sat at one of the plastic tables and took a large bite of my sandwich. Andy would love these. In college, we'd often visited a deli for Italian subs, but they weren't as good. But he only came to New York that one time. Afterwards, all I ever got was a card at Christmas, one that always featured a bright star—what he thought *I* was. He'd moved on, and for some reason, that bothered me.

Wiping away a trail of oil running down my chin, I turned my thoughts to matters more pressing than romance. I needed to let Lisa and Michelle know I would be gone for a while, find a flight, and pack. I was going home, but not as the star Andy and everyone else believed me to be.

How had I let God down so badly?

Chapter 2

After landing in Atlanta, my first order of business before going home was to stop by the hospital to see Andy. The pneumatic door whooshed open to the hum of many voices like a brook tumbling over rocks. I stepped around a wheelchair in the middle of the walkway, its passenger a young woman with a newborn in her arms. As I reached to press the call button for the elevator, another hand collided with mine.

"Oh, I'm sorry, I— Morgan? Is that you? Why, it is."

Andy's mother, a modern version of Aunt Bea from Mayberry, enveloped me in a hug. Her dangly copper earrings tangled in my hair. Laughing, she slipped the earring out of her ear. "Andy's going to be thrilled to see you, dear. And relieved." She untangled her jewelry from my hair. "Your mama told me she asked you to come help out. We can't thank you enough."

"It's the least I could do considering it was my mother who caused the accident." The door opened to a full elevator. We managed to squeeze in and rode in silence to the third floor.

When we got to Andy's room, Mrs. Wayfield went in first. She wanted me to be a surprise for Andy, so I waited outside the doorway.

"Memaw! You're here!" A little girl's voice rang with delight.

I peeked through the crack between the doorjamb and the hinges. The little girl jumping up and down had to be Andy's niece, the one he was raising for his late sister—she looked exactly like her. I pulled back, not wanting to be caught.

"Glad to see you too, sugar. Let me look at you. Why, you've grown another foot since I last saw you."

"No, I haven't, Memaw. See? I still only got two. And they're in new shoes."

I couldn't wait any more. I slipped inside the room. They stood at the bedside, hiding Andy from sight. "And they're inside the cutest shoes I've ever seen."

Mrs. Wayfield put her hands on her granddaughter's shoulders and pulled her back from the bed so Andy could see me. "Dear, look who I found in the lobby."

Andy. He still had the power to make my heart dance. His hair stuck up every which way, giving him a boyish appearance in contrast to his five o'clock shadow.

His hand reached out and I moved toward him. When our fingers touched, a spark rippled up my arm and quivered across my shoulders. I drew closer, my gaze fastened on his lips. Whew! Was it hot in here? I forced my attention off his mouth.

He grinned. "You're a sight for sore eyes." Then he squinted, like he always did when something seemed weird. "That's a dumb saying, isn't it?"

He always could make me laugh. I bent down to kiss his stubbled cheek, but he turned his head and my lips caught the corner of his mouth. I nearly melted.

Clearing my throat, I straightened. "And I see you're still getting all the attention, Andy."

The little girl giggled. I turned and pointed to her feet. "I meant what I said about your shoes. Where did you get them? And do you think they have any in my size?"

Giggling again, she stuck out one foot and pointed her toe. "Uncle Andy got 'em for me at Merry-Go-Round Shoes." She looked me up and down in frank appraisal. "I'm Cassie. What's your name?"

A hospital volunteer swept in and deposited a vase of roses on the bedside table. As soon as the woman left, I leaned down to Cassie. "Morgan. I'm an old friend of your uncle's."

Behind me, the click-clack of high heels crossed the floor. "Well, I'm a *very close* friend of Andy's, and I don't remember ever seeing you."

If life were a cartoon, icicles would have fallen from those words. I turned and peered into the eyes of a haughty, beautiful brunette—a *young* haughty, beautiful brunette. What was she to Andy?

I held out my hand. "I'm Morgan James. It's nice to meet you."

"Vanessa Owens." She dismissed me with a sniff and rushed to Andy's bedside. And people called New Yorkers rude?

She ran her fingers over the vase of roses. "I see you got my flowers." Her words slid out all syrupy. "Darlin', Daddy wants to come see you tonight if you're feeling up to it. Shall I tell him it's all right?"

Gak. The girl purred. Just how old was she? She couldn't be more than eighteen or nineteen. What was Andy doing with a girl almost a decade younger than himself? I glanced at Mrs. Wayfield, whose lips clamped into a tight line.

"Uh ... if he has to, I guess. I'm not really up to visitors."

Vanessa swept her gaze over Cassie, Andy's mom, and me. "Well, if everyone would leave and let you rest, you'd be better a lot quicker. Mrs. Wayfield, I'm sure Cassie needs a nap. It was ... pleasant meeting you, Megan."

"It's Morgan."

"Goodbye, Morgan."

The automatic blood-pressure machine pumped up the cuff on Andy's arm, turning his fingertips red. He grimaced. Vanessa made no move to leave. I got the message, but I couldn't understand Andy. He'd never been able to abide rudeness.

Well, don't ever let it be said that Morgan James couldn't take a hint. The blood-pressure cuff deflated with a whoosh. I picked up my handbag, but before I could make good my escape, my conscience pricked. If Vanessa and Andy were an item, maybe she'd simply been overly worried about him. Maybe she knew my mother caused his accident. Maybe her bad manners were due to that.

I decided to take the high road and flashed her a smile. "It was nice to meet you too." I waved at Andy. "See you when you're home."

Vanessa's eyes narrowed, her gaze pinning me like a fifth-grade science project. "Why?"

Then again, maybe not. I glanced at her hand. No ring, so she wasn't Andy's fiancée, in spite of having laid claim to him. He'd changed if this was what he liked in a woman now. And if it was, Vanessa could have him.

Andy rose up on his elbows. "Morgan's going to direct the play for me."

Vanessa raised her chin and looked down her perfectly sculpted nose at me. "But I'm the star in that little play. I can direct it."

A bell dinged. A voice paged Dr. Patil.

Little play? My proverbial claws were about to come out. That script took a lot of sweat and sleepless nights to write.

Mrs. Wayfield rose and took Cassie's hand. "I think it's time we leave. We'll see you in the morning, son."

I wasn't about to stick around either. "I'll go with you, Mrs. Wayfield. Bye, Andy." I took Cassie's other hand.

Winking at me as I held open the door, Mrs. Wayfield said in a loud voice, "Cassie, did you know that Miss Morgan is an actress on Broadway?"

An aide scurried past us, her rubber-soled shoes squeaking and squishing as she walked. The door clicked shut behind us before I could hear Vanessa's reaction—or see her expression. I no longer had the right to ask what role Vanessa played in Andy's life, but you can bet I wanted to.

Cassie peered up at me with wide eyes. "Are you really an actress, Miss Morgan? A real actress on a real stage?"

Ah, the soothing power of a fan. I smiled. "I really am."

A phone rang at the nurse's station down the hall. Cassie skipped ahead, her tight curls bouncing against her cheeks, and pushed the button for the elevator. "I want to be an actress when I grow up."

She mashed the "1" button and looked up at her grandmother. Mrs. Wayfield shook her head and pointed to the "L" button. With a straight forefinger, Cassie circled the button and punched it. She had a dramatic flair, all right.

"Would you like to be in the play I'm going to direct for your uncle?"

Her sweet face lost its glow. "There's no part for me. Uncle Andy said so."

I squatted to look her in the eyes. "I'll tell you a secret. I wrote that play, and I can write in a part just for you." I glanced up at her grandmother, whose vigorous nodding tickled me.

"You can?"

Cassie threw her arms around my neck, nearly knocking me over. I braced myself.

"I can and will. I'll have the new script ready tomorrow night." I rose, embarrassed when my knees cracked loudly.

"Oh, thank you, Miss Morgan. Did you hear that, Memaw? I'm gonna be in the play!"

She danced around in delight until we arrived at the lobby. The doors slid open and cold air blew in sharp contrast to the warmth of Andy's room. A couple, each carrying a potted poinsettia, swept past us into the elevator.

Through the lobby windows, the trees bent in the wind and rain hit the panes. Andy's niece ran to the lobby's Christmas tree, in the process of being set up by volunteers, and inspected the ornaments.

I slid my purse higher on my shoulder and pulled out my umbrella. "I guess I'll be seeing you when I come over to talk with Andy about the play."

His mom laid her hand on my arm. "Andy is being released in the morning. Why don't y'all come for dinner tomorrow night, dear."

I wanted time with Andy, but things had changed. "Are you sure I won't be interrupting Vanessa and Andy?"

Mrs. Wayfield lips stretched into a sly smile. "Oh, I'm counting on it."

Chapter 3

My parents' house, white with dark green shutters, sat in the apex of a circular driveway. Mama had the wrap-around porch decked out for the holidays. Wreaths graced each window, and the traditional Christmas pillows lay resplendent on wicker rockers.

Before I could even turn off the engine, the front door opened. Mama looked younger than her fifty-one years. It had to be the laughter. The Bible said it was good medicine, and Mama, being a believer, always partook. The delight I felt in being home, greeted by my mother, surprised me. Home was so different than New York, yet …

I turned the engine off and jumped out of the car, banging the door shut behind me. Mindful of the fluorescent-pink cast encasing her broken wrist and held in a paisley scarf-sling, I settled into Mama's one-armed hug.

She pulled back to give me the mama-once-over.

"Do I meet your standards?"

"Just looking for changes. Last time, it was—"

"And just look at you, Mama. Not a gray hair yet." They wouldn't dare.

Mama patted her hair and grinned. "Did you stop to see Andy?"

"I did." I opened the back door of the rental car and pulled out my suitcase. I wanted to ask her why she'd never mentioned Vanessa Owens, but I didn't want her to think I was … What was I, anyway? Maybe I needed to figure out how I felt about him, first. "Considering what happened, he looked pretty good."

He looked wonderful.

Mama glanced inside the car at the empty backseat. "Is that it?" Finding nothing else, she shut the door and hooked her good arm through mine. "Then let's get this show inside. Your daddy's in the family room. He'll join us as soon as the last quarter of the Falcons game is over. Supper's about ready. You hungry? I can't wait for you to see how I redecorated your old room."

In Mama's rapid-fire speech, she lassoed me at "redecorate." My childhood room. Is this what I'd worked so hard for—to come home a theatrical forever-bridesmaid, the second banana? I had to win the lead in *Bloom!* As we headed inside, I crossed my fingers and sent up a silent plea.

My suitcase bumped over the threshold. "If I know you, Mama, you've made the room HGTV-worthy."

The foyer was no longer celery green but a warm coffee-with-cream color. A new deacon's bench sat on the right with a basket on one end, filled with a newspaper, some mail—junk by the looks of it—and the dog's leash.

"Where is Oliver?" The dog was usually at Daddy's feet.

"In the yard. I wanted you to get settled before I let him in."

Cheering blared from the TV as I went to greet Daddy. He wrapped me in a warm bear hug. Some things never changed. I was home.

"Now, close your eyes, sugar." Mama took me by the hand and led me up the stairs and down the hall, then with the flourish of a game show host presenting first prize, said, "Taa-dah!" It was easy to see where I got my drama genes.

The room, now in satiny white, cream, and beige, was a startling contrast to the bright yellow and turquoise paint from my teens. But the monochromatic color scheme was lovely and relaxing. A pop of remaining turquoise drew my attention. It was the old teddy bear Andy won for me at the county fair. I oohed and ahhed over her work, then she left me to get settled.

I sat on the bench at the foot of my bed and checked my phone for messages from my agent, Frank Cotswold—Cotsie, as I affectionately knew him. A lone text from the manager of the restaurant where I waited tables asked what time I was coming in. I sent a reply to remind him I'd already cleared a leave of absence. Then I sent another text to Cotsie, alerting him I was in Sugar Hill and to call me the minute he heard anything from *Bloom!*'s casting director.

After hanging my clothes in the closet and plugging my phone charger into the wall, I headed downstairs to the kitchen to help with supper. Home cooking would be nice for a change. The aroma of fried chicken greeted me, but not the sizzle of it frying.

Mama pulled her head out of the fridge. "Oh good, you're here." She waved to a packed shelf. "Fetch that covered blue bowl, please. The women's ministry has made sure I don't have to dice or fuss for the next couple of weeks."

I lifted the bowl, peeking beneath the cover. Tiny pieces of celery and green onion peeked back. "Is this Miss Pugh's potato salad?" Southern women learned from the cradle that the best gesture of solace for a troubled neighbor was a plate of hot fried chicken and a bowl of cold potato salad. In a real crisis, they threw in a large banana pudding. As far as I was concerned, we were in crisis mode. I opened the fridge again, rooting past the dill pickles, sweet tea, and leftover pizza. Ah, there it was.

With nothing to do but plate it up, we had supper on in no time. Daddy joined us at the island, asked the blessing, and we dove in. The fried chicken was as good as I remembered, the potato salad had the vinegary snap I loved, and the decadent banana pudding filled the nooks I'd saved for it. Laughter brought it all together into harmony—that and Oliver watching to see who dropped the first tidbit for him to snap up.

I let my eyes feast on Mama and Daddy. I may have greasepaint in my veins, but I had home in my heart. The question was could the two ever be aligned?

Daddy patted his belly, picked up the TV remote he'd set beside his plate, and stood. "Thank you, ladies." He kissed Mama's cheek, and with Oliver following him, went back to his TV, while she and I lingered over coffee.

"Tell me about this latest play." She patted her lips with a napkin. "It's something new, you said? Anything I've heard of?"

I stirred sugar into my cup, the spoon clinking against the sides. "It's called *Bloom!*"

She frowned.

"It's by a new playwright," I added.

Mama motioned for the sugar. "Ah, so with a new playwright, is it off-Broadway?"

"Yes, but it's the lead." I pushed the bowl toward her.

She paused, one hand on the bowl. Her gaze zeroed in on my right eye, then my left, then back to the right again. What was she looking for?

"But you were in a supporting role *on* Broadway. Why are you going backwards?" My mother never wasted a breath. There was no beating around the magnolias with her.

"It was a very *minor* supporting role, Mama." She didn't understand how it worked. "That first year, I was lucky to get a walk-on in a production so far off Broadway, it was in Poughkeepsie. It took two years to get my first speaking part, and then it was only two lines. I've paid my dues. It's past time."

"Your performance in *Hello, Dolly!* was excellent." She drank the last of her coffee and set the cup back on its saucer.

I got up, retrieved the pot from the Mr. Coffee next to the sink, and refilled our cups. Mama hadn't bought a Keurig yet. She always believed a full pot of coffee was more hospitable.

"But it wasn't the lead, and I didn't even get a mention in the reviews."

She ran her finger along the edge of the banana pudding bowl, collecting a dollop of whipped cream. "Is that so important, the reviews?" She sucked the cream off her finger.

"A good one can influence auditions that will move me away from off-Broadway—and on to better parts. I'm tired of working three jobs just to get by in New York. If I don't start getting leading roles …" I picked up a slightly soggy vanilla wafer from the bottom of the pudding.

Mama wrinkled her nose. I wasn't sure if it was over the cookie or what I'd said. "And that's your goal?"

"It's every actor's goal."

Without a word, Mama stared.

"Okay, maybe not *every* actor, but it's mine. And I believe God gave it to me when I left Sugar Hill." I ran my fingers through my hair, jerking out a couple of snarls, then twisted and secured it with a barrette I had in my pocket.

Mama tilted her head, watching my every move. "And if you don't obtain it?"

I'd avoided looking that far down the road. Now Mama forced me to face the possibility. "Then I've failed. I didn't use the talent God gave me, and I let Him down." *And He let me down.* I didn't say that out loud though.

Mama used her good arm to push up from the table. "Then I'll be praying you don't let Him down."

"Thanks."

I think. She was so in tune with God, I wasn't sure what she'd pray. I only hoped she and the Lord wanted the same results I did.

She handed me a plate to load in the dishwasher. "Is Andy getting out of the hospital tomorrow?"

"That's what Mrs. Wayfield said." I picked up a cup and dumped the dregs into the sink. "I'm supposed to go over there tomorrow night for dinner and to discuss the staging, but …" I set the cup upside down in the machine's upper rack. "Vanessa Owens is going to be there."

"Oh? Why?"

Closing the dishwasher, I tried to appear unaffected. "Well … actually I don't know—to guard him, maybe? She's very territorial about Andy."

"Really?" Mama picked up a dispenser next to the sink and squirted hand cream into my hands. "Interesting."

I massaged the almond-scented lotion into my hands and then hers, carefully avoiding her cast. "What do you mean?"

"Andy isn't dating her. He's not dating anyone."

My hands stopped their rubbing. That wasn't the impression I'd gotten at the hospital, with her draped all over Andy. "How do you know that?" And did Vanessa know it?

"Miss Owens inspires the gossips. I've heard plenty without trying."

"So what does Andy have to do with her?"

"It's a bit delicate. Her daddy is chairman of the deacons. He's also on the personnel committee and the only dissenting voice about hiring Andy. Sam

Owens is not a fan of the worship music."

Mama slid onto a barstool, propping her feet on the crossbar. "He's very vocal about preferring the old hymns and how they should be played. Vanessa, on the other hand, was a fan of Night Star. On Andy's first Sunday, she let him know she owned every one of his CDs." She patted the stool next to her for me to sit. "That girl manages to be everywhere he is. She can't sing a lick, so she joined the drama ministry. Unfortunately, she thinks acting is throwing her arms around and speaking in an affected, melodramatic voice. I'm guessing she thinks her daddy's position opens all doors."

"And Andy gave her the female lead in *Three Men and the Baby*?"

Mama's upper lip twitched. She thought this was funny? It wasn't. Not one bitty bit.

I dropped onto the stool next to her. "So let me get this straight. I have to direct a groupie who can't act or sing but is starring in a musical? Oh, Mama-mine, what have you gotten me into?"

Chapter 4

Feeling like Daniel at the mouth of the lion's den, I walked past a car I assumed was Vanessa's parked in Andy's driveway and rang the doorbell. I was here to do business, not engage in a romance. So why was my stomach filled with the chorus line from *Cats*?

The door burst open and Mrs. Wayfield tugged me inside. "Come in, dear." She turned her head and shouted over her shoulder, "Andy, Morgan's here."

Andy's dachshund, Tuppence, danced around my feet until I bent and petted her. Mrs. Wayfield shooed her away with her apron. "They're in the den."

Of course. The lions roared as I trod the narrow, carpeted hallway, past Mr. Wayfield's study to a wide set of double doors.

Andy sat in a wheelchair with his broken foot in a non-walking cast, straight out in front of him supported by a padded brace. Vanessa, wearing jeans so tight they looked like they'd been painted on, wedged herself between the cushion and the arm of the sofa. She couldn't get any closer unless she sat on his lap.

Andy's face glowed with welcome. But was it for Vanessa or me? I gave myself a mental shake. It didn't matter. I was here on business.

If only my heart would listen.

He reached out and squeezed my hand. "Thanks for coming. I'm so over my head directing a play. There's a notebook on the hearth for you." He gestured to a large binder by the fireplace. "It's got the script and my pathetic blocking notes, plus the tech designs. We've been in rehearsals for three weeks already."

Only three? Why did amateur groups always cut short rehearsal time when they needed more than professionals?

He withdrew his arm from Vanessa's clasp. "We can go through it now if you like."

Okay, he was all business too. My heart did a nosedive, but I told it this was for the best. I sat on the hearth and opened his production book.

Vanessa glared. "I still don't know why we need her. I directed the children's Christmas play last year."

A muscle near Andy's eye twitched. It always did when he tried not to laugh. What happened during that play that tickled his funny bone?

"Morgan is a Broadway professional, Vanessa. She has experience in every aspect of a production. Besides, she wrote the script. No one knows it better than she does."

"Well, I have my own ideas about ... wait a minute." She snapped her attention directly to me. "Really? You've acted on Broadway?" She jumped up and joined me on the hearth.

I wasn't sure how it happened, but I went from *persona non grata* to potatoes *au gratin*. "I have. I mean I do."

"What do you have planned for us? And can you help me? I want to be an actress more than anything, but ..." She glanced at Andy. "Well, I know I don't have any experience, but ... but I *feel* it."

Ah, now I understood. Andy was out of the picture, and I had become her new focus. What an incredibly fast allegiance shift. Still, I recognized her enthusiasm, although I started younger—at Cassie's age. That reminded me. I might be about to stick myself between the first dropped line and a wardrobe malfunction—I took lines from Vanessa and gave them to Cassie. I wondered if—

Tuppence jumped up, barking as Cassie flew into the family room. "Miss Morgan! I thought I heard you." She plopped down beside me. "Did you show Uncle Andy my lines?"

Vertical creases appeared above Andy's nose and his left eyebrow rose. I swallowed, suddenly uncertain of his reaction.

"There aren't any lines for a child." With a frown of confusion, Vanessa slid the stylistic gold heart on her necklace back and forth.

Cassie raised her little chin and grasped my hand. "Yes, there are. Miss Morgan wrote some for me."

"She did?" The creases in Andy's forehead smoothed out as he glanced at me. "Thanks, Morgan. You've made her very happy."

What about you? I dug deep for some mental discipline. Andy's reaction didn't matter. The play mattered.

"I think that's grand." Vanessa winked at Cassie. "I wish I'd started as young as you."

Cassie stared at Vanessa, turned her eyes on her uncle, bounced her gaze to me, then back at Vanessa. "Huh?"

"Come on, y'all," Mrs. Wayfield called from the dining room. "Supper's ready."

Vanessa jumped up, holding out a hand to me.

Tuppence scrambled to get out of our way as Cassie took my other hand. "You're sitting by me, Miss Morgan."

"Where do you want me, Cassie?" Vanessa asked.

Andy's niece pointed to the chair opposite mine. "You're there."

"Oh, good." Vanessa plopped down.

I felt like a blue ribbon at the county fair.

As the dishes were passed, Vanessa plied me with question after question about the plays I'd been in, how long it took to get a part, and the best acting schools.

When the pot roast came my way, I served myself a portion, adding a spoonful of gravy to my potatoes, then tucked into my supper. "This is wonderful, Mrs. Wayfield. I really miss home cooking."

"Can't you cook?" Cassie asked, her eyes large with surprise.

"I can but rarely have the time to, sugar." I laid my fork down. If Vanessa wanted to be an actress, and by her intensity I believed she did, she ought to know what it was really like. But did I really want Andy to think me a failure? "When you're starting out, you work two or even three jobs to make ends meet."

Cassie's eyes widened. "Wow." She slid a chunk of meat off her plate and held her hand beneath the tablecloth. Tuppence delicately took the tidbit.

"Cassie." Andy's mouth twitched. He didn't quite have stern down yet.

"Oops." She wiped her hand on her pants. "So how come you gots to work so many jobs?"

"You can't get a regular job and go to auditions. You need part-time work so you can trade with other people if you want to get off for an audition or the run of a play. Most of us wait tables."

Vanessa drank it in as if I'd offered cold champagne instead of lukewarm water. I guess it did seem romantic. It did to me when I was eighteen. It would be interesting to see how much ability she possessed. And Cassie. This gig might be fun after all.

After dinner, Vanessa sat quietly while Andy explained what he'd already accomplished with the cast before the accident. "They've got their blocking nailed down, unless you plan to change it."

By the calendar, then, I had five weeks left until the performance weekend. We might be able to pull it off, but it would be tight. Tomorrow night was my first rehearsal with them, and I planned to thank God in my prayers for Vanessa's turnaround. Having her think I was her golden ticket to stardom might be a good thing. At least, I hoped it would be.

Chapter 5

I tapped my fingers on the steering wheel to the music of the Zac Brown Band. I hadn't been home more than two days and already I'd reverted to country music instead of show tunes. I thought I'd rooted out the country girl in me. The last strains of "Goodbye in Her Eyes" twanged as I drove into the church parking lot.

A moment after I stepped into the auditorium, the house lights dimmed and the stage lights came to life one after the other. Excellent. The lighting crew was checking all the spots. I moved down the aisle to the front of the room. The sanctuary would seat twelve hundred, and Mom told me they'd already sold out for all three nights of the production.

From what Andy said, most of the cast knew their lines and had some acting experience. My biggest worry was Vanessa. One bad actor could ruin a performance for all.

I'd worked all night on the new script, printing it out early this morning. Would Vanessa revert to her former behavior and pitch a hissy fit? My palms grew moist. Most likely, she'd believe I'd done it for spite, but I'd prayed before I rewrote it, asking the Lord to help me truly like her.

The rewrite made the script stronger and provided a part for Cassie. I hoped Vanessa would see that. If she were part of Andy's life, then surely she had a soft spot for his niece. Who wouldn't? Cassie was adorable.

I dropped my briefcase on the front pew and studied the assembled cast, counting thirty-four. Good. That meant we had several of the stage crew in attendance. In front of the platform, Vanessa stood in a small group, chatting. She glanced over her shoulder at me, but I couldn't read her expression.

Cassie arrived with Mrs. Wayfield and dashed up to give me a hug. "Do you have my part, Mith Morgan?"

I gestured to my briefcase. "It's in there, sugar. If you'll sit a moment, I'll get started, then you can hand them out to everyone. Will you do that for me?"

"Yeth ma'am." Her little face split with the cutest gap-toothed smile.

"Cassie, did you lose a tooth last night?"

She stretched her lips to show me. "And I got a two dollarth for it from the toof fairy."

"You're a lucky little girl. All I ever got was a quarter." I straightened up. It was time to get this show going. "If everyone will come front and center, we'll get started. First, I need the sound engineer to get me wired. And who is our stage manager?"

As soon as I was outfitted with a wireless microphone so I wouldn't lose my voice, I was ready. The volunteer stage manager, Karl, sat beside me with his notebook open. I pulled the new scripts from my briefcase and handed them to Cassie.

"Cassie is going to give everyone a new script."

Voices erupted from around the room.

"I already learned my part."

"I've marked my script for the props."

"Why is there a new one?"

Vanessa put two fingers in her mouth and spit out a whistle that would've made an NFL coach proud. Everyone stopped and gaped. "Quiet, y'all. Miss Morgan knows what she's doing, so y'all just listen up." She nodded at me.

"Thank you, Vanessa. Now, for most of you, the parts won't change at all, except for a few stage directions. There has been an addition of a few lines for a couple of children." I'd added another little boy as a brother to Cassie's part so no one would blame her for the changes. "Tonight, my plan is to meet all of you, find out your roles, and do a run-through of the first act. I want to see how you're coming along. It's ambitious, I know, so let's get started."

One by one, they told me their name and role or position in the crew. Since some had joined the church after I went off to college, I introduced myself, explained my degree in theatre, and my professional experience. Just before I called for places, I asked if anyone had a young boy about seven years old.

Alan—rather Bobby Adams who played the part of Alan the seeker—offered his son. "Trey's taking acting lessons."

That was great news. "Thank you. For tonight, will you read his lines too, please? All right, all those in act one, scene one, on stage, please."

A few among the amateur cast had a lot of experience and did quite well. Unfortunately, poor Vanessa was not among those. She delivered her lines in a loud, unidentifiable accent and an abundance of gestures. I hoped with coaching, she would drop the affectations. She had a good voice, and I made a note in the margin of my script.

As we got closer to Cassie's first line, the muscles in my neck tensed. When she opened her mouth, Vanessa spoke the line in tandem with her, except Andy's niece was a natural, adding the right amount of emotion to her words.

"Oh, is that one of the ones that goes to Cassie? I'm sorry, I'd already memorized it." She marked it out in her script, which she wasn't using. That was a good sign.

"I'm delighted you have your lines memorized, Vanessa."

She stood taller, and I realized she lacked confidence. Knowing I could help her with that delighted me.

"I took that line because it segues into the part I wrote in for her. Now let's continue." I picked up my pencil and jotted another note about adding vocal warm-up drills to the next rehearsal.

We made it through the rest of the act with relative ease. After scheduling the next scene, and a cue-to-cue rehearsal with the tech crew, I called an end to the evening. Vanessa paced upstage with her phone to her ear. I sat on the front pew, writing notes.

A few minutes later, Vanessa dropped down on the other side of my briefcase. "You really are good at all this." She gestured toward the stage. "I love everything about the theatre. I want to learn it all. If only I could get my daddy to understand how important it is to me."

I set my production book aside. "Does he not support the play?"

"Oh, the play, sure, but that's because we've always done one. He thinks it's fine to act in a church play, but not on a professional stage. He's always telling me stories of casting couches and the horrible morals of actors. It isn't really like that, is it?"

"That's highly exaggerated. Maybe back in the thirties and forties, but not now. Women are wiser and stronger."

"That's what I told him, but ... maybe, would you talk to him?"

After what I'd heard about her daddy, I had no desire to speak with him, and I doubted he'd listen anyway. "Let me work on an idea and we'll talk later. Right now, it's time to leave."

At that moment, I didn't know if she'd respond to coaching, but she had the desire. Sometimes, that's all that's needed, and I planned to give it my all.

Chapter 6

With tomorrow being Sunday, there weren't any rehearsals tonight. Andy and I sat in his living room at the table his mother had set up for us by the fireplace. She had the air conditioner set so low, it was chilly enough for a fire. Tuppence curled up into a ball next to Andy's feet.

As much as I tried to keep my feelings disciplined, I found myself staring at Andy instead of the script. The firelight reflected in his eyes and shadows danced in his hair, making my heart flutter.

He glanced up from his production book. "What?" He brushed a hand over his mouth. "Do I have some leftover dinner on my face?"

"Oh, uh … no, I was … thinking. About when you had that New Year's Eve gig in New York." Right. I was having visions of kissing him. At least I could blame the fire for the heat in my cheeks.

"Man, that was something, wasn't it?"

"I was so excited to see you again and show you New York." I'd had it all planned. I'd show him around, the opportunities for him. I dreamed he'd find an apartment near mine. "You never did tell me why you left so quickly."

"Hives."

"Hives? I don't get it."

One side of his mouth lifted in a heart-breaking grin. "I'm allergic to big cities. I've always told you I'm a small-town country boy."

An ember popped in the fireplace. "But you toured all the big cities. Did you get hives in all of them?"

"New York was the first time."

A glimmer of hope rose.

"After that, I took antihistamines."

The dream bubble I'd so carefully hidden yet continued to nurture—the one where Andy realized he couldn't live without me and moved to New York—burst. It would never work. We'd never work.

I blinked against the tears that suddenly stung my eyes. Reality was I was here to work, not flirt. If only I could convince my heart.

I turned the page in my production book. "Here's what I thought would be good action for Cassie and Trey."

Andy stared at me with an unreadable expression before studying the blocking. He only disagreed with me on one place. His point was valid and I made the adjustment. We discussed the music and the soloists.

"Andy, you're so good at this. Still, I can't understand why you left the band."

"After I got Cassie, I couldn't stay on the road and I couldn't take her with me. The poor baby had a hard time getting over her mama and daddy's death, and every time I left, she thought I wouldn't come back. So when the church offered me the job, I jumped at it."

"You don't miss being in the band?"

"Yes and no. I love being a worship pastor. I just wish—"

"Wish what?"

He ran his hand through his hair and a sigh rose from deep inside him. "Vanessa's father … no, forget I said anything."

I laid my hand on his wrist. "We've been close since we were kids. You can tell me."

"It's a delicate situation." His voice lowered to a whisper. "If I didn't have Cassie, it would be easy to leave or maybe stand up to Mr. Owens. But I have to think of my niece. Her life needs to remain stable right now." He leaned over and rubbed his leg at the top of his cast. "I bite my tongue a lot." He gave me a rueful grimace.

"I guess I can understand that." Poor Andy. The situation was more than delicate. My guess? It was explosive, and he always took the high moral ground. I wanted to wrap my arms around him. Instead, I glanced at the mantel clock. It was going on ten. Tuppence yawned and stretched.

"Is that it?" Andy asked as I closed my script.

"Actually, there's something else." I took a deep breath and let it out slowly. "Tell me what Vanessa's audition was like that made you give her the lead."

He leaned over the side of the wheelchair and picked up the fire poker. I rose and pulled the screen aside for him to break up the logs. "No one else tried out."

"Nobody?" Suspicion rose in my knower. My grandmother on my daddy's side used to point to just beneath her ribcage and say, "That's your knower—the spot where God places discernment."

Andy shook his head. "Her daddy put out the word that she wanted the role. That's the dynamics around here, Morgan. Deacon Owens heads the finance committee, is on the personnel committee, and chairs the deacon board. He's a wealthy man who's not afraid to wield his power."

My knower was right, but I couldn't connect the dots. "I grew up in this church. It was never like this. What happened?"

Andy avoided my gaze, leaning down to pet Tuppence. "Chalk it up to a personality conflict. But back to Vanessa's audition, what could I do? I was stuck. I couldn't tell her thanks but no thanks."

"I guess not." I understood more now, but I definitely needed to give her private coaching lessons and hope she had some talent. "Could her performance hurt the event's reputation? Your mom said y'all sell out each year."

Andy's smile disappeared. "Our reputation isn't really at stake." His brows drew together. "Yours is. Sam sent a press release today to the AJC and all the other newspapers, announcing that you're the author and director. I'm almost sorry I let your mama talk me into letting you come. It would have been better to cancel the pageant." He winced and shifted his weight in the wheelchair. "Vanessa's daddy would have had my hide though, if I'd canceled."

The Andy I knew wouldn't allow himself to be manipulated. "Why do you stay? You wouldn't have any trouble finding another church. It wouldn't have to be far away. And Cassie seems like she's very well-adjusted now."

He gazed at the fireplace. "She's fine as long as things are status quo. Besides,"—he turned his attention back to me—"I love Sugar Hill. I was raised here, and want to live my life here. Cassie just started kindergarten and is happy. I can't see risking a move because of my pride."

Chapter 7

"Mith Morgan, Trey ithn't where he belongs." Cassie pointed to her script while Trey stomped his foot.

"I don't wanna be back there. I can't see my grandpa."

Who said little boys weren't divas? I put my arm around his little shoulders. "Trey, sweetheart, you're taller than Cassie. If you're in front of her, nobody will see her." A grin pulled at my lips. "They'll think her voice is you."

With a look of sheer horror on his face, he moved slightly upstage of Cassie.

"All right, everybody, let's try this scene again from line thirty-eight, page twelve."

Cassie's pickup line fell right on the heels of Trey's. I wondered if a talent for music gave her an edge on timing. Hers was perfect. The rest of the scene went as smoothly as possible for where we were in the schedule. I called an end to rehearsal, and the actors left the stage to gather their belongings from the front row seats.

"For those who haven't yet, I want those lines learned. You're off script by next rehearsal." I held my hand up at a couple of protests. "You won't have them all completely memorized, I know, but you'll get them quicker without the crutch, so no scripts next time. I'll have someone calling lines."

I caught Vanessa's arm as she started up the aisle. "Are you free to have lunch with me tomorrow?"

Her look of delight made me glad I asked. "I sure can."

"Great. I'll pick you up at noon. See you then."

*

Vanessa stirred her iced tea, tasted it, and wrinkled her nose. "They don't make a decent sweet tea here." Huffing her displeasure at the server, she snatched three packets of sugar from the holder, ripped them open, and dumped them into her glass. Her spoon clanked against the sides as she stirred. Shades of her daddy—from what I'd heard of him—displayed themselves in her personality at times.

"It must be hard not to have everything live up to your expectations."

She rolled her eyes. "You have no idea, Morgan."

Oh, I thought I did. Though she missed the irony of my words, I didn't want my mouth to overload my tail, so I hushed. It wouldn't serve any purpose to antagonize her just because her behavior sometimes left much to be desired. If she had talent, and that was a big if, then New York would straighten her out fast enough.

She studied the menu with the intensity of a gaffer fine-tuning his sound and light boards. When the gangly server appeared, she closed it with a snap. "I'll take a BLT, with turkey bacon."

"Uh, we don't have turkey bacon." The poor boy had no idea what he was up against.

Vanessa's eyes circled the world again as she reopened her menu. "You order, Morgan. I have to choose again."

I winked at our waiter. "I'll have a Greek salad, please."

"Yes ma'am." He brightened as he scribbled my order.

Vanessa finally ordered a veggie burger, and the kid left us.

After a few minutes of small talk, I smoothed my napkin in my lap. "We need to have a talk."

"Oh dear. Have I done something wrong? If I have, I'm sorry." Her quicksilver personality was mindboggling.

"No, you haven't done anything wrong. Although ..." I decided to take a chance. Maybe no one ever told her about her manners. "You were rather short with our server."

She blinked, then her face turned red. She blew out a breath. "I've got my daddy's temper and lack of patience, I'm afraid. Mama says I need to work on my people skills."

At least someone was honest. "Anyway, the reason I invited you today was to talk to you about private coaching."

Her head tilted to the side. "Coaching? Like in gymnastics?"

"Sort of. I mean drama coaching."

"Really? You'd do that for me?"

"That's what I think you need, Vanessa. You're wooden on stage."

She frowned. "What do you mean by wooden?"

Our server returned with our order. As he placed Vanessa's in front of her, she apologized. He smiled and nodded, obviously pleased, before leaving.

As I speared a Kalamata olive, I explained how coaching differed from lessons. "If you ever go to acting school, then you get lessons on every aspect of the theatre and acting. In our coaching sessions, we'll concentrate on this play and this script."

"When do we start?"

I loved her enthusiasm. I hoped I could have a positive effect on her whole personality. "We have very little time, so we'll start tomorrow morning and work every day for two to three hours."

*

Vanessa and I decided not to tell anyone about our coaching sessions. Her first rehearsal was nothing short of miraculous. Never had I encountered anyone so wooden change so dramatically—pun intended. The girl had raw talent, and like well-prepared garden soil, what was planted took root. With the one-on-one attention, she stopped overacting and looked to me for direction at rehearsals.

When I gave her a character interview sheet, she read it, then looked up at me in wonderment. "I feel like I've been in a dark room and you just turned the lights on for me." She learned how to climb inside the head of the character she was playing, look at the world through her eyes, and then react as she would.

All Vanessa had needed were the tools—which I provided. What an amazing feeling. I had helped create an actor. Had God felt like that when He created the world? I knew, of course, the two didn't compare, but I couldn't help the rush of delight in her metamorphosis. Even the other cast members noticed and showered her with compliments.

I'd worked with her every day for the past two weeks, and with one practice left before the dress rehearsal, I was confident she would pull it off—unless nerves got the upper hand.

Chapter 8

Mama was in the sunroom, drinking her morning coffee and reading her Bible. Ever since Daddy turned the back porch into an all-seasons room, she spent her morning quiet time there, enjoying the solitude and sunlight that streamed through the windows. In the kitchen, I sliced a raisin bagel in two and popped the halves in the toaster. After slathering it with butter, cinnamon, and sugar, I picked up the coffee carafe and a cup and joined her.

Mama slipped a bookmark I'd made in kindergarten between the pages of her Bible. "Mornin', darlin'. What are your plans today?" She held up her cup for a refill.

"Another coaching session with Vanessa." I took a bite of bagel and quickly wiped the butter trailing down my chin.

"How's she doing?" A half smile on her face, Mama handed me another napkin.

"Much better than I expected."

"I've always said you'd be an excellent coach."

"Let's just say I uncovered some hidden talent."

"Don't sell yourself short, Morgan. Your acting talent is honed, but anyone who could take that girl and turn her into anything remotely resembling an actress is downright amazing."

I sipped my coffee, testing its heat. Coaching was beyond satisfying, I gave her that, but amazing? "It was fun. She was like a bucket of polymer crystals soaking up every hint I gave."

A cardinal landed on the bird feeder and eyed us through the window before indulging in his breakfast. Great, now even the birds were giving me the mama-once-over. *What are you up to, God?*

"Has Andy seen her perform since the two of you started working together?"

"He doesn't know about it. I want it to be a surprise."

"I hear he gets his walking cast today." Mama changed topics faster than a tornado changed direction.

"He does, and he'll see Vanessa perform tonight. I'm hoping he'll be pleased by her ability."

"Hmm."

"What does that mean?"

"Better he be pleased with you, sugar."

She was like a dog with a bone. "There's no future there. I'm going back to New York, and big cities give him hives."

Picking up her Bible, Mama slowly rose from her chair, then as if an afterthought, she faced me from the doorway. "Are you sure Broadway is what you want—where you're supposed to be?"

"It's all I've dreamed about since I was ten years old." The cardinal had his fill and flew to a nearby tree to preen.

She tapped her fingers on her Bible. "Search your heart, Morgan. Look deep for the joy." She set her Bible back on the side table, turned, and went through the doorway.

Now, what did she mean by that? She knew I loved to act. A good performance brought me joy. The cardinal hopped back to the bird feeder and stared at me through the window.

As much as coaching Vanessa did?

That was different.

The bird ruffled its feathers.

What about when you wrote the script?

That was amazing. It seemed like God filled my heart and it flowed out my fingers to the keyboard.

And when you direct?

That was really cool. My third year in New York, I guest-directed a college production of *Singing in the Rain*. The newspapers reviewed it and gave "the director" kudos.

The cardinal flew off. I picked up Mama's Bible and opened it to the bookmark. The passage was about finding God's will.

Great. Mama and God were ganging up on me. If I weren't supposed to be a Broadway star, why had God given me the talent and the desire? I was more confused than ever.

My cell phone vibrated in my pocket, but it was just an email. My agent always called, so it wasn't him. The doorbell rang. I waited a moment, then not hearing Mama, I went to the door.

Andy stood on the front porch, a black walking cast on his foot and a guitar case in his hand.

"Hey, Andy. Glad you could ditch the crutches. What's up?"

"I want to go over something with you—get your opinion."

About what? I wondered. "Sure. Go on into the sunroom. You want something? Coffee? A Coke?"

"Coke sounds great."

He was strumming a beautiful melody as I entered with his drink. "What's that tune?"

"It's one I'm hoping you'll want to use in the play. I'd really like to write original music for the entire production."

That would be a dream come true. I'd thought about asking him yet never got the chance. "But there's not a lot of time left before the performances."

"Not for everything, but I've got one ready, and we've been working on it to surprise you. Then I thought I'd better let you in on the secret." His gave a sheepish grin. "In case you didn't like what I'd written."

Smart man. "Play it for me."

The melody was haunting, and the words pierced my heart. How could I not love it? It was as if he had laid open my heart, read what was inside, and put it to music. I smiled through the tears I felt forming. "You still have the golden touch in songwriting."

He lifted his eyes from his guitar and found mine. "As you do with playwriting." Bands of light from the sun cut through the blinds and cast a glow around us, doing strange things to my vision.

"So what do you think?"

That I'm hopelessly in love with you.

I swallowed, shoving down the unbidden words. "I love the song, Andy. It's perfect and it will touch hearts. I hope you write more. Maybe we can find a publisher."

"I've put some feelers out but didn't want to move before I knew how you felt."

Couldn't he see how I felt? Then my own words to Mama rang in my ears: "There's no future in that. I'm going back to New York, and big cities give him hives."

Best he didn't see. I set my glass on the coffee table. "Do you miss the band?"

"Sometimes." He strummed softly as we talked. "I miss jamming with the guys, but we've got some good talent at the church. Some stayed after practice the other night. We played and talked until close to midnight. What about you? Are you missing New York?"

No. The revelation hit me hard. I had to look forward, not backwards. I picked up a throw pillow and hugged it to my chest. "I'm enjoying my time here. It's a nice vacation."

"A working vacation."

I forced a laugh. "It is that."

"But that's all? No thoughts of moving back?"

A cloud crossed the sun, and the glow left the room, but it was for the best—my vision cleared. "My future is in New York, Andy. Broadway doesn't live in Sugar Hill."

He nodded and set his guitar back in its case. "I guess I'll see you at rehearsal."

I walked him out. The set of his shoulders looked lower than when he came in. I hated myself at that moment, but I was sure God had set me on this path. I had to remain true.

Chapter 9

Country music thrummed through the auditorium's speakers. I picked up the microphone lying beside me on the pew, tapped its screen and listened for the resulting thump, then waved to the control booth. "Karl, let's try washing the entire stage in green, please."

His voice echoed back to me over the sound system. "You thinking like an 89 or a 389 green, or more like 2004 green?"

For a volunteer, he sure knew his stuff. "I'm thinking muted and dreamlike to promote introspection, so definitely not Christmas green or too light like fresh grass. It needs a little gray."

"I know just the one."

"Thanks, and cue the computer to sound FX track eleven. I want to hear the accompanying music."

A second later, eerie green washed over the stage, and replacing the country twang, a flute played a lonely, haunting melody. I shivered.

Wow. That was exactly the effect I wanted. How tremendous it was to impact reactions with lights and sound—to entertain people while presenting a crucial message. The late director Betty Hamm once told me, "Drama brings life to our stories. Drama brings Christ's stories to our eyes. Drama uses our senses and draws us in. Then, when we least expect it, drama touches, teaches, and transforms us." She was right. People let down their guard when they think they're being entertained.

Joy filled me and overflowed.

"How's that?" Karl's voice boomed from the control booth.

"Perfect, Karl. Thanks."

Look deep for the joy.

Mama's words rose like heartburn. She didn't understand the joy in an audience's applause. I imagined the joy in seeing my name on a Broadway theatre's marquee.

Bloom! starring Morgan James. A thrill zipped through my veins.

The house lights came up and broke the spell. I sighed and picked up my production book to look over the trouble spots I wanted to key in on tonight. A music cue, a quicker scene change in act two, and costumes—ack! I still needed to meet with makeup and wardrobe.

"Solving last-minute problems?"

Talk about sound effects. Andy's voice sent a quiver down my spine. And straight to my heart. I feigned a casual smile. "I didn't hear you come in."

He dropped down beside me, surprising me. I scooted over to give him a little room. "Are you sticking around?"

"Do you want me to?"

"Definitely. I have a surprise for you."

"Oh? What's that?"

I gently elbowed his side. "No way. You'll have to wait and see."

The auditorium door opened, and Vanessa sailed down the aisle. I hadn't seen her with Andy since I began working with her. I braced myself but she breezed past us with a mere wiggle of her fingers and hurried backstage.

I swallowed a throat-blocking knot of hope and tried to sound merely curious. "Hey, buddy, I noticed Vanessa isn't as chummy lately."

"Vanessa?" He blinked and shrugged. "What do you mean? Is something wrong?"

Men can be so oblivious. "She blew in here and didn't even stop to say 'hey.'"

"Is that a problem?" He pointed to a Fresnel spotlight. "Is that new?"

"I don't know. Forget the lights, Andy. Did you two have a fight?" Would her performance be affected?

His attention snapped from the spot to me, his brows drawn tight. "Why would I fight with Vanessa?"

Twenty-nine and he already had dementia. "Maybe because your girlfriend got mad at you?" I popped a TicTac into my mouth and held the little box out for him.

"Girlfriend?" He laughed and took a mint. "Honey, Vanessa isn't now, nor has she ever been, my girlfriend."

I raised my eyebrows high. "Does she know that?"

"Well now, it was a problem for a while. Then a couple of weeks ago, she stopped bothering me. So yeah, I guess she does know. Or she found greener grass." He chuckled. "Why?" His shoulder bumped mine. "Did it bother you, thinking I liked her?"

I wasn't ready to go there. "I thought you'd lost your marbles, going after a girl ten years your junior."

He chuckled, low and soft. "You didn't need to worry. I couldn't give my heart to any other girl when it belongs to you. Always has. Always will."

Air rushed into my throat, along with the TicTac. I coughed, sputtered, then swallowed the mint whole.

"Well?"

The challenge in his eyes made my mouth as dry as the Arizona desert I once visited. I loved him. There was no use denying it, but I'd be back in New York before Christmas. Pain pinched my heart. I desperately needed a diversion from this conversation. "It's—"

"Hey!" Vanessa stood center stage, hands on her hips, and glared at us. "Are we ever going to start rehearsing tonight?"

I never thought I'd be grateful to that girl for anything, but her timing was impeccable. I pushed upright against the hard pew back. "Yes. Places everyone. We're going to do a full run-through."

As the house lights went down, I snapped on the small conductor's light attached to a music stand and flipped to page one in the script. "Prepare to be amazed, Wayfield."

*

When the last line had been delivered and the house lights came up, silence echoed in the auditorium. Every member of the cast had surprised themselves with their skill. I leaned over to ask Andy what he thought, but he wasn't there. I'd been so caught up in the play, I never noticed him leave. Twisting, I glanced over my shoulder. He stood in the rear of the auditorium talking with Pastor Paul and Vanessa's daddy.

I turned back to the assembled cast. Vanessa's portrayal of her character made me suspend disbelief. I'd solved the problem of Vanessa's lack of a singing voice by giving her solo to Jenny, whose rich alto voice showcased the song to perfection and made me weep. Cassie and Trey would steal the hearts of the audience. Everything came together perfectly.

Satisfaction filled my soul all the way down to my toes. I closed my production book and stood. "High-fives to every single one of you. You've smoothed the rough spots to a polished gleam. Now go home, get some rest, and take extra good care of your voices. Don't forget, six o'clock sharp tomorrow night for dress rehearsal."

Everyone scattered. I picked up my purse.

"Morgan?" A grin stretched across Vanessa's face. "I'm nearly busting with excitement. Daddy just told me I've been enrolled at NYU in the Tisch School of the Arts. Daddy has a good friend on the board. He pulled a few strings and I'm in. I'm going to New York!" She danced a little jig.

"Not until after the pageant is over, I hope."

"Silly, I'll start in the spring semester." She slid the heart on her necklace back and forth. "I owe it all to you for coaching me. When Mama watched me rehearse last week, she said she saw the difference too." Vanessa wiggled in delight. "Anyway, she talked Daddy into enrolling me."

I laid my hand on her arm. "I'm proud of your accomplishment, and you were a delight to coach. Keep that attitude of always learning and you'll do well."

"Thanks, Morgan." She slung the long strap of her cross-body purse over her shoulder. "See you tomorrow night."

I retrieved the rest of my things and followed her up the aisle. In the narthex, Andy waited. He opened the door for Vanessa, said good night, then turned back to me. "Can I talk you into a cup of coffee?"

I was always wound up tighter than a tick on a dog after a rehearsal. Some down time sounded good. "Sure, if you promise it's decaf and throw in a slice of pie."

His eyes danced and he executed a royal bow. "At your service, madam." He held the door as I swept through, laughing.

It was a short walk to The Squire's Pie Shoppe. Actually, it was a short walk to anywhere in downtown Sugar Hill. Unlike New York in wintertime, our breath didn't leave clouds of steam in the night air. Still, it was chilly. Christmas weather in Georgia. The streetlights were decked out in their holiday attire. Green and gold garlands tied with red bows had been strung with colored lights from each lamppost and across the road, through the three blocks of downtown.

The shops seemed to be in competition for the most used. Even The Suite Spot, Sugar Hill's business incubator, proudly flashed a display. The town Christmas tree towered in front of the city hall. Rockwell would have loved Sugar Hill.

We strolled—well, I strolled, Andy gimped along in his walking cast—by Bishop's Five and Dime. It pleased me to see Bryce and Cecily resisted the one-dollar name. So did Pfingsten's Toys. I'd gone to school with both Jesse Pfingsten and his wife, Lacey. Their store window sported a new generation of nose prints. I'd come back tomorrow to do a little Christmas shopping.

Inside Squires, the owner and resident baker, Pam, emerged from the kitchen to greet us. "I've got my tickets. I can't wait to see Cassie in *Three Men and the Baby*. I purely can't imagine little Morgan having written it."

She set our plates, laden with huge slices of pie, in front of us. "Why, I remember when your mama and daddy would bring you in here after school when you were a little thing, for my fresh peach pie. You always knew the day the peaches were ripe enough. Seems to me you were about Cassie's age then." She chuckled and went to chat with another customer.

Andy took my hands and asked a blessing. After his first bite, he paused, with his fork in the air.

"What?"

"Never mind. Eat your pie first. Then I want to ask you something."

After his declaration of me holding his heart forever, what I'd wanted when I was eighteen, I was now afraid of happening. I loved him, but I had a path to follow. What would I do if Andy asked me to marry him now?

Chapter 10

I took a bite of pie. Pam Squires couldn't make a bad pie, but that bite turned to dust in my mouth. My heart pounded and every nerve pulsated enough to electrify Atlanta. Andy happily devoured his rhubarb.

We both reached for our coffee cups at the same time. We were so alike in so many small ways. If only—

"Morgan ..."

Here it comes. I don't want to break his heart, Lord. My own is tearing apart. But I have to hold on to my dream. I can't give up now.

I shoved another bite into my mouth to stall. "Hmm?"

Andy leaned forward, his eyes sparkling. "After watching what you've managed with Vanessa and the others, Pastor Paul and Deacon Owens would like to offer you the position of creative arts director for the church."

I blinked. That certainly wasn't what I'd expected. I swallowed the pie—and my pride. What was I thinking? That he couldn't live without me? Heat crawled into my cheeks, and it wasn't from the coffee.

Wait a minute. What was *he* thinking? He was the one who always pushed me to excel, to reach for the stars. Now he wanted me to give it all up?

His hand rose like a traffic cop. "Don't answer yet. Think about it. Pray on it, Morgan. See if this might be what God wants for you."

God or Andy? Boy, if my mama was in cahoots with them on this, I was in trouble. Using the tines of my fork, I pushed a chunk of piecrust to the plate's edge. "I'll let you know after the last performance."

He reached across the table, his little finger crooked like when we did a pinkie swear as kids. I linked fingers and forced a smile, but my heart quivered like it knew it was about to be broken.

*

Mama and I strolled down Main Street, enjoying the Christmas decorations. It's funny how Sugar Hill, a blip on the map halfway between Norcross and Gainesville, remained such a tiny town. Yet here, we had the best of both worlds.

Big city—well, not New York City-big, but relatively so—and small-town living.

I sucked in a lungful of crisp air. "I hadn't realized how much I missed this."

Mama's smile had its told-you-so slant, but she refrained from voicing it. I didn't tell her about Andy's job offer. That would only add charcoal to her grill, and I didn't want to be mopped and barbequed.

We stepped into Bishop's Five and Dime, and 1950 stared me in the face. On black-and-white checkered linoleum floors, wooden cases displayed merchandise, inviting one to pick up items of interest. Glass cabinets lined the walls, filled with more expensive wares. Bishop's hadn't changed since my grandmother was a little girl. Delight quickened.

At the end of one aisle, I stopped dead in my tracks. "Why is the lunch counter from Suhoversnik's Drug Store here, and why is Leanna working it instead of being at the pharmacy?"

"They closed the drug store last year—too hard to compete with the national chains," Mama said, her voice wistful. "The lunch counter was all that kept the store afloat. Anyway, Leanna's daddy was ready to retire, so he suggested it. It seemed like a natural move given that she and Cecily are cousins."

"I'm glad they're still around. Leanna makes the best burger this side of the Mississippi, and I plan to have one for lunch." I waved at her. She plopped down her spatula, ran out from behind the counter, and, squealing, grabbed me in a hug. I shouldn't have been surprised at everyone's friendliness, yet I was. New York had jaded me.

Mama suggested we finish our Christmas shopping, then stop back for burgers when we were done. In New York City, everything was so far apart, I had to get a taxi or hop on the subway to get from one errand to the next. But here, by the end of the day, I'd be laden with bags, feet sore, and happily sated with one of Leanna's deluxe cheeseburgers and fresh homemade French fries.

"See you in a while," I told Leanna and resumed my wandering down the aisles, looking at the merchandise. I wanted a small trinket for each of the cast members. A pin for the women, maybe, that spoke of their character. I hadn't a clue what to get them, but with the variety of things available, I was certain to find something.

Mama's laughter carried from the back of the store where she chatted with Cecily. On the top of one display case sat a jumbled array of costume jewelry. In one corner, I found a miniature Oscar charm. It was perfect for Cassie. I'd get it, then check with her grandmother to see if she had a charm bracelet. If not, I'd come back and get her one. Soon, I had all the women and most of the men's gifts selected. And here I'd been thinking New York could beat Sugar Hill for variety. Silly me.

I wanted to get something for Andy, but what? It couldn't say too much, since I wasn't sure I could give him what he really wanted. If he'd told me I held his heart five years ago, I never would have gone to New York. But he didn't, and I did. And now I was on the edge of seeing my dream become reality. Oh, why did life have to be so complicated?

Chapter 11

A sharp, cold wind blew in from the north, signaling a nor'easter. A large Styrofoam ball rolled and skittered across the church parking lot, coming to rest next to a crepe myrtle decorated with Christmas lights. Cindy, one of the teens, dropped her strand of lights and chased after the ball. Two other similar ones had been painted white and were skewered to the church lawn. This one, I was sure, faced a similar fate and would join the others to make a snowman. Sugar Hill rarely if ever saw Christmas snow, and never enough to make a decent snowman.

I waved at the kids, turned off the engine, and reached for the door handle. A spark of static electricity zapped me, and foreboding pumped gas on top of the barbeque I'd had for supper. I swallowed a threatening burp. Theatrical people were a superstitious lot, and tradition had it if dress rehearsal was a disaster, then opening night would be a smash hit. I hoped the cast knew that. In weather like tonight, tension would be high and tempers short.

Inside the church auditorium, the crew bustled about, doing last-minute adjustments and final light and sound checks. As soon as they were ready, I gathered them and any cast members already present for prayer. That wasn't done corporately in New York, on or off Broadway. I usually prayed alone while putting on my makeup. Here, standing with them and holding hands felt like a hug.

I let Karl take the lead and his eloquence calmed my stomach. I knew Who was in charge. When Karl finished, I added a request for those members of the audience who would see and hear of the Savior's birth. I prayed for hearts to be softened.

A screech hastened our amens. Lettie the prop mistress, a twittering sparrow of a woman, ran onto the stage. In her hands lay several chunks of what had been a king's crown.

"What happened?" I examined the pieces.

"I don't know. I came in and it was on the floor like you see it. It was fine when I left last night." She clicked her tongue, *tsk*ing several times. "It's ruined."

"I'm sure it's not." I put my arm around her shoulder and walked her toward the wings. "You're so talented, I'm positive you can fix it."

She stopped, tilted her head to the left, then the right, and back again as she eyed the fractured crown. She looked up at me with wide eyes. "Oh. I think maybe I can. A little hot glue, a couple of new jewels ..." She slid out from under my arm and flitted backstage, chirping to herself as she left.

One disaster averted, or mended to be exact. I crossed my fingers against any more. With everyone ready, I took my place in the front row with a notepad and pen, then nodded to Karl.

"Clear the stage," he bellowed. Those not in the opening number scurried off behind the curtain. "Places."

Karl signaled me and I nodded to Andy. He turned to his orchestra and the overture began. The curtain rose and—

Where was Daryl?

A heartbeat later, he ran into the scene. He covered with a well-place ad-lib, making me chuckle. The music swelled in a delightful arrangement of "It's the Most Wonderful Time of the Year" as the cast, armed with shopping bags, scurried in and out of the storefronts.

The choreography was wonderful. The execution ... not so much. They forgot one important rule—don't break the fourth wall. I had invited guests to the dress rehearsal, and all the grandmas were intent on seeing if their grandchildren were in the audience—the very reason I invited them to come that night instead of opening night.

Cassie wore a long flannel nightie as Liz, her stage mama, walked her into the scene. I held my breath as Liz tucked her into bed. The next part had been added just a week ago, and Cassie was so young I wasn't sure it would work.

After the prayer, Liz said goodnight and left the stage. On cue, Cassie rose to her knees and peered out a window. The music began and without looking away, my darling Cassie sang "Happy Birthday, Jesus" without missing a word. Her adorable lisp enhanced the song. If she did this well during the performances, she'd steal the show.

*

Tradition held. Dress rehearsal was a disaster.

Everyone except Cassie and Vanessa forgot lines, missed cues, and couldn't remember the blocking. Even the stage crew used the wrong backdrop for the three kings' procession. A forlorn and tragic-looking lot assembled on stage for the postmortem. Like most casts and directors, we'd grown close, and if they were like any troupe I was ever part of, they felt they'd let me down. I had to show them it wasn't true.

"Jenny, what's Zehmira's speech right after introducing herself?" Jenny had flubbed those lines.

Not missing a beat, she recited with a heavy Jewish accent, "We run an inn. In Bethlehem. Bethlehem! Not exactly the center of attention. You see, Bethlehem is about five miles from Jerusalem—just far enough off the beaten path to make us out of the way. We don't get a lot of visitors. Now, an inn in Jerusalem! Oy, that would have been something. But, Meshulam the Clueless says to me, 'Zemmie, we'll build our inn in Bethlehem.' Oy, we get by, we get by; but no, we are not wealthy people."

Jenny sat down with a satisfied grin.

"See? You know it. You simply let nerves get in your way. Your accent is perfect and adds that spark of humor I love. You'll do fine." Her accent was more Brooklyn than true Jewish, but it was the humorous touch I wanted for that part.

She lifted her head, and as if sewn together, her eyebrows raised in partnership with her lips. She got it—that illusive belief in one's ability.

"What about me, Miss Morgan?" Trey looked like he was about to cry. "I'm sorry I tripped during the first song."

"Oh, Trey, you did great, sweetie. You recovered so well, the trip looked planned. I'm going to owe you a double-dipper ice cream cone."

He glowed. My words were true though. He was too young to be nervous. Of course, he waved to his grandmother after he regained his balance, but I'd expected that.

By the time I completed the postmortem, everyone's mood was bright and upbeat. They believed in the message they would present and in themselves once again. I remembered the first time I felt that belief, but it paled in comparison to helping Jenny and the rest of the cast.

Wow.

As everyone went home, I couldn't help pondering how I felt. The gratification over these new friends' metamorphosis, and having a hand in it, filled me with deep satisfying joy. Basking in the feeling, I gathered my production book and purse and started up the aisle. Halfway, I turned and looked back at the empty stage, lit by a single bulb. How would going back to New York and being onstage myself compare?

Later, I tossed and turned in bed trying to will myself to sleep, but I kept seeing Andy's face, alive with love. My heart "squoze," like little Cassie said. Heaven help me, I loved her too.

But I'd come too far and worked too long to forsake the dream. I punched my pillow and buried my head. Yet, like a hungry mosquito, a nagging thought

refused to leave me.
 Would realizing the dream cost me love?

Chapter 12

My phone rang early. I grabbed it, once again hoping it was Cotsie with news about *Bloom!* but saw Andy's name in the display. My heart skipped a beat, then made up for it with a funny little double time.

"Hey." I rolled over, trapping my cell phone between my ear and the pillow.

"Hey yourself, sleepyhead. Toss some clothes on and let's go get breakfast."

"Okay. Give me twenty minutes."

I tapped off, tossed the phone in my purse, and slipped into the shower. Twenty minutes later, I had on the barest of makeup and damp hair, but I was dressed and ready.

Andy stood at the bottom of the stairs as I came down. His eyes followed my every step. "How can you look so beautiful this early in the morning?"

It took all I had in me not to jump over the last three steps and into his arms. "My hair's still wet." I got to the bottom of the stairs.

He didn't move but wrapped his arms around me. "It smells good. Coconut."

I leaned back. His face was stubbly around his dimple where he missed shaving. Mercy, I loved this man. My eyes fastened on his lips and then his lips fastened on mine.

Oh my.

"Ahem."

We jumped apart.

"Morning, Mrs. James." Andy's slow smile spread over his red face.

I couldn't help laughing. "We're going to breakfast, Mama."

She folded her arms below a knowing smirk. "Mm-hmm."

Andy grabbed my hand, and we ran out to his car, giggling like teenagers. Seemed to me, we did that a few times when we actually were teens. We talked about nothing and everything as we drove to breakfast. He was the only boy—man now—I ever let see the real me. With any other man I dated, I was on guard the whole time. Andy was, among other things, a sweet relief.

We found an open table inside the Joshua Tree Diner. I hadn't had their *Huevos con Nopalitos* in a long time, so when Beulah Smythe, who was part of the cast, poured our coffee, I ordered without even opening the menu.

"I wondered when y'all would get around to comin' for breakfast, Morgan." Beulah scribbled our orders on her pad.

"I haven't had any really good Mexican since the last time I was home. That's one thing they don't do well in New York. But if you ever want the best hot pastrami, you've got to come visit me. My apartment is above the greatest Jewish deli on this earth."

She pursed her lips like she sucked a lemon. "Sorry, sugar, but I can't imagine anything enticing me to leave Sugar Hill to visit New York City. Even you." She marched to the kitchen. Beulah never was one to mince words.

Andy and I hid our chuckles behind our coffee cups. Then we chatted for several minutes about the play. I told him how much I loved directing and how gratifying it was.

"I'm really glad you asked Mama to call me. I wouldn't have experienced this otherwise."

He set his cup down. "Have you thought about the job offer? I already told you that you still have my heart. If you came back to work—"

"Here you go, Morgan." Beulah set my plate down. "Careful, it's hot."

Relief made my arms weak. My emotions were raw after last night, and I'd cry if we got into this now. I swallowed the lump in my throat and dove into my breakfast. I was disappointed. It didn't taste like I remembered. Maybe they had a new cook or maybe it was just me, but my breakfast, like my dream, now tasted bitter. I laid down my fork.

Andy frowned. "Something wrong?"

Not trusting my voice, I shook my head and took a sip of water. "A bit of pepper in my throat. Andy, about the job ... I told you I'd give you my answer after the pageant closed. That's next weekend."

It was only a short reprieve. What was I going to do? It seemed wrong to give up on my dream. Still, Cotsie hadn't called. Maybe I wasn't good enough to carry a leading role. I couldn't understand what God was doing. I'd kept myself pure like the Bible said. I didn't do the things that would make me fit in. I avoided parties—except cast parties at the end of a run—and I didn't drink at those. I kept away from all appearances of evil, working hard at being a light for God.

So why have you withheld leading roles from me?

He didn't answer.

I watched Beulah refill Andy's coffee. His banter was cheerful, but I knew better. I'd bruised his heart. Beulah raised a disapproving eyebrow at my still full cup.

I wasn't pleased with myself. Andy had planned a fun morning. He deserved better than me—someone without a crazy dream.

The sound of glass shattering echoed from the kitchen, but for me, it was the sound of two hearts breaking.

Chapter 13

I had promised to take Cassie shopping to buy her uncle and memaw Christmas presents, and even though I hurt Andy—not to mention my own heartache—I couldn't let her down. I swapped cars with Mrs. Wayfield so Cassie would have her booster seat, and we headed out, singing "Jingle Bells."

"You're tho much fun, Mith Morgan. I wish you didn't have to go back to New York. Couldn't you live here and commute like Trey'th daddy?"

I glanced at her through the rearview mirror. "Where does his daddy work, sugar?"

"In Gainethville."

"Ah, well, Sugar Hill to Gainesville is a thirty-minute commute. New York is twenty-two and a half hours away."

Her little face grew contemplative. "You couldn't drive, then. What about flying? You could do that."

Lord, I don't want to break her heart too. Help me here.

I pulled into a parking space in front of Bishop's. "You know, if I took a plane every day to work, I wouldn't have any money left over to take you out to lunch."

She jumped out of the car and grabbed my hand. "I'm gonna order a cheethburger and a chocolate shake."

Thank you. "That sounds delicious. Now, let's go shopping."

She pushed open the door. "Charge it!"

Laughing, I asked, "Where did you hear that?"

"Wilma Flint-thtone and Betty Rubble." She tugged my hand. "Come on."

She was quite the little shopper too. She picked up a variety of things, examining each one thoughtfully, before putting it down. "What are you looking for, Cassie?"

She shrugged but then squared her little shoulders. "I'll know it when I thee it."

I stifled a giggle. She sounded so adult. I let her wander, occasionally pointing out an item I thought Mrs. Wayfield would like.

Toward the back of the store, she stopped with a gasp. "That'th it." She stood in front of a glass wiener dog oil and vinegar set. "They look like Tuppenth."

"They're adorable, and your memaw will love them."

She chose a letter opener with a guitar handle for Andy.

"You're terrific at finding the right gifts, Cassie. I'll have to consult with you for my parents."

We paid for her things and Cecily wrapped them for her. After a fun lunch, I took her home for a nap. She protested until I told her I was taking one.

"All good actors take a nap before a performance."

*

The cast gathered around me for prayer. I asked God to open the hearts of those who would watch our performance. "Let them see You, Lord, and let their lives be touched and changed by what we do. It's for Your glory. Amen." How I loved this part of working with the church cast. I'd grown nearer to God during this time at home, and I savored the relationship.

"Five minutes, everyone," Karl said. "Places."

I left the backstage and took my seat in the front row. I found myself as nervous as I had been my first time in a Broadway play. At the same time, I felt wrapped in peace. I whispered a thank-you to God as the house lights went down and the curtain went up.

Singing, the cast sailed through the choreography of the opening song with ease. My heart soared with them. They wove in and out, carrying their shopping bags and glitter-laden packages. Not one was dropped nor one step missed. I released the breath I'd been holding. The scene change went without a hiccup, and I came close to jumping out of my seat when Jenny nailed every word in her monologue. The audience laughed in all the right places.

However, it was Cassie who stole the first act. She remembered every line and never once looked to the audience to find her memaw. She was a natural actress. Even her lisp was endearing. I saw quite a few wiping away tears while she sang her solo.

When the lights came up for intermission, I went backstage and into the green room, where everyone had gathered. Andy limped in a moment later. He told them how great they were doing, then looked to me. I guessed my grin looked dopey because he laughed.

I wrinkled my nose at him. "I can't tell y'all how proud I am at this moment. If I do, I'll cry and then some of you would, and that really messes with your makeup." They laughed as I had hoped. Just then, I felt my phone vibrate in my pocket. I pulled it out and glanced at the display. Cotsie's name blinked at me.

My heartbeat accelerated. "Excuse me. I have to take this."

I turned and walked into the hall outside the green room. "Hey, Cotsie."

"Morgan! Congratulations, sweetheart! You won the lead in *Bloom!*"

Adrenalin shot through me. "I did? Really? The lead?" My voice squeaked and tears of joy and thanksgiving filled my eyes. I *was* good enough! "Really?"

He laughed. "Yeah, kid, it's for real. Rehearsals start on Monday. Can you get back?"

Monday? "I'll be there. Tell them yes and ... and thank you." My hands shook and I had to press the off circle three times. I spun around and bumped into Andy.

I bounced on the balls of my feet. "I got the part. The lead. I finally got a lead role, Andy!"

I don't know what I expected—at least a high-five, something. But he didn't move. He didn't hug me in congratulations. He stood there frozen, except for one side of his mouth that rose halfway as his shoulders slumped. "I guess you won't be taking the job here."

That was all he could think of to say? My euphoria wilted. "Come on, Andy. I've worked hard for this. Can't you be happy for me?"

"You've been happy here, Morgan. You love directing. Look what you did with Vanessa. That's where your talent lies."

I felt like he'd slapped me. "Suddenly you decry my acting ability? I have a dream, Andy. A dream God gave me." I folded my arms across my chest like Cassie did when she got mad.

Andy shook his head. "If it's what you really think God wants for you, then—"

"What God wants or what you do?" I wished I could snatch the words back. Andy recoiled as if I'd spit on him. I reached out. He backed up. "Andy—"

"Five minutes," Karl called. "Places everyone."

For a moment longer, Andy stared as if he no longer recognized me. Then he gave a curt nod to Karl, turned his back, and disappeared down the steps to the orchestra pit. I couldn't move.

"Morgan, get to your seat." Karl nudged me. Like an automaton, I obeyed, but guilt accompanied me.

I told myself I shouldn't feel guilty. He hurt me too. The stars he encouraged me to grab were finally within my reach. Why couldn't he be happy for me?

After the final curtain, the audience swept forward to congratulate the cast, Andy, and me. I tried to push down my own hurt and be happy for the cast over their success. I pasted on a smile and turned the admiration back to the cast. But inside, my heart was breaking.

Chapter 14

Somehow, I got through the final performance. My bags had been stuffed in the trunk of the tiny rental car and the gas tank read full. No stops after the final performance. In the commotion of the cast accepting congratulations and the picture-taking, I managed to give Cassie a hug, told her I was proud of her, then I slipped away unnoticed.

As I drove to the airport, I didn't know whether to cry or shout glory. My heart alternately soared with the thrill of winning the lead in *Bloom!* and broke over leaving Andy, Cassie, and Sugar Hill behind. I dozed on the plane, but awoke when a bad dream made me cry out.

"I hope you aren't running away from something, dear." A soft but wrinkled and heavily veined hand touched my arm. It belonged to my seatmate, Elsie.

"Actually, I'm running *to* something. I've got the lead role in an off-Broadway musical."

"Really? Hmm." She stuck her forefinger between the pages of a romance novel. "You sure? That dream didn't seem to make you happy." A frown furrowed her brow in stark contrast to her twinkly blue eyes.

"I—" The dream had vanished. I squirmed against the plane's seatbelt. "How strange. A moment ago, I remembered it vividly, but now…" I smiled and shrugged.

Elsie leaned forward and glanced out the window. "Yes, dreams have a way of doing that. Sometimes, we get to keep them only for a season."

"What do you me—?"

"Please return your seats to an upright position and close your tray tables."

I wasn't sure what Elsie meant, but it didn't matter anyway. I couldn't wait to get back to Broadway and the energy of New York City, where the night lights glittered and sparkled. As soon as the plane stopped, I jumped out of my seat and opened the overhead storage. A Stetson rested on top of my bag.

"Can I help you?" a deep voice asked.

I glanced over my shoulder at the hat's owner. "Well, thanks, Cowboy."

He settled his hat on his head, then hefted my bag.

"If you're in town for a while, be sure to stop by the Cherry Lane Theatre and see me in *Bloom!* I'll leave a ticket for you at the box office."

"Looks like you're blooming now." He chuckled, touched his fingers to his hat, then hoisted down Elsie's bag and his own. He gave me his name for the ticket, and once we were off the causeway and into the terminal, I said goodbye to him and Elsie.

I hurried to catch a cab. The pneumatic doors split wide and ushered in an icy blast. How could I have forgotten this frigid weather in the span of six weeks? Or the constant odor of exhaust fumes? I coughed as I raised my hand for a taxi.

By the time I got to my apartment, it was closing in on one o'clock and I had to be at the theatre by two. Not bothering to unpack, I took a quick shower, changed, and grabbed my winter coat from the closet. I left a note for my roommates, telling them I was back but had gone to the Cherry Lane Theatre.

Once there, I paid the cabbie and turned to look at the marquee. It listed the current performance, *Legendary Lives*. I knew it was too soon for any mention of *Bloom!* but still … I'd hoped to see my name. I checked the side windows, but the only playbill was for tonight.

A cold wind slapped a piece of newspaper against my ankle. Before I could reach down and peel it off, the wind shifted and it fell away on its own, coming to rest in the gutter. Overhead, a canopy of gray clouds covered New York. I shivered and hurried inside.

I stood for a moment, letting my eyes adjust to the dim light as I slid out of my coat. A side door opened and the director, Stephen Castleman, strode out. With his nose buried in a script, he almost plowed into me.

"Watch where you—oh. Sorry, Morgan." He rolled the script and stuffed it under his arm, then reached for my hand. "I'm glad you're back, my dear. Cotsie wasn't sure when your plane was getting in. How was your flight?"

He was already walking away from me. In the short time I was gone, I'd forgotten how fast everyone in the theatre moved. And how little they truly seemed to care.

Stephen glanced over his shoulder. "You coming?"

"Yes. And my flight was horrible." I followed him. "We crashed in the Adirondacks."

"That's nice, my dear. Hey, Rosenblum! Did Trundle deliver?"

I'd worked with Stephen before. It was only a walk-on, but had he always been this way? Or was I simply over-tired from lack of sleep? I was no diva, but I thought I'd get—what? What *had* I expected?

I went to the green room and found a pot of coffee. Some caffeine would rid me of whatever it was bothering me.

By four o'clock, we'd blocked act one. Stephen called an end to rehearsal, telling us that tomorrow the choreographer would work with us on the musical numbers for act one. As we filed out, the *Legendary Lives* cast arrived in a flurry of coats and hats and hollered hellos.

Excited to see my friends, I lingered a moment to tell them I was back, but they hurried past me with barely a nod or a wave. Not one said "hey" or "good to see you." Not even a "where have you been?" No one had missed me.

And then I was alone in the lobby.

I'd never felt so invisible.

Chapter 15

The next few days blurred into one another. Always before, I'd delighted in the challenges of learning new choreography, developing my characterization, and memorizing lines. Now there was a blatant absence of that electrifying thrill. I was empty and unfulfilled.

After sharing a supper of Chinese takeout with my roommates, Lisa left on a date and Michelle to her job as a Starbucks barista. I wandered out on the fire escape—our New York City equivalent of a back deck. The clouds had broken up, but there were so few stars to be seen. It sure wasn't a silent north Georgia sky with a million twinkling lights blazing overhead.

Here, the only lights were neon. Televisions shrilled loudly through walls that were too thin, overpowering my own TV, while sirens blared every hour somewhere in The City That Never Sleeps.

And the smells. In Sugar Hill, flowers and pine trees invited deep breathing. Okay, maybe not near the chicken farms, but everywhere else. Here, I lived above the best Jewish deli in the city and the only aroma I could detect was smog.

I searched the sky. "God, what's wrong with me? You finally answer my dream and it's not what I expected. I thought this was what you wanted for me. I thought it was my heart's desire. But now, I don't know what to think anymore."

That small voice I only heard when I ran out of answers finally whispered, "You've been following the stars in your eyes and missed what I have especially for you—what I planned long ago—to give you your heart's desire."

My hands tightened on the railing. I saw it now. I thought I couldn't give up the dream, so God gave it to me, showing me He knew best. Too bad I'd been a putz, so stubborn, hanging onto that dream, when God clearly showed me what I really loved.

Or should I say *whom* I truly loved. Andy. I'd hurt him badly and didn't know if he'd want me back in his life, but I knew what I had to do. Forget *Bloom!* I was going to bloom where God wanted to plant me.

I grabbed my cell and called Cotsie. He answered on the first ring. I lifted my chin and dove in. "Tell Stephen I want out. I'm not right for the part. I'm going home."

"What? Are you crazy? We worked hard for this. I worked hard for this *for* you. Have you been smoking pot with your roommates?"

"One, my roommates don't smoke anything. And two, Cotsie, I appreciate all you've done for me. You're a sweetheart, but I want to direct."

He snorted. "Fine. I'll find you a theatre in Poughkeepsie and you can direct."

I couldn't help but laugh. "Sweet Cotsie, you're all bluff and I love you. I'm going home to Sugar Hill, Georgia."

And the man I love. If nothing else, I could open an acting studio or get a job teaching drama at the high school. That idea struck a chord in my heart and I felt like warm oil had been poured over my head.

"I can't understand you, kid, but should you change your mind, you know where to find me. Stay as lovely as you are, Morgan," Cotsie said with a catch in his voice, "and you'll do well, child."

"Thanks. You stay well too. I promise I'll send any good talent I find to you. In fact, keep your eyes open for a nineteen-year-old named Vanessa Owens. She's coming here for the spring semester at Tisch. She's good, Cotsie, and she'll be great one day."

"Thanks, kid."

Next, I made a list of things to do. I had to check with my roommates see if they wanted Vanessa for a third. I needed to close out my bank account, not that there was a fortune in it. Then I had to pack my things and see if I could get a flight home. It was only three more days till Christmas. I called the airlines and managed to get a noon flight on Christmas Eve. I called Mama and told her I was coming home.

"You're what?"

"I'm coming home to stay. My flight gets in a little before supper time on Christmas Eve, but I'll rent a car."

"You can't."

"Why not? I drove from the airport when I came home a month ago."

"No, you can't come home *now*."

"Mama, what in the world is wrong with you? When I left, you cried because I was leaving. Now you don't want me?"

"Of course I want you, sugar. Just not now."

"Oh, is your sister coming for Christmas? You need my room?" I pulled a Diet Coke from the fridge and popped the tab, grabbing a paper towel when it foamed up. Michelle must have dropped that one. "That's okay, I'll stay with one of my friends."

"You can't do that. What about your play?"

"I quit, Mama. I realized that wasn't what God wanted for me."

"Oh dear."

Oh dear? "Mama, what is wrong? You didn't cause another accident, did you? Is Andy all right?"

"Of course not. And he's fine. I've got to go. Bye." The line went dead.

She hung up! My mother hung up on me. I called her back, but she didn't answer. After dropping my phone on the table, I took a long drink of Coke, then trudged down the hall to the bathroom. At this moment, a bubble bath called my name.

Now that I'd made my decision, I felt euphoric. As I lowered myself into the tub, I remembered what the woman on the plane said, that sometimes dreams were only for a season. Would I have come to New York if I hadn't dreamed of being a Broadway star? It was where I got my training—the finest available. Maybe God did give me the dream after all, but for His reasons, not mine.

I shook my head. My thoughts sounded like Mama. I needed to get some sleep. I had one-third of an apartment to pack up and arrange to be shipped home.

Chapter 16

By dawn Christmas Eve day, everything had been packed and the boxes picked up by UPS. All that was left was my suitcase. Lisa and Michelle had both spoken with Vanessa and liked her, so I didn't feel like I'd left them in the lurch. Having a little time before my cab came, I brewed a cup of tea and took it into the living room. I wouldn't miss this place—my roommates, yes, but the apartment, no. It was so tiny.

The doorbell rang. It was still too early for the taxi. I set my tea down and went to the door, peering through the peephole. A worn brown leather bomber jacket over a blue—wait a minute. New Yorkers wear wool or cashmere overcoats, not leather bom—

My heart flipped inside my chest. That jacket—it was Andy! I fumbled with the half-dozen locks and yanked open the door. "Andy?"

With a bouquet of magnolias in one hand, he held his arms open wide. I didn't waste a second—I jumped into them.

"What are you doing here?" Mama's strange conversation echoed in my ears. She knew about this.

He silenced me with a heart-melting kiss. When my toes touched earth again, I pulled him inside. "Why aren't you at home with Cassie?"

"She pushed me out the door. Morgan, I've quit my job and come here to be with you." He dug his hand into his pocket and pulled out a tiny blue velvet box. "I … we, Cassie and I want you in our lives forever. Will you marry me? Us?"

"What about your allergies?"

"I'll take Benadryl."

"Oh, Andy. This is too funny." I kissed him.

"Funny?" he asked between kisses. "Proposing is funny?"

"No, silly. And yes, I'll marry you. I love you." I slid the ring on my finger and placed the flowers in a glass of water. "What's funny is that I quit the play to come home—to be with you in Sugar Hill."

Andy dropped onto the sofa. He patted the cushion next to him. Cuddled in his arms, I explained. "The glitter, the sparkle that was the city was gone when I got back. The thrill of acting didn't come close to the joy of directing and coaching." I dug my fingertips into his ribs. "And don't you dare say 'I told you so.' I realized I didn't want to spend my life wondering what might have been."

With his knuckle, Andy raised my chin and gazed into my eyes. "So we're a pair of jobless, homeless people hopelessly in love." He kissed my right eyelid.

"Yeah, but it's Christmas Eve. Miracles happen on this night every year."

"They do?" He kissed my nose.

"Yep. You're here and that's a big one after I was so stubborn."

"Yeah, well, you weren't the only one." He kissed my lips, curling my toes. "We both got our own agendas in front of God's."

I drew my feet up. "So what now?"

"I got an offer from a church in Woodstock. But what do you want, Morgan?"

"What God wants, and I know exactly what that is—the starring role in your life."

He laughed and hugged me tight.

"I know that's a bit sappy, but hey, I'm an actor." It was my turn to kiss him. "But God's given me another dream." I turned to face him. "I want to teach drama in high school or maybe open an acting studio. We'll see which door God opens."

"Sounds like the perfect plan to me." He pulled me to my feet. "I hear your cab. Let's go home."

Hand in hand, we raced down the steps to the taxi. I couldn't wait. I was anxious to see the bright stars back in Sugar Hill. New York City had its benefits, but they sure couldn't do a night sky.

God was watching over us, and there was a cancellation on my flight. On the plane, I leaned my head on Andy's shoulder. A very nice woman had exchanged seats with him when he told her we'd just gotten engaged. A sigh of deep contentment escaped.

"Happy?" Andy asked and kissed my forehead.

I tilted my head so I could look in his eyes. "It's more than that. It's a deep-down joy of knowing love and God's will. It doesn't get any better than that."

Andy squeezed my hand and I looked out the plane window. It wasn't night. No bright stars blinking in the sky, but I could imagine stars twinkling in God's eye as He winked at me.

Acknowlegments

Acknowledgements for *Ice Melts in Spring* by Linda W. Yezak:

Kay Arthur doesn't have a clue how much she influenced this novella, but her book *His Imprint, My Expression* provided amazing guidance through the maze of questions raised in my story and how to answer them. Jerry Jenkins also has no idea how much he helped, but after taking his course about writing for the inspirational market, I learned the elements of Christian fiction and how to boldly weave the Gospel message into my story. This novella is different from anything I've ever written because of the influence of those who didn't even know they influenced me.

But there are others who deserve my gratitude:

To my Caffeine Dream Team, my precious group of friends and supporters, my general love and thanks for all you do for me. Special thanks to team members Cindy Huff, Kimberli Buffalo, Cecilia Pulliam, Pegg Thomas, Sylvia Stewart, Kassy Paris, and Lora Mayfield. Each of them edited, encouraged, and helped me improve the story. God bless y'all!

To Mom for listening and Billy for his patience, thank you is not enough. You also have my undying love and devotion.

To my God and Savior, it never ceases to amaze me what a deep interest You take in my writing and my fictional characters. May my humble works bring glory to Your Name.

Acknowledgements for *Lillie Beth in Summer* by Eva Marie Everson:

A huge thank you to Word Weavers Page 6—our beloved Bruce Brady, Carey Clark, Cynthia Howerter, Penny Hunt, and Susan Simpson—who helped critique this little novella of mine. Another thank you to Cynthia Howerter, who took time out of her busy life to serve as my critique partner. Cindy, your opinion means the world to me, and your eagle eye is amazing. And to Megan H. Dice for her "thumbs up" on the concerns I had of the medical nature. And, thank you, Dennis Everson, for allowing me to "hole up" in my office ... All. The. Time. (or so it seems ...)

A double "thank you" to Bruce Brady for graciously allowing me to use his line spoken to me one month before his home-going: *I'm going to live forever; it's my address that's going to change.* I will miss you forever, Bruce. And to my brother Van Purvis who unknowingly handed me the line: *She's already gone, she just hasn't left yet.*

Thank you, Eddie Jones, publisher of Lighthouse Publishing of the Carolinas, for taking on this project ... and to Jennifer Uhlarik for agreeing to be our editor extraordinaire!

Thanks be to God, who breathes the stories in my heart and then allows me to tell them. And for seeing to it that I had such a fine Southern upbringing.

Acknowledgements for *Through an Autumn Window* by Claire Fullerton:

My heartfelt gratitude to Eva Marie Everson for inviting me into this wonderful project. And thank you to kind editor, Jennifer Uhlarik, for playing fair. It was a pleasure working with you. To Tama Dudley Harris, thank you for being my role model for female friendship. To my agent, Julie Gwinn, thank you for your continued support. To my husband, Bill Feil, thank you for always lending an ear as I craft my stories. And my everlasting gratitude and appreciation to Memphis, the city on the river, where I had the privilege of growing up.

Acknowledgements for *A Magnolia Blooms in Winter* by Ane Mulligan

Thank you always and forever to my critique partners, Michelle Griep, Elizabeth Ludwig, and Patty Smith Hall. You brainstorm me out of pits and bogs, and keep me sane. I wouldn't want to do this journey without you.

My wonderful editor, Jennifer Uhlarik. Thank you for your brilliant editing. You make me sound so good. Hugs!

Eva Marie Everson, my co-author and acquisitions editor. You were my first mentor, then my first editor. How fun to close this circle and be co-authors in this collection.

Thank you, my friend, Karl Wagner, for your expertise in theatrical lighting. You're always my #1 go-to person.

To my husband for believing in me and my stories, for helping me brainstorm ideas, and for eating more ham sandwiches than a man should while I'm on deadline. I love you.

To the Lover of my soul, Jesus, thank you for whispering to my heart. All the glory is Yours.